TILTING
AT
WINDMILLS

TILTING
AT
WINDMILLS

JOSEPH PITTMAN

POCKET BOOKS
New York London Toronto Sydney Singapore

POCKET BOOKS, a division of Simon & Schuster, Inc.
1230 Avenue of the Americas, New York, NY 10020

ISBN: 0-7434-0737-7

For my parents,

GERARD AND ROSEMARY PITTMAN

AUTHOR'S NOTE

Stories come from the most curious of places. At a crossroads in my life, I pondered what else was out there. On a train ride that hugged the Hudson River, I stumbled across the phrase *tilting at windmills* in the novel I was reading. The reference, of course, had nothing to do with a windmill, but it made me wonder. Life's better now, more rewarding. Still, this story grew out of a certain period of my life. They say writing is therapy, and if so, I owe this book a lot of money for sessions too numerous to count.

I've got some people to thank, notably Elaine Koster and Emily Heckman, agent and editor, respectively. Windmills spin, and so does life, sometimes dizzyingly, and I've got these two ladies to thank for giving me the chance to experience that wonderful feeling. Thanks also to Phil Mann, for sharing his knowledge of the public relations industry; Tom Ebersold, for his expert computer advice; and Michael Cravotta, for always knowing this day would arrive. Lastly, my appreciation to Amy Pierpont, Christina Boys, and the gang at Pocket Books.

The village of Linden Corners doesn't exist. Rather, it is a composite of the many wonderful small towns that have popped up to enrich the Hudson River Valley and upstate New York. Nor, as far as I've been able to discover, is there one of those wondrous windmills in this beautiful region, though its history indicates the idea is not improbable. So let the mind wander, and let the imagination soar, not unlike the wind itself.

Fortune is guiding our affairs better than
we ourselves could have wished.

—CERVANTES, *Don Quixote*

I spend too much time raiding windmills . . .
And maybe anyway the wind blows,
it's all worth waiting for . . .
World without end couldn't hold her.

—TOAD THE WET SPROCKET,
"Windmills"

PROLOGUE

Seasons came and seasons went until countless years had passed and the men who had crafted her, labored in the hot sun to build the magnificent windmill, were like the wind itself, blown into the past, into the memories we coin as history. As for the windmill, it was allowed to fall into disrepair for too long a time, and the once-heralded landmark—a classic token of a lost era—became nothing more than an eyesore to a generation that no longer embraced its ancestry. There was talk, and not just once, of tearing down the old windmill.

Until she came along. The woman who loved the windmill and restored it to its former beauty and grace. At last, the wind would again pass through its sails, a familiar friend returned to define an otherwise lost landscape. She thought it sacrilegious to deprive the windmill of its true purpose, and by restoring its spirit to the building, she breathed vibrant new life into the community around it. She could never know, though, never imagine, that her love for the creaky old structure would inspire a sense of mutual caring and nurturing—even love—among the townsfolk. But it would, even in the face of awful tragedy and sorrow. The windmill would generate an invisible power of healing—and would bring together two most unlikely souls.

The sound was the hollowness of artificial life. The smell was the antiseptic odor of life held in the balance. The staccato beep of the heart machine, the lingering hiss of the breathing apparatus. No, she wasn't gone, but neither was she fully here. Rather, she lay dreaming in her own private world. Her eyes were closed, her mouth, too—around a small tube.

Seated beside her, he thought he could detect a smile. In reality, the plastic tubing had caused an upswing of her lip, a false sign of consciousness. Otherwise, her features were devoid of animation; she had little color, too. What did register was an inner warmth, and that passed through her hands, her strong but somehow delicate fingers, to his. Entwined forever, like their lives.

It was after midnight and even though visiting hours were long over, he remained, not ready to leave her side. He was waiting for a sign. For all the words he'd spoken, aloud, silently, those tender expressions of love he had whispered into her ear, she had failed to respond. He assumed, and perhaps not wrongly, that she did not detect his presence.

"Hang in there. Please."

It was not the plea of the desperate or the wallowing of the guilty. He spoke merely with a sense of hope.

"Mr. Duncan? Maybe you need some rest."

He was about to protest to the duty nurse who had appeared. But doesn't everyone put up an argument, only to eventually relent? He was too tired to argue. So with a simple kiss to the still woman's forehead, mindful of the bandages and bruises, he left the room. He was not yet ready to leave the hospital; the wound was still too new and answers too few. He was about to ask the nurse to page her doctor when the doctor appeared around the corner. He held a chart and was closely examining it.

"Dr. Savage?" he asked.

The kind man, an elderly soul with a comforting sawbones appearance and a stethoscope dangling, proplike, around his neck, stopped, offered a smile.

"Still here, I see." Then, with a gentle touch of hand to shoulder, he repeated the nurse's instructions.

"Get yourself some rest. There's nothing you can do now. Little we can do, except monitor her progress. The surgery went well, yes, but it's too early for predictions. She's not ready to wake; her body knows what's best right now." He paused, as though thinking of what else to offer, something positive. "There's a little girl?"

He nodded, and understood. Excusing himself with thanks that sounded as hollow as her breathing had, he left the hospital and drove the twenty miles along blackened roads back to the farmhouse, where he hoped he was needed.

There was that word again. Hope.

A*s it turned out, he was needed.*

Cynthia, her closest neighbor and friend, had stayed with Janey, the aforementioned little girl, who was now in bed but wary of sleep, of the dark, even at this late hour.

He entered the dimly lit room and was grateful that it fit his mood and hid his emotions. Easing down on the soft mattress, smoothing the rainbow-patterned quilt, he stared at the curious and sweet seven-year-old. He gently brushed her blond hair out of her eyes, smiled when it fell back in protest. It was a bit wild and unruly, not unlike this precious little girl. Snuggled deep into her bed, she appeared the picture of calm. He knew, though, she was scared.

"How's Momma?"

What to say? "She's doing what you should be doing."

"You mean sleeping."

He nodded.

"I want to see her. I didn't get my good-night kiss," she said with the barest hint of a pout. She wasn't a pouter by trade.

"Just so happens, I brought a kiss home from your mom," Brian said, and bent down to kiss the girl on her forehead. He imagined his lips as a conduit, keeping alive the unbreakable connection between mother and child.

The soft touch brought a comforting smile to the little girl's lips. "I'm not very tired. Will you tell me a story?"

"Sure," he said, knowing she was beyond tired and that once he began the story, she'd slip into dreamland, where, hopefully, the violent memories of today would fail to reach her. "What kind of story?"

"A girl story," she insisted.

Cynthia was standing in the door frame. Brian turned to her for help. "What's a girl story? Like one about a princess?"

Cynthia smiled when Janey said, "Yeah, yeah, where the beautiful princess falls in love and is quite happy in the end."

Brian thought first of "Sleeping Beauty," then dismissed it as quickly as the idea had come to him. Not the time for such a story. So he opted for a story of love in the face of great odds and made sure it had a happy ending, because Janey needed to hear one and so did he. But as his voice spoke the words as they came to him, his mind played a different dialogue, a true story of how he'd met his own beautiful princess and fallen in love. Did they have an ending, one in which they would both be, as Janey had stated in her very grown-up way, "quite happy"? That was still to be decided, and it did not wholly depend on her mother's waking. It depended, too, on the power of love, of life.

Eventually, Janey drifted off to sleep. Outside, crickets sang their lullaby, and the wind lay dormant now.

*T*hirty minutes later, Cynthia left for her own farmhouse and husband and her own life, leaving Brian alone on the back porch, staring up at the starry night, the sky so still and different from that which had radically changed everything earlier this day. Yesterday now, he mused, remembering the hour. The view was different tonight, the landscape so suddenly changed, so empty. He journeyed off the porch and through the high late-summer grass, the cold dew stinging his bare feet as he reached the crest of the hill. From there, he stared down, and the sight he wished to see—the mighty and magnificent windmill—was only a figment of his imagination. Tonight it was mighty and magnificent only in its wreckage.*

Here, in the shadows of the night, as the windmill lay in ruins, a jumbled mess of broken, torn, scorched wood, Brian Duncan tried to shut out the horrible pictures that came to him and instead tried to focus on the good, the wondrous, the other events of the recent past, when life had suddenly and inexplicably changed forever. Dropping to the grass, staring ahead but not really seeing, he hoped with all his heart that she would awake.

Understanding the complexities of love, the tragedies of life, was never easy, and he hoped, too, in his tale of yesterday that there lay a clue. Because what was tomorrow, after all, without someone to share it with?

PART ONE

MARCH

ONE

For the first time in weeks, my alarm sounded and woke me from a deep sleep. Instinctively, I reached over and slammed down the snooze button. Even still, I remained awake and excited. Today there was purpose. Today I would reclaim the life I'd been forced to put on hold.

Reclaim. That was a good word, inspirational and fitting for this morning on which, after a short sabbatical, I found myself returning to the pressures of my hard-earned career. Willingly, eagerly, and with determination.

From my vantage point on the bed, I could see outside the window. Rain pelted the sidewalks, the fire escape, the window itself, and no doubt people below as they journeyed to work on this dreary Wednesday. It figured my first day back would not be made easy; the rain always seemed to bring Manhattan to a screeching halt. Weather be damned—my mood was upbeat, and not just because I was finally going back to work.

Madison was expected back, too. Maddie.

The alarm rang a second time and again I hit the snooze button, fearing I might possibly fall back to sleep. I'd been doing that a lot lately—but I had the excuse of being among the bedridden. I'd been sick. *Past tense,* I thought with grateful silence, having heard only yesterday my positive prognosis. I tried to share my good news with Maddie, who was away on an important business trip in St. Louis. Her phone rang four times before the hotel's service picked up. I left a message, feeling certain that all had gone well with the presentation and that she was out celebrating with Justin Warfield—her boss and, incidentally, mine as well.

I checked the clock—8:07, just three minutes before the alarm would go off again. This was New York time, Eastern Standard, and too early to call anyone here, much less someone in the Midwest. Sharing our mutual good fortune, as well as learning when her plane was due, would have to wait.

So, the rainy weather notwithstanding, I had two good reasons for getting up this morning—the return of my health and the return of the woman I loved. I threw back the blankets and got out of bed, flung my thick robe over my T-shirt and boxers, and padded into the living room. I opened the blinds and looked out at 83rd Street. Yup, a crappy day was brewing, but it wasn't going to bother me.

For the next hour, I busied myself with the mundane. Showered, shaved, brushed my teeth, and ran a comb through my dark brown hair. Staring at myself in the mirror, I was still thrown by how skinny I looked. Not that I was ever overweight, but with my six-foot frame, losing more than a few pounds really showed. I'd been forced to cut fatty foods and alcohol from my diet, and now I was barely pushing 165 pounds. For the past six weeks I'd been out of commission, recovering from a particularly intrusive case of hepatitis, which had attacked my liver and my life. I was wracked by bouts of sheer exhaustion, loss of appetite, and a host of other symptoms that basically came and went whenever the hell they felt like. No medicine, no pills, just lots of rest and the patience of a saint. It was my first "real" illness, not a cold or some kind of influenza, a real virus with a nasty kick, and if it taught me one thing, it's that I'm not a kid anymore. The time had arrived (my doctor proclaiming it long overdue) for me to start treating myself better: diet, exercise, the clean routine for a healthy working machine. No more doughnuts on the run for ol' Brian Duncan—now I ate grapefruit in sections and whole-grain cereals, and it was a change my friends wouldn't believe. Sometimes if you're not willing to change your bad habits, something comes along and forces the issue. They call them cosmic two-by-fours. And I had been smacked head-on.

Enough. Point is, I now had breakfast dishes to clear away, and I did so, and then decided it wasn't so early that I couldn't go ahead and call St. Louis. The number was by the phone. I quickly punched in the digits, and soon the phone was ringing at the Adam's Mark. A moment later, I was put through to room 809.

Maddie picked up the phone on the third ring; there was a slight delay before I heard her murmured hello.

"Hey, it's me."

"Hi, Brian." Her voice sounded groggy. I'd called too early. "What time is it?"

"Nine here. I guess eight your time." I paused. "Let me guess—I'm your wake-up call."

Levity was dangerous when Maddie lacked sleep.

"It was a late night. Umm, Brian, can we talk when I'm back?"

"Sure. Can I pick you up at the airport?"

"Brian—you know Justin's arranged for a limo."

"Right—sorry. Guess I'm eager to see you. How about dinner? I've got—"

She interrupted me. "Look, Brian, I'm half asleep. It's been a busy week and I need to catch up on some sleep. I'll call you—tomorrow. I probably won't be back until late tonight. Thanks for understanding."

"Okay, 'bye," I said, and quickly added, "I love you."

Not quickly enough. She'd already hung up, and my words hung dead in the air.

I replaced the receiver and thought for a second that something seemed off about our conversation. Not until I was dressed and on my way out the door did it hit me. She hadn't asked about my health. My health. I tried to pinpoint what had caused this giant setback.

Back in late January, the public relations agency that employed me, the well-respected Beckford Group, was among a select few agencies up for a big lucrative health-care account. Our president had chosen to wine and dine the prospective new client's representatives and he'd brought along his top two people, namely me and Madison Chasen, a fellow account director who happened to be my girlfriend of three years. The restaurant had been our choice, and so Maddie had picked Sequoia, one of Manhattan's newest and, in her words, toniest restaurants. This was surprising new vocabulary territory for her, and it showed how modern this classic Southern belle had become. Me, I was from the suburbs of Philadelphia and knew little about the posh and the privileged, and that suited me fine. If Maddie was the social climber of our happy couple, I was perfectly content holding the ladder.

Justin Warfield, our fortysomething president, had been wooing this particular client for months, enticing them with our past success in the field of health-care public relations. He also liked the idea of a get-to-know-each-other dinner, because he knew it was the personality of the agency that would seal the deal for us. Entertaining clients over an expensive meal had won Justin many accounts, and he was certain it would yet again yield the same lucrative results. Dinner was a big hit, with Dominick Voltaire and his team of associates walking away feeling even better about us than before, and we'd felt good about the possibility of their choosing the Beckford Group to handle the multimillion-dollar launch of a new hypertension drug. Everyone went home in the best of spirits and quite full from the meal.

Me, I went home and puked my guts out.

When, three days later, I was still out of the office on sick leave and thinking I had the flu, I went—actually, was dragged—to the doctor's office. Either the oysters I ate were contaminated or the person handling the oysters wasn't practicing good hygiene; the doctor was fairly certain I'd contracted hepatitis A. Not a fatal disease, but one that could lead to complications if not properly monitored. For the weeks that followed, I took a short-term disability leave from the office and lay about my apartment like a miserable wreck, staring at the television. Between intermittent naps, I also worked on providing Justin and Maddie with brilliant ideas on how to get the powerful Dominick Voltaire to sign with us. And just this past Sunday, they'd flown out to St. Louis to make the final presentation—without me.

What a difference a few days makes. Just as Justin and Maddie were wrapping things up, the doctor proclaimed me well enough to venture out—but said that I should still take it easy. The office was my first destination.

Now, as I tried to hail a cab outside my Upper East Side apartment, the irony was not lost on me that, here, on my first day heading back to the office, the virus gone from my system, I'd missed the presentation I'd worked so hard on. Justin and Maddie, I knew, made a formidable team, and so I had little doubt that the client was bowled over by the plans. Our plans.

Finally, luck came my way and a stray cab stopped. I climbed in, and told him 50th and Broadway. Home to the Beckford Group, where I'd made my living for the last seven years. I was eager to catch up on the latest office gossip.

The latest news, it turned out, was my return, and I spent much of the day educating folks about the particulars of my illness. It was the last topic I wanted to discuss, but maybe hearing someone else's misery helped my colleagues enjoy their own good health. Or maybe they cared. I did manage to squeeze in some work, and by the end of the day, I was exhausted.

My doctor had warned me not to overdo it—the virus was gone, but now came the crucial healing period. The best thing to do was go home. I'd heard the good news from St. Louis—Justin and Maddie had secured Voltaire, ensuring millions for our small agency. If there was one damper on hearing this good news, it was hearing it all secondhand. After all the work I'd done, I might have expected to get the first phone call, or for Maddie to have told me this morning. In fact, she'd said very little.

In the six weeks since I'd been sick, I felt Maddie begin to drift away, in direct opposition to the plans we had hammered out at Christmas. Plans that included taking our relationship to the next level—moving in together when my lease was up this coming summer. Then came the Voltaire account and my sudden contagious status. And our quality time waned liked the long days of August.

Truth was, though, I hadn't expected to fall in love, and not with Maddie. Madison Chasen, graduate of New York University, had worked for two high-powered agencies before coming aboard at age twenty-seven as an account director, my equal and three years my junior. Still, we weren't competitive; instead, we gravitated toward each other, professionally at first, until one weekend at her Southampton share, we'd fallen drunkenly into the pool first and then her bed second, and on waking sober the next morning, we'd found we had little regret and a great deal of passion left. She'd been working at Beckford for only four months when we became an item. No one cared, Justin Warfield in particular. He knew we were both workaholics and that we didn't mind the late-night hours as long as we were together.

Spending time together. For the past few weeks we'd spent little time together, and little of that could be termed quality. What I needed was to feel her in my arms again, to know we were all right and still on the course we had charted, and these thoughts were occupying my tired mind when a knock came at my office door. The day had gotten away from me—I noticed it was five-thirty. One of our junior associates, Bill Ettman, was standing in my door frame with his suit jacket on. He looked ready to leave.

"Hey, Brian, the gang's going to McHale's for drinks. What do you say—wanna join the party? First day back and all, I think you owe us all a round."

Bill was a nice guy with an easy familiarity with the entire sixteen-person staff and clearly the group leader when it came to out-of-the-office activities. Trouble was, they all wanted to drink, celebrate our windfall, and my body was telling me no way, no how. One of the many shitty aspects of hepatitis—you can't drink. Not for six months, the doc said, and I took him at his word. And there was nothing worse than being the only one sober among a group of silly drunks. So I declined the offer.

"Thanks. I'd better not. I've overstayed my welcome anyway. Told myself two hours, max, and here it is—oh, shit—eight
hours later."

Bill was about to leave when I called him back.

"What's up?" he asked.

"What time are Justin and Maddie due back—any idea?"

He checked his watch. "If the plane's on time, they should
be landing soon. But don't expect them at McHale's. Bet they're
plenty tired. We'll have another celebration, probably tomorrow.
You in tomorrow?"

I already knew I wouldn't be. "Today was a trial run. Gotta
give myself the rest of the week. Next Monday, for sure. Life re-
turns to normal soon, and I for one can't fucking wait."

"I hear ya," he said, and then was gone. The beer was calling.

The office cleared out soon after, reminding me of the old
days when just me and Maddie and a bunch of take-out cartons
from Westside Cottage remained. I gathered my jacket, flicked
the light off, and before I left, stole one last look at my office. Se-
cretly I was pleased no one had been using it in my absence, not a
temp or some junior upstart who needed the view for creative
purposes or some such lame excuse. Being away, paranoia sometimes creeps in and you begin to wonder if work goes on without
you.

On my way out, I passed Maddie's darkened office, a rare
sight. Her desk, piled high with paperwork, reflected her work-
load. I missed her a great deal, and I couldn't wait to see her
again.

I should have gone directly home, no passing Go, no collecting
two hundred dollars, and certainly, no stopping at Maddie's
Upper West Side place for a surprise visit. But that's where my
feet took me when a new wave of paranoia overtook my better

judgment. And on my way, I should have purchased one of those small collapsible umbrellas from the vendor hawking them on the street corner. Only five bucks (ten once the rain began), and I was staring straight into a dark sky threatening to purge.

It was now six-fifteen and the streets and sidewalks of Midtown were flush with cars and people going every which way they could and, more often, where they shouldn't. Horns blared as people crossed against the light, all in a hurry to be anywhere but where they were this moment. I dodged a quick-turning cab, passed another umbrella vendor without stopping, and headed uptown. Maddie lived just off the park in a brownstone on West 76th Street. She'd started with two roommates, whittled it down to one a couple years ago, and, six months later, had the place to herself. Unless I was there, and I often was. Hers was a two-bedroom main-floor apartment with a big bay window and flower boxes and the sweet smell of a woman's touch, a noticeably sharp contrast to my East Side studio. She'd often asked me to move closer, but I'd stood firm. I liked my place, and I liked my rent, too. So we ended up spending a lot of time at Maddie's. I had my own keys.

I began to feel droplets of rain, big wet ones that spotted my suit jacket, and I was still fifteen blocks from Maddie's. I searched out a cab, but all the available ones dried up at the slightest hint of rain, suddenly off duty and racing homeward. What possessed me to walk these twenty-five blocks, I didn't know—not exactly what I should be doing, healthwise. The walk had utterly worn me out. Luck, though, played on my side, as the M10 bus came up beside the curb. I hopped on with a few others, sliding my MetroCard in the slot. Traffic was nasty, and in fifteen minutes, we finally hit 76th Street.

A minute later, I had crossed the street, gone halfway down the block, and climbed the stoop. I unlocked the outside door, and then Maddie's front door, letting myself inside.

The first sound I heard was, in fact, no sound. Then I detected noises from somewhere within the apartment, and I almost called out Maddie's name. But she couldn't be home, not yet, and for a moment I wondered if it was her cleaning person. Or maybe the sound was deceptive, drifting downward from the upstairs neighbor.

I'd barely moved into the living room when the muffled sound came again, and I realized, no, it was not the neighbor. Concentrating on the noise, I almost tripped over a suitcase that had been placed in the middle of the floor. Whoever was here, I could have spooked them but good. But then again, my stealthy behavior here was going to spook someone eventually; maybe it was better to announce my presence. I continued down the hall, despite an inner voice telling me to do the complete opposite.

Maybe she got home early; maybe she was on the phone. Maybe I should turn around and leave.

The sound of voices intensified as I approached the end of the hall. My stomach was tight with tension and threatened an angry growl. *Please,* I began telling myself, *let Maddie have given her place to a friend for these few days. Please.*

The door was half open. My palms had gone dry, as had my mouth. Finally my eyes caught the first glimpse of human activity. There was no doubt that the woman lying on the bed was one Madison Laurette Chasen, the woman I loved. I knew her sound, recognized her rhythm. I even recognized the man she was with, and although I'd never seen him in such a state of, well, undress, there was little question whom she was, uh, merging with. Justin Warfield. The boss. Or was that The Boss? Though it appeared their professional relationship had taken a decidedly more personal tone. They were clearly enjoying themselves, their slick, sweat-coated bodies indicating that they had really gotten down to business. And in all their excitement, they failed to notice me watching their every move—and what moves they were. Justin's eager thrusting, Maddie's willing squirms. Her pale skin in stark contrast to his olive tone. His mouth suckled her generous breasts; her fingers hungrily grasped the hair on his back. *Beauty and the Beast* without the music.

I'd seen more than I wanted, more than I needed, but I couldn't get my feet to move. I was frozen in place. Let's just say that if I'd been a judge and they'd been an Olympic event, they'd have earned high marks. But did I wait for the conclusion of their program? Was it the short program or the long? And what then? Act shocked, upset, surprised, disappointed, pissed off? Did I applaud? I was fresh out of gold medals.

As I stupidly stood there, what bothered me most, I think, was the familiarity they seemed to have with each other's bodies, the sense that they knew where to touch and when to touch in exchange for mutual pleasure. A thrilled cry escaped from Maddie's lips, and suddenly I found that my feet would move again, so I made a silent escape from the bedroom. They'd never even noticed me.

I stopped in the kitchen to throw water on my flushed face. For some reason, I opened the refrigerator, saw a bottle of champagne on the top shelf and nothing much else. Maddie wasn't a shopper, a stupid detail to recall. I considered taking the bottle, depriving them of their celebratory bubbly, and then feared they might realize someone had stopped by for an unannounced visit. Did I really want to risk discovery? Their passionate exchange shook the apartment, and I found myself grabbing the neck of the bottle and making a mad dash for the front door. Not only had I seen enough, now I'd heard enough.

Outside the droplets were gone, replaced by a steady sheet of rain. And of course, no cabs, and no umbrella man either—and no buses in sight. They all seemed to be washed down the gutter along with the best relationship of my life.

I opened Maddie's trash bin and threw in the chilled bottle of champagne. It cracked against some other glass, and the crystal liquid spilled all over the inside of the can. *Nice-smelling garbage,* I thought, not without some irony.

By the time I got home, I was soaking wet and numb. There was one message on my machine. Surprise—it was from Maddie.

"Hi, Brian. Our afternoon flight was canceled because of the weather. I'm hoping to get a later flight, but who knows? I'll call you tomorrow. Sorry about this morning; I wasn't very awake. Hope you're feeling better."

I nearly laughed. Of all the days to get out of bed.

Just this morning I'd been so hopeful about reclaiming my life. Now, I was left with altogether another option: Could I restart my life? And if so, how? And with whom?

As I deleted her message, an idea began to form, and for a brief second I found myself trying to smile. I failed.

Two

An optimist might suggest that at least I had something new to worry about, a new distraction in a life that for six weeks had been consumed with issues of health. The new question that presented itself was a real easy one: When exactly did my girlfriend start sleeping with my boss? The choices were two—before my illness, which I immediately discounted, or during it, most likely in a hotel room in St. Louis where a connecting door between suites opened onto temptation. I suppose the *when* was irrelevant, really, leaving me to concentrate on the *why*. On that point, I came up shockingly empty. Of course I hadn't spoken with either Maddie or Justin since my discovery, and truth be told, the longer I put it off, the better, since I had no idea how I was going to handle this little situation.

The week had ended by this point, Thursday and Friday passing in a blurry self-imposed seclusion, the only communication with the outside world courtesy of the answering machine. Maddie had left me a message each day.

Thursday's went like this: *Beep.* "Brian, hi. It's Maddie. Well, I'm back, finally. The gang tells me you stopped by the office yesterday. I guess that means you're feeling better. Anyway, it's three o'clock; just had a quick lunch before the next meeting. Hope I didn't wake you. 'Bye."

And then Friday's went as follows: *Beep.* "Hi. It's me, Maddie. Remember? Did you call? I think my machine must be broken. Anyway, don't forget that we have theater tickets for Saturday night. *The Lion King*—remember, we bought tickets like a year ago. Hope you're up for it. I miss your arms around me. Feeling better? 'Bye."

I ignored both messages, deleted them almost immediately. Okay, I played them each a second time, standing over the machine with my arms crossed and my jaws clamped so tightly my teeth ached. Maddie, I had learned, was very good at this public relations profession. Tweak the truth until it served your purpose.

I returned neither call.

I awoke, though, from a dream on Saturday to the realization that I had to act as normal as possible, not wanting Maddie to know that something was wrong. I had to take the next step; I had to call her. So I waited until ten o'clock when I knew Maddie would be out at the gym, no doubt working off the lunches of the past week. Though she'd seemed to have gotten a hell of a workout already during her Wednesday-night bedroom aerobics. Her answering machine was working just fine. The message I left was innocence personified.

Beep. "Hi. It's Brian. Sorry I haven't called. Had a doctor's appointment and then came home and slept. I'm still feeling down, and don't think it would be wise to go to the theater tonight. Take a friend; have a good time. I'm dropping by the office Monday. I need to see Justin."

Before I explained why or lost my nerve or left an expletive-filled piece of my mind, I hung up. The rest of the day passed in silence, until five when my friend John called. We made plans for later that night. Me, Chinese takeout, videos with a friend. Maddie, a hit show, and a randy companion who would treat her to dinner and then treat her as dessert. No doubt they'd feel the love tonight.

So curtain time arrived and so did my friend John Oliver. I let him in, grabbing a package of goodies from his arms, a bunch of white cartons from First Wok, videos—*Beavis and Butt-head* and *The Incredible Mr. Limpet* (with Don Knotts!), and a six-pack of beer. I popped a bottle for John, grabbed a Coke for myself, and we settled down to eat.

"Sorry," John said, lifting the beer to his mouth. "Forgot you can't drink. Bummer."

Bummer indeed. I could have used a good stiff drink.

John is one of my closest friends, a guy I met back in college who happened to move to New York about the time I did, and we'd been in touch ever since. We both shared an appreciation for dumb movies, and tonight he'd brought two that had somehow escaped me. A lot of people tend to write John off as a dumb jock because he's a big guy, but really he's an astute, thoughtful person, and at this time in my life, he was very much appreciated.

Between bites of egg roll, he asked after my health, my job, and my girlfriend, and it wasn't until that last topic did my voice betray me. I had wanted to keep the developments of the past week to myself, but I guess that wasn't going to happen.

"Looks like things with Maddie aren't going so well," I said. "What's the trouble?"

I hesitated. If we got into this, we'd never get to the movies, and believe me, watching the cartoon antics of two pubescent idiots was preferable to opening up this can of worms. "Just going through a rough patch. What with my being sick and her being so busy with work. Gearing up for the new account has tapped everyone's time and energy, but looks like it's been worth the effort. The Beckford Group landed the gig to launch Voltaire's hottest new drug. It's going to mean millions. Anyway, it's taken a toll on our relationship."

"*Sounds* legit," he replied.

"But . . ."

"But? You mean like, sounds legit but it's total bullshit? Yeah, that's what it sounds like, and when you're ready to spill your guts, I'll listen. But . . ."

"But?"

"But right now, let's watch some stupid movies. I recommend *Limpet* first. You have never seen anything like this, promise." He put his hand to his heart, like the Boy Scout he once was. Except now he lacked sincerity.

We grabbed more to drink (he was doing a bang-up job on the beer all by himself) and watched the story of mild-mannered Don Knotts becoming a fish and helping the government during World War II. The distraction worked—for the first time since Wednesday, my problems slipped from my mind—and I was able to enjoy the evening. We put in the second video and laughed for eighty-seven minutes straight, and then continued our night of idiot TV with *Saturday Night Live,* even suffering through the sketches after "Weekend Update." At one o'clock, John cleaned up our mess, grabbed the last of the Sam Adams, and plopped back down on the sofa.

The apartment was, for the first time that night, quiet.

And so I spoke up.

"Maddie's screwing the boss."

John was in mid-drink, and he choked. Took a minute to recover.

"Jesus, Brian—you can't just come out with a statement like that . . . without warning."

"Think how I felt when I saw them together."

"Saw them how? On a date, in public, holding hands, that kind of thing?" His voice was hopeful, but I shook my head.

"Mid-fuck. Her bed."

"Maddie and that prick Justin Warfiend?"

John had met Justin many times when he'd come by the office and he'd always been less than taken with the big boss, and always called him Warfiend.

"What'd she say?"

"Say? No words, really, just a lot of grunting and oohing and ahing. They were quite taken with each other."

"No, you idiot, when you confronted her. Surely you interrupted . . . of course you didn't, not Brian Duncan. Jesus, Bri, you find your girlfriend and your boss doing the horizontal hokey-pokey and you don't stop them? What—were you afraid he might fire you?"

"No, you jerk. Look, words didn't exactly flow to my tongue—I think I swallowed them all. So I hightailed it out of there. And no, I haven't spoken to her. But I guess come Monday, I'll have to—it's my first official day back. Maybe there'll be too much work."

"Brian, she's not just your coworker—she's your girlfriend. You'll have to talk about it. She'll know something's wrong immediately and you'll 'fess up—you always do. Brian, you're not one to keep things—you know, problems—all bottled up. Though the fact that you managed to keep it secret for three days amazes me." He paused. "So, what are you going to do?"

I shrugged. "Haven't really decided."

"I don't envy you. Your eggs are all in one basket and now one has cracked, and it's making them all rotten."

"What?" I said, and started to laugh.

"Hey—it made sense in my head. Maybe it's the beer. Anyway, I gotta pee—and then I gotta go."

"Yeah."

John left ten minutes later, saying that if I needed to talk— anytime—just call. I thanked him, and I closed the door, grateful for his friendship. He was right, I do usually talk about the things that bother me, and keeping a secret—not spilling my guts, as he'd so graciously put it—was out of character.

But I'd stay out of character for a while longer, because I hadn't exactly been truthful with John when I'd said I didn't know what I was going to do. The idea had come to me after Maddie's second message, that darling claim of having missed my arms wrapped around her. Come Monday morning, I'd take action. The element of surprise would indeed be on my side. John wouldn't believe it, nor would Justin.

As for Maddie, not in her wildest dreams would she think Brian Duncan capable of such a move.

I guess I fell asleep shortly afterward. Sunday passed with excruciating slowness. Monday wouldn't come soon enough.

Or maybe I could have waited some more, given the curve this beautiful spring morning threw me. Justin and Maddie, I found out, had sure been busy those six weeks I'd been gone.

That's not how the morning began, though. I woke with confidence, with the knowledge that I had control. I was about to exert a power move, so I was dressing for the occasion. I donned one of my better suits, a slate gray three-button suit from Hugo Boss. I straightened my Joseph Abboud tie, tied the laces of my Cole Haan shoes. Yeah, I was in my corporate battle wear, ready to head into the enemy camp. I had easy access thanks to my electronic card key, the nineties' Trojan Horse.

I arrived at the Beckford Group's nineteenth-floor offices at eight-thirty and found the place already buzzing with activity, mostly of a social nature, with everyone asking about the past weekend while brewing pots of coffee. The smell of muffins and bagels emanated from the staff kitchen. That was a good sign, since it was Justin's routine to bring these goodies every Monday; it meant he was already in.

I dropped my leather attaché in my office, then headed down the hall to Justin's corner office. His secretary was not at her desk, probably off getting a muffin or something, and so that gave me free rein to just walk in on the boss. It seemed to be a new habit.

This time he was alone.

Justin was standing behind his desk. He was on the phone, yammering on about something with the smooth, easy tone that usually won over whomever he was talking to. He saw me and waved me in and began wrapping up his call. As I waited, I watched this man whom I'd grown to trust, this man who had given my career the spark it needed. I'd always admired his sharp look, the Armani suits, the slicked-back black hair and natural tan of his skin, all of it lending him an air of confidence. Now, I thought he just looked sleazy.

"Hey, look who's back—the prodigal account director," he said, as he put down the phone and extended his hand. I reluctantly shook it, noticing that it was only the start of the workday and already he'd rolled up his sleeves, exposing arms thickly covered with curly black hair. It took all my concentration not to punch the ape.

Instead, I said, "Hey," back.

"Have a seat. I've a spare second before the announcement."

"The announcement?" I asked. "What . . . ?"

He flashed bleached teeth. "You'll have to wait like the rest of them." He was characteristically unctuous and I wondered what was going on. He didn't give me the chance to ask. "So, Brian . . . hey, how're you feeling? Guess you're back full time—and none too soon, because there's a shitload of work to do. I hope you're up to the challenge, 'cause we've got big plans at the Beckford Warfield Group. Big mondo plans. And you're a part of it—hell, you're our creative genius."

The added name to the corporate banner didn't escape me. "Beckford Warfield?"

He grinned like the Cheshire cat's dentist. "All in good time."

He was distracting me from my own agenda. "Uh, Justin, there's this little matter—"

He held up a hand like a crossing guard, and I stopped. His secretary, Laura, had popped in.

"She's in?" Justin asked.

"She's in," replied Laura with simple efficiency.

"Who's 'she'?" I asked as a follow-up.

"You've got no patience this morning, do you, Bri?"

"I've spent the past six weeks being patient."

"As well as being a patient." He laughed at his lame joke, then added insult to injury by saying, "Get it?"

Hilarious.

"Well, follow me and you'll get all your questions answered," he said, and he was up and out of his chair, rolling down his sleeves and throwing on his suit jacket, all in one smooth motion. Then he was gone, rocketing down to the conference room, a man on a mission. I was slow to follow and wondered if my sabbatical from the corporate pace had lessened my tolerance for it.

When I got there, I saw I was one of many. In fact, he'd assembled the entire sixteen-member staff inside the conference room, a nice-size room with classic furniture and a great view of Midtown Manhattan. Everyone was anxiously standing about, eyes focused on Justin. Mine included. I hovered near the back, a virtual stranger in these familiar surroundings. Just then the "she" Justin referred to shot through the door frame. Not all that surprisingly, she was Maddie.

And she looked great. Healthy glow, professional attire, she was vibrant, and despite my feelings, I felt my heart do a quick dance. Love is a tricky emotion to quell, even in the face of betrayal. She didn't help matters any, though, by going directly to Justin's side. As they stood next to each other, it was clear they were the envy of the room, beautiful people in positions of power. Maddie looked like she'd never been a part of me.

Madison Laurette Chasen. A Georgia-bred beauty who'd worked hard to successfully rid herself of her Southern accent, a woman who'd worked equally hard at mastering her career, if the pale beige Donna Karan suit was any indication. Her hair, a lustrous and thick golden blond, absolutely radiated, even in the artificial glow of fluorescent lights. Here was a woman who would not be denied her ambition, who surged forward with clear goals and the smarts to reach them. Why, then, had she gone and done the predictable? Why had she fucked the boss?

The answer, it appeared, was unfolding before me.

"A couple of announcements, folks, before we begin this exciting new work week," said Justin with the ease of a born leader. "As you all know, Franklin Beckford, our beloved chairman, has not been in the best of health lately and has cut back his hours dramatically. He has decided now to permanently step down as chairman. His only regret is that he cannot be here to tell you all—he and his wife, Suki, have just left on an extended trip. Clearly, Franklin wants to enjoy himself, as he's wanted to for some time. The announcement last week that we landed Voltaire Health Group's account sealed this agency's financial future, so Franklin felt he could retire on this very high note.

"So, as of today, I am assuming the responsibilities for the company and therefore have been named the new chairman."

The gang broke into spontaneous applause, and I joined in, though hardly with the effort I would have given, say, last Tuesday. He enjoyed his moment before shushing us and proceeding to his next announcement. He was renaming the agency the Beckford Warfield Group, and this was also met with hearty applause—and with whistles. All in all, a lot of energy and noise for a Monday morning. Justin must have put something in the coffee.

Once again, Justin quieted everyone down, the chairman quickly assuming command of the ranks. I'd already stopped and had my arms crossed over my chest. There was more to come, I sensed, as everyone focused in on the person standing beside the newly appointed boss. Maddie looked confident on the surface, but I could tell, as someone who knew her well, that this was just a façade. Maddie was nervous.

And that's when it hit me. Like a ton of bricks.

"Technically, I've already made two announcements," Justin said, "but those are intertwined, so we'll just count them as one. Which leaves me with still one more announcement. Colleagues, I ask you, when the president gets promoted to chairman, does that not open up a position for a new president? Of course it does, and I'm happy to say that the perfect candidate is someone we know, we respect, we love. Our own—anyone for a drum roll?— Maddie Chasen."

For the third time in ten minutes, the room was full of applause. This time, it was more raucous, the obvious support for a person from their ranks succeeding beyond anyone's hopes. Maddie had played the game and been rewarded, a shining example now for inspiring hard work in others. I saw not one person in the room who looked disappointed in this news. Yet had I seen myself in a mirror just then, I'd have seen plenty of disappointment. No one, though, was paying me any mind. They had gotten used to my not being around, and guess what—they'd have plenty more time to get used to it.

I slipped out of the conference room undetected and returned to my office.

So far, the morning had not gone as planned. I still had to talk to Justin. I still had to quit.

Time dragged as indecision racked my nerves and butterflies danced in my stomach. My plan, if I went through with it, was twofold. First, find the guts to face Justin. Second, avoid running into Maddie. Twenty minutes passed when I finally made up my mind to confront Justin, and that's when I looked up and saw him standing in the doorway.

"Hey, sorry to cut you off before, but . . . well, it was important that we tell everyone together, and quickly, before rumors started. I like my staff to know what's going on. But anyway, it's your first day back—an exciting one, too." He paused, and I guess he was studying my face, because the next thing he said was, "You don't share the excitement?"

"No, it's not that. It's . . . great news, for you. Sorry about Franklin, though it sounds like he's got the better end of the deal. Get all the money from a buyout and travel the world . . ."

"I get the sense that there's a 'but' to your less-than-pronounced enthusiasm."

Isn't there always a "but"? As in life is great, but . . .

"We need to talk," I said.

He gave a quick nod of his head. "Okay. Shoot. What's up,

big guy?" Here it comes—the supportive boss, the pal who signs your paychecks.

"Maybe you should come in."

"Okay."

"And close the door."

He did so, and then sat down in my guest chair. A case of role reversal that I hoped enabled me to keep control of the situation.

"Are you all right—healthwise?"

"Yeah. I mean, I still get tired here and there and I've got to make sure that I get lots of rest. But it's pretty much out of my system. It's just . . ."

"You're happy for Maddie, right?"

"Couldn't be happier," came my monotone reply.

"So then what's the problem? Do I have to force it out of you?"

"It's not easy to say this, Justin, not after so many years here."

"Whoa. Stop right there," he said, again halting my conversation with his upraised hand. "You sound like a person who's getting ready to quit. And that's not possible. Brian Duncan is my star, and he's back after a stint on the disabled list, but hey, come on—it's back to the game and let's win some. You know what I'm saying . . ."

His face sank as he realized his sports analogy wasn't working.

"I'm sorry, Justin, but it's something I've got to do."

"Got to?"

"Have to."

"You've got another job offer? You know I'll match it—hell, I'll better it."

"There's no other job. I'm taking a break."

"A break? From working? Christ, Brian, you've just had a

six-week break, which, may I remind you, was a break with full pay."

"It's not like I was off seeing the world, Justin. I had a pretty major illness. And now . . . and now I'm not sure I want to return to the daily grind of nine-to-five, put on the shirt and tie and be creative on demand. There's got to be more to life, more to—"

"What does Maddie say about this?"

He surprised me by mentioning her. "Nothing. I haven't spoken with her."

"Oh," he replied, suddenly uncertain. "Look, Brian, I'm not sure where all this 'more to life' stuff is coming from, but if you're not ready to return to work, I'll give you a couple more weeks. Get the rest you need, and then come back. Maybe six weeks wasn't long enough for you to recover and it's the sickness that's hampering your decision process. What do you say? We need you, Brian, more than ever since landing Voltaire. It's going to be high pressure launching this new drug and we need the best creative mind in the business. And that mind happens to be yours. Hell, it's how we landed the account in the first place, all your great ideas. So come on, take two weeks—go somewhere and lay in the sun—and then come back refreshed and ready to work. Hell, I'll even spring for the airfare. You can't pass that up, can you? Consider it a bonus for helping us land Voltaire."

"That's a generous offer, and anyone would jump at the chance. You're being very accommodating, Justin, like you have been during these past six weeks. But I just can't accept. I realize this is unexpected, but I've already made my plans and they don't include the Beckford Group—pardon, the Beckford Warfield Group."

I didn't mean for it to sound snotty, but that's how it came out, and suddenly Justin's eyes widened and his nostrils flared in anger. "Aha. Pieces are falling into place." He stood up, placing his hands on my desk and leaning in close. "Listen, Duncan, I've got no room at this agency for petty jealousy. So your girlfriend just got a major promotion. So what? Are you afraid of Maddie's success? Jealous that she beat you to the top? Pissed off that I didn't give the job to you because you've worked here longer?"

"No, no, Justin. You've got it wrong; that's not it at all. Maddie has nothing to do with my leaving . . . well, her promotion doesn't have anything to do . . ." I stopped, realizing it was futile. This was why I wanted to talk with him earlier, but how was I to know the morning would unfold with such drama? Clearly Justin thought my decision to quit was related to this morning's shakeup, that I was leaving out of jealousy and anger and some petty, childish revenge motive. Which I wasn't. I was quitting because the boss had screwed my girlfriend and I didn't feel like dealing with it. Wasn't it easier to just remove yourself from the situation?

"Well, Duncan? I'm right."

I shook my head. "No, Justin, you're not. Except you're going to think what you think and there's nothing I can do to change that."

"You know, Duncan, I'm disappointed in you. When you first came to work for this company, you brought a sense of freshness, determination, the idea that nothing would stop you, nothing would bring you down. Now look at you, quitting because you got passed over for a job you weren't ready for, maybe wouldn't ever be. Some people are born to play the corporate game, driven people like myself and Maddie. Then there are those who are afraid to roll the dice. They fail. You, Brian—you failed."

Any number of replies came to me, none of them suitable. I just remained quiet and let Justin head for the door. He opened it, then turned back for one last moment of melodrama. "Don't think you're getting off easy, Brian. After your living off my goodwill for the past six weeks, I'm expecting two weeks' notice."

"Expect what you want, Justin. Just don't actually count on my being here."

"Get the hell out of this office."

Maybe his words were meant to hurt me or intimidate me. Instead, I smiled, a great big shit-eating grin that pissed him off even more. He stormed away, and I began the process of packing my personal items.

For the moment, I felt great personal satisfaction. Forgetting, of course, that I'd just thrown away everything I'd worked for. My job, my security, the woman I'd once loved.

But what I had in return had no price tag. I had my self-respect, and if that's not something to build a new life on, I don't know what is.

Of course, escaping the confines of the Beckford Warfield Group with my newfound self-esteem intact was quite another matter. First I had to get to the elevators, and that entailed sneaking past Maddie's office. And really, can you still call it self-esteem if you're using the word *sneaking?*

Not ten minutes had elapsed since Justin had stormed out of my office, and I'd managed to gather up my few belongings. I began to make my escape to freedom. Hopefully the word wasn't yet out and people would not stop me to express whatever they felt. As I walked down the corridor, past cubicles and busy workers, no one looked up, no one bothered.

As I approached Maddie's office, my feet kept walking, but my eyes couldn't avoid a peek inside. My mind filled with all sorts of excuses about what I was doing and why I was leaving. My tongue, though, felt thick and unable to form words, and that was just as well, since Maddie's office was empty. I'd been holding my breath, and I let it out in a rush of air.

Seconds later, I reached the bank of elevators and pressed the DOWN button. While I waited for the indicator button to light up and ping, I heard instead the click of heels against the marble floor. Distinctive, deliberate heels. Maddie's heels. Coming my way.

Staring at her reflection in the glass of the elevator door, I waited for what she had to say. She didn't look particularly pleased.

"Weren't you even going to congratulate me?"

THREE

Perhaps I was foolish to think I could escape confrontation for a second time. Standing before the bank of elevators with a box of my personal belongings—the box itself a beacon of retreat—I couldn't delay this face-to-face with Madison Laurette Chasen. Well, nearly face-to-face, since I'd yet to turn around and face the obvious hurt that was in her voice. Already she had assumed the role of victim—a role I'd already claimed.

So I turned around, my shoes making a screeching noise against the hard floor. No one took notice. Everyone nearby had cleared the area, and if I were smart, I'd have done likewise. Maddie wore a stern expression on her otherwise lovely face and her arms were crossed; she was defensive and angry. She stood four feet from me. We were like two opponents ready for battle. A referee would have been a nice buffer—a down elevator even nicer.

"Well?" she asked me. I still hadn't responded to her question, and wasn't sure if I was going to.

Finally, in my best monotone, I said, "Congratulations."

"Can you say it and mean it?"

I seriously considered her question before answering with a definitive "no."

"So Justin's right—you're leaving because you're jealous. Christ." She let out a short, unattractive snort, accompanied by a flick of her lustrous golden hair. Aggression and beauty, wrapped in one conflicted package. "Were you even planning on telling me, the woman you're supposed to love? Or were you waiting for Justin to distribute an 'all concerned' memo? God, Brian, I can't believe that after everything we've been through, you'd pull a stunt like this."

"A stunt? It's anything but a stunt. And anyway, this isn't really the place to get into this, okay? As for Justin, he'll believe what he wants; he always does. What surprises me is the nearly biblical effect his words have on you. He says it, you believe it, like it's some fucking eleventh commandment. Honor your boss. In some circles, they call them yes-men. Or yes-women."

Her nostrils flared at the suggestion that she was incapable of making up her own mind. She fired back with equally stinging words. "Better than being a quitter. Jesus, Brian, we used to be a team."

Just then, the elevator arrived and the doors opened. I made a move toward them. The box was getting heavier.

"Can we talk later?" Maddie asked.

I hesitated, reminding myself to be strong, to just get into the elevator and let the doors close on her. But I held the doors—glad no one else was inside the car—and stole a last glance at her, this amazingly beautiful creature who had shared my life for so long. Now, I saw a picture to admire but nothing beneath. "Later? That's not a good idea, Maddie. It's better here, better now."

And I stepped into the empty elevator.

"Brian?"

The way she said my name, her soft voice suddenly shaky and betraying her lost Southern roots, made my knees waver. I knew this approach, usually so sultry and successful with me. Slowly I closed my eyes in an effort to resist Maddie's persuasive powers. Her next words would dictate my next move.

"Brian, I love you."

The words sank into the pores of my skin, and briefly my heart swelled, more out of regret for the past, for all we'd shared. Maybe she thought those words would melt my heart, make me reveal the truth behind my actions. I felt words flowing to my tongue, the wrong words, those that would tell all that my eyes had witnessed. I wanted to ask her how she could have slept with Justin, but then, as soon as the image of them came to me, the urge passed. My eyes opened and they were dry. "No," I said. "No, you don't."

Timing is everything, and the elevator doors seemed to know this. They closed and the car fell quickly, as did my heart.

A minute later, back out on the streets of New York, I realized I'd done the unthinkable and was now free and clear of any and all responsibility. The next step in life would be anything I wanted. I grabbed a cab, headed uptown. Traffic was light and we jerked onward. Forward motion—that was good.

*   *   *

All I'd avoided telling Maddie, I revealed instead to John. He deserved to know what I'd done and why and what my plans were, even if they were sketchy in my own mind. So that's how, later that day, he came to stand in my foyer with an incredulous look on his face, his chin halfway to the floor. I'd called him just over twenty minutes earlier. He'd been at work, halfway across town. And now he was here.

"You did what?" he said as I opened the door and let him in.

"Like I said on the phone, I quit my job."

"You quit your job."

"Gee, do you notice an echo here? And I haven't even moved out of my apartment yet."

His eyes widened in further shock. "You're moving out?"

"Away," I said, correcting him. "Moving away."

"You're moving away?"

"What exactly do you call an echo that repeats itself? Isn't that redundant?" I laughed a bit. "I think you need a drink—and since you finished the beer the other night, we need to go somewhere. I dumped all my booze weeks ago—wasn't doing me any good."

"You dumped your booze?" he said, about to explode from too many shocks. He backed up, double-checked the number on my apartment door, and said, "Brian, is that you? Are you in there? Where am I?"

Truth be known, it was the reaction I'd expected. Disbelief. My best friend couldn't believe what I'd done, but then again, neither could I. However, the deed was done and there was no going back. All of me thinking, *Why should I, anyway?* I was absolutely thrilled, overcome with a sense of freedom that surely defined the concept. After thirteen years of continuous corporate culture, I'd cashed in my personal stock options to pursue God only knew what.

John gathered his wits and entered the apartment. "Let me

see if I've got this straight. You marched into Justin's office and announced you were quitting your job. Just like that, after six weeks of being on sick leave and, well, leaving them to deal with the pressures of this new client, one you were instrumental in getting?"

"Actually, I did it in my office."

"And then you say, 'That's it; I'm outta here.' No notice?"

I shook my head with nonchalance. "None. Oh, he asked for two weeks, but then things got ugly and he threw me out. Man, John, it was great, like a movie. I walked out, never to return. Even got the little trinkets off my desk."

Overwhelmed, he dropped to the sofa. "Fuck me."

I patted his shoulder and said, "Well, it's probably words to that effect that brought about this whole situation."

"But . . ."

"Yes?" I asked, an eyebrow arched.

"But . . . whoa, wait a second. This doesn't compute—no way. You're Brian Duncan. The most responsible man on the planet. The guy who finds a nickel on the sidewalk and then takes out a classified to track down its owner. The guy who helps little old ladies across the street . . . and waits until a telemarketer finishes the pitch before hanging up . . ."

"Hey, John?"

"What?"

"Shut up."

He considered this a second, then offered up his usual solution for conundrums. "Come on, Bri, we're going for a drink. I don't know about you, but shit, I need one."

Twenty minutes later, we were settled at the short oak bar of a place called the Gaf, located on East 85th Street, a few blocks from my apartment. We'd gone there often in years past because they had good scotch (which John liked) and good Irish stout (which never failed to thrill me). Today John ordered up his scotch, a double, and I had a cranberry and seltzer and tried to blot out the wonderfully rank smell of stale beer that tempted me toward medical truancy.

We spent a couple hours there, he happily drinking away, the alcohol lessening the shock value of all that I'd done as our conversation took many turns. The first drink calmed him; the second made him curious about what my plans were. Another drink brought about a near-drunken rant of enviousness, and the next prompted a lecture about my out-of-character gumption. To shut him up, I offered up my apartment as a sublet, and he quickly agreed to take it, since he was overdue for new digs anyway; he still played the roommates blues. Finally, the talk wound its way to Maddie, her betrayal, her attitude toward my impulsive action this morning. The fact that she hadn't owned up to her part in these developments set off a heated debate between us.

"Are you ever gonna tell Maddie you saw her and Justin together?"

"Nope."

"Shit, Brian, why not? It's the best part of revenge, you know, the confrontation."

"I'm not in this for revenge," I said, trying to come up with the words that would best explain my actions. "Look, John, I'm taking this as an opportunity, and a golden one at that. For me and Maddie, it was either get married or end it, and I thought marriage wouldn't be so bad, really. We were certainly talking about it—you know that. Who knows, though, maybe she was having second thoughts. Whatever the reasoning, her decision to sleep with Justin was a conscious one, something she wanted to do. So let her get the promotion and let her get on with her life. And in the meantime, let me get on with mine."

"Which entails what, exactly?" he asked, his words starting to slur. Still, he ordered up another drink and so did I, just seltzer with a fresh wedge of lime.

I shrugged off his question. "Who says I need to know now what I'm going to do? Pack up my apartment, hop in my car, and head out onto the open road. Destination unknown. Maybe somewhere along the way something will catch my eye, make me stop and see what it's all about. But really, that's not what's going to happen, John. What I want, what I'm searching for, well, it has to come from within. This time away is supposed to allow me to explore all that's churning inside me. Think about it: For the first time since college, John, I'm free of responsibility and can do whatever I want." Then I laughed at my nonchalance. "Of course, my bank account's going to suffer for a while, but I figure six months ought to give me enough time to start answering some of the questions I've got. After that, we'll see."

He sucked down more of the scotch, then looked at me with bleary eyes. "You know what I think?"

"No, but if tradition counts for anything, you're going to tell me."

He pointed an accusatory finger at me. "You're running away."

I laughed, a defensive move. "No, I'm not."

"Yes, you are."

"No, John, I'm . . . Christ, before we get into a pissing match, let's drop it. Okay?"

"You're so eager to drop it because you know I'm right. Do it once, do it again," he said with the knowledge of years.

"John, you don't know what you're talking about," I said.

"At least face some reality, Bri. Come on—when *you* fall in love, you fall hard. When love doesn't work out, well, you fall even harder. If things had worked out with Lucy years ago, you'd probably have two cars, two kids, and a big fat mortgage now—the American dream. But it didn't work, and what did you do? You ran here, to New York, and sought help from yours truly. Now, listen to me again, and believe me, I can be this honest with you because, well, 'cause the booze helps. But listen up: You can't run away again."

"John, dredging up history is pointless. Lucy and I . . . we were just grown-up kids who didn't know anything about being adults. And it's completely different. I wasn't running away then; I was—"

"Aha!" he screamed out. We caught the attention of the other people in the cramped little bar, curious looks indicating that they thought someone had had too much to drink. I tried to encourage John to leave, but he protested by draining his scotch and asking for another. I waved the bartender away.

"Thanks," I said, tossing down thirty bucks on the bar, and, with my friend in tow, I exited the bar.

It was late, past ten. We'd been there for four hours, and John was pretty drunk. Good thing I'd chosen the Gaf, so close to John's place. With lots of help from me, we wove our way down the street, crossed Second Avenue against traffic, and soon found the entrance to his apartment building.

"You need help going up the stairs?" I asked.

"No, you run along," he said. "It's your pattern."

Deflecting his stinging comment, I helped him with his keys and got him inside the building. I turned around and headed down Second and toward home. It was a cold night, crisp and clear, and I enjoyed the brisk walk, liked the way the air cleared my mind after hours in the stuffy, dank bar. There were places that had nights like this all the time, where you could actually see the sky and the stars.

Thoughts kept creeping into my mind. One in particular— John's theory about how I always run from my problems rather than face up to them. Had I once? And was I doing it now? Was it really my place to talk with Maddie, to confront her with her betrayal? Or was it hers, to realize her mistake and come running to me? Nothing was making sense, and I wondered if maybe I were drunk on bar fumes. I tried to push these troubling, doubt-ing thoughts away—and found I couldn't. They were firmly lodged now in my brain: Brian Duncan just running away.

Before long, a week had passed and I was ready for the next brave step. I packed, put things in storage, notified family and friends, and finalized all the necessary details. Putting your life on hold while you go off to find yourself is no easy task. I was up for it, though, enjoying the physical challenge while suppressing the cerebral. There would be time for mind games later.

Before I knew it, Friday morning arrived. D day. Departure day.

I awoke for the last time in my apartment, and for that sin-gle moment everything felt normal. As though I were going to work, making weekend plans with Maddie, and generally going about the routine I'd conditioned myself for these past thirteen years. But the two suitcases near the closet stood as reminders that nothing was the same, nothing would be as it was. The job was gone, so was a certain woman, and come tomorrow, so was the apartment.

I had only a few second thoughts. I was leaving the comfort I'd known, intent now on my trek into the vast unknown. Fear didn't begin to describe what I was feeling as a heaviness settled into my chest like a bad case of heartburn and nausea nestled in the pit of my stomach. Emotions I hadn't felt in years toyed with my system, and as a result, my blood was on fire and my body was alive.

Thirty minutes passed while I made my final preparations, that one last sweep of the apartment to make sure I'd taken everything I wanted from my previous life, any objects that might ease the solitude that would be my constant companion on the road. There was one particular item in my desk drawer that, at the last minute, I took out and slipped into my jacket pocket. I thought fleetingly of Maddie, wondered if I'd hear from her, then dismissed it. My attention was drawn to the window, where I saw people on the streets rushing to work, dressed in suits and carrying briefcases. In jeans and a turtleneck, wearing sneakers and a brown leather jacket, I was dressed for the future.

I grabbed the two suitcases, and with my heart suddenly full of an odd mixture of sadness and joy, I closed the door behind me, listening for that final turn of the lock. Its click lingered in my mind as I went down the stairs. Once out in the cool morning air, I realized I'd been holding my breath and so I let it out. A cold breeze washed over and invigorated me. Winter, it was clear, was still hovering, but spring was coming. Hope springs eternal indeed.

My car was parked in the garage across the street, so it was a quick, no-nonsense walk with my heavy load. I'd packed only clothes, figuring any mementos would only bog me down with weight both physical and emotional. Besides, you don't have to pack memories. They never leave you.

Some even meet you head-on.

A surprise guest was waiting for me in the garage. She was sitting on the trunk of my black Grand Am, her feet resting on its fender. In her hands I saw a tissue, which she used to dab at the corner of her eyes. She was dressed in an attractive package of denim and lace.

"Is Justin allowing casual-dress Fridays?"

Maddie said, "This doesn't strike me as a moment for flippancy."

"This isn't much of a moment for anything," I replied, standing before the car with the suitcases still in my hands, hoping she'd get the hint that as long as I held them, she was holding me up. But she wasn't giving up easily, and so I cleared my throat to help along my hint.

She got off the car at last, enabling me to open the trunk and

drop both bags onto the carpeted floor beside the emergency repair kit. It helps to be prepared. Except at this precise moment, I
wasn't. Not for this.

"Brian, don't you think I'm owed a better explanation? For
all of this—us. Brian, for us?"

I wasn't budging. "Shouldn't you be at work?"

She wrapped herself in her arms. "I've never seen you be so
cold. There's nothing in your eyes."

"The new president of a corporation has important responsibilities, and I'm sure your underlings at work need your expert
guidance."

"That's your third reference to work. Why won't you talk to
me—the person, the woman—not the title? Dammit, Brian."

"Maddie, what are you doing here? And how did you know to
find me here—now," I asked, hoping we could dispense with this
scene quickly and painlessly—okay, quickly. I wasn't sure how
long I could keep up this distant attitude. Truth was, inside I was
melting at the sight of her gleaming hair, the resonance of her
voice. She was a beautiful woman, nothing could change that, but
my feelings went far below the surface, deep down to the heart.

"Don't be mad at John—I forced him to tell me."

"John. Great. My best friend sides with . . ." But then I
dropped it. It was irrelevant at this point. I guess that in the face
of true friendship, his actions were justified. He was looking toward the long run.

"Take me with you," she blurted out.

I couldn't help it—I laughed. And I instantly regretted it. I
was angry, yes, but cruelty had no place, not between two people
who had once shared their hopes and dreams, their inner souls
with each other.

"I'm sorry," I said. "Look, Maddie, let's just leave it as is, before either one of us says something hurtful. This . . . whatever
you call it . . . my leaving, it's something I have to do for myself.

If I stayed, I wouldn't be the man you want me to be. He doesn't exist anymore."

"That's why I want to go. Let me know who you are, who you've become."

"Maddie, there's no way you could give everything up now. You'd call it a vacation, and in two hours, you'd be checking your messages. This is no vacation, not for me."

"Then what is it?"

"It's life, and it's vital I do this. Alone."

"I think you're running away," she stated, and for a second I was shaken to the core. Those were John's words, too, and again doubt crept beneath my skin. Was I really running away? Or had John used this line on Maddie in an effort to get me to change my mind? Was now the time to tell Maddie everything? But if I did come clean now, at this crucial moment, would I still be able to leave, to say that final good-bye, or would the flood of memories we'd created draw me close to her, to where I'd be unable to resist her? Silence enveloped us—indecision on my part, uncertainty on hers—and for a moment I saw the woman I'd fallen for, had come to love. It was a nice way to remember her.

"Good-bye, Maddie," I said strongly, confidence taking over. It worked. Maddie let me go, no more explanation needed.

We'd loved each other, planned a future.

But people change and so do their plans, and sometimes things are never the same. You can't relive the past; you can't re-capture its mood. Life is a series of new memories, and new adventures, and I for one was ready for them.

One last stop, and it seemed predestined, because I found a parking space right in front of the building. In New York, you find hidden messages in the details.

I was on 47th Street, a street I'd walked or crossed many

times, but only one time in particular did the street leave any lasting impression. The month had been December, just last year, less than three short months ago. Snow had covered the sidewalks of New York, pretty, white litter that drifted down from the sky and still seemed fresh on that cold morning. Maddie and I, we'd been playing tourist in our own backyard as we visited the Christmas tree in Rockefeller Center, window-shopped along Fifth Avenue, and contemplated taking in a matinee. It was a Wednesday and the office was closed for the holiday week. There were any number of streets we could have taken, but 47th, going west, would take us directly to the half-price TKTS booth where we could see what Broadway had to offer on that beautiful winter's day. So we headed west, strolling arm in arm down the diamond district, lost in our own world. We stopped in front of a tiny shop called Eli's Jewelers and I pointed to something glistening in the window. A not tiny piece of diamond surrounded by three others on a gold band, it sparkled in the bright sunshine and I thanked the weather or maybe even God for giving the ring that extra sheen.

"Oh . . . oh, Brian, it's beautiful. No, it's more than that. It's . . . indescribable. There's no word in the English language . . ."

She turned to me.

"Now you know the problem I have every time someone asks me about you. I become utterly speechless."

"Oh," she said, and leaned in until our lips touched. We were lost in each other and could have been anywhere rather than in this wintry urban wilderness.

The blaring sound of a taxi horn broke us apart and we laughed. People passing us smiled, the holiday mood vibrantly alive on this diamond-laced street. I told her then that the ring would soon be hers. But it was official—we were now unofficially engaged, or pre-engaged, or, forsaking a label, merely two people very much in love.

That day, we did see a show, we did walk hand in hand
through the drifts of snow in Central Park, and we did make
love the night long. And we did see nothing but the brightest
and most intoxicating future imaginable. The perfect life, marriage, children. She wanted three kids, and I said how fine that
sounded. Maddie wanted boys, and wasn't that wonderful, but a
special little girl would, I thought, bring out the untapped father in me. So with these hopes and dreams shared, I took the
next step. The next morning I went back to Eli's and bought the
ring.

Now, with the memory of that day so bittersweet in my
mind, I entered the little jewelry shop. The ring was in my
pocket. The tinkling of a bell alerted the owner, and he smiled at
me with recognition. His brow furrowed. This kindly old gentleman had been in business too long a time, and he knew a
wounded heart when he saw one.

"My boy," he said, and clasped his hands in genuine concern.
There was little else to say.

I removed the box from my pocket and set it on the counter
without opening it.

"I bought this . . ."

"New Year's Eve, I remember. Figured you needed it for the
evening's celebration. Not so?"

I shook my head. "Change of plans."

"Let me get my paperwork—I'll be right back."

He left me, and I stole a quick glance around the small shop.
The last thing I wanted to see was a giddy couple hovering over a
selection of engagement rings. I was shaky still from having seen
Maddie, and I wondered if any good at all had come of our seeing
each other again. She'd given me one last chance to explain my actions. For her, too, it was the moment to come clean, and the fact
that she hadn't done so told me I'd made the right decision. Maddie and I were not destiny's couple.

One day, though, one day in the future, we'd have to confront the truth, settle the past before we could move on. Or was that all psychobabble?

"Here we go," the man said, a thick file marked DECEMBER in his frail old hands. "Only February is thicker," he confessed.

"I've changed my mind," I suddenly announced.

"Eh? What's that?"

"I'm holding onto the ring."

He was very confused. Join the club.

"I can't explain it," I said, and that much was the truth. "Something is telling me to keep it."

He smiled, showing his teeth. "Hope?"

I shook my head. "More of a talisman. For my journey."

"Eh?"

"It's okay—I don't especially get it either. But someday, maybe I will, and someday, perhaps I'll return and we can do business." I picked up the ring box and quickly pocketed it. "Thanks."

"Life, my boy," the old man wisely said. "Always we must tilt at windmills. But they turn, and they turn, and you live. Remember."

I left the jewelry store, my wallet empty but my heart somehow richer, and it was that exact feeling that took me through the crowded streets of New York City, through the Lincoln Tunnel, into New Jersey, and onto an empty road that held nothing but hope and, somewhere, someplace, my future.

FIRST INTERLUDE

Brian slept little that first night, and by nine o'clock in the morning, he was back at the hospital. Annie lay in the slightly arched bed, silent and still in the sleep of the wounded. Her vital signs had stabilized, that was good, and the color had returned to her cheeks. That instilled within him hope that she would wake sometime soon. Perhaps today.

He'd left the farmhouse that morning under a cloud of controversy, Janey insisting she was going with him. She simply wanted to see her mother, that was all. Cynthia and Brian had exchanged worried looks, confused about what was best for Janey, and in the end had found themselves agreeing: It was too soon. Let Annie wake, let her be able to talk to her girl, assure her she was on the mend. Janey, wise beyond her years, had relented—for now, she said—freeing Brian to leave without guilt.

Except he wasn't guiltless. Sure, maybe when it came to Janey, but Annie, that was an altogether different story. Was it his stubbornness, or hers, or just the fates or the hand of God or a freak accident? He could debate this for all eternity and probably not come up with a satisfactory answer. Perhaps, for now, it was best to let go of blame and concentrate on what was. His healing could wait; Annie's could not.

He was back at his post, beside her bed, watching her sleep. She wasn't breathing, not on her own, and maybe wouldn't for a while. As a result of the accident, Annie had punctured a lung. The surgery had staved off further damage, but they had to wait for a positive sign of recovery. The other bruises were more obvious, especially this next day, purples and reds that stood pronounced on her forehead and cheeks and on her hands. Still, there was something about her, a glow of life, and that gave him—yes, he couldn't think it enough, not in this crucial period of recovery—hope.

"Janey sends her love," Brian said. "Actually, she wanted to bring it herself, wrapped in a tight bow, no doubt, and sparkling with glitter." Maybe he was wrong in not bringing Janey to her mother's side. The hospital staff, though, had their own rules, and if Janey had to follow Brian's, Brian had to follow the hospital's. Loving people and wanting the best for them was never easy but always worth it.

"I was thinking, Annie, of the first time we met. First time I met Janey, too. Could it really have been only six months ago? Seems like I've known you forever and Janey since she was a baby. She's grown so much, even from that first moment we met—you remember, by the windmill."

Just then a beeping filled the room, startling Brian. Fear struck his heart as he realized the machine at Annie's side was blaring and he didn't know what it meant. He knew it didn't signal anything good. He was about to call for a nurse when the door to the room burst open and a team of nurses entered, one rushing to Annie's side, another to the machine, while the third ushered Brian outside, ignoring his protests and questions. In a blur, a handful of white-coated figures flew past him and into the closed ICU.

"Annie . . ." he said, her name a whisper on his lips.

Impossible minutes passed; he tried to watch through the glass until a nurse finally pulled a curtain across it. What, he wondered, could have gone wrong, so swiftly, so . . . awfully? It took fifteen endless minutes before anyone emerged, and thankfully it was Dr. Savage, her attending physician, wearing that same comforting expression and stethoscope.

"She's fine, Mr. Duncan—for now. We've got her stabilized."

"What happened?"

He hung his head in silence, in contemplation. "We're not sure—yet."

"What do you mean, you're not sure? How about an educated guess? My God, we're talking about a young woman's life here. She's got a daughter who needs her. We need to know, Doctor. Is Annie going to make it?"

He grimaced, as though reluctant to share his thoughts. "Are there next of kin?"

"Only her young daughter. Her parents are gone; there's no one. I'm the closest you'll get. Tell me, please."

"We're . . . we're concerned about a possible, uh, infection. But we're monitoring her very closely."

"An infection? What kind?"

"In the damaged lung. What pierced the lung was not one of her ribs. It was a piece of rusted metal. We believe we've cleaned the wound thoroughly."

"So what you're saying is, we wait?"

"Time heals," he said, "or it plays its hand. We do our best, but we're human. I'll be honest with you, Mr. Duncan: Annie has suffered a

grievous injury. Complications with these kinds of injuries are hard to predict. But we're anticipating and we're watching. I'm sorry. Right now, it's the best I can offer."

Brian wasn't satisfied with Dr. Savage's vagueness.

"I'm not going anywhere."

Dr. Savage nodded agreeably. "Stay as long as necessary. But don't forget who needs your help more."

*B*rian stayed all day, sitting by Annie's bedside, holding her hand and telling her how strong she was, how strong Janey was, too, how alike they were, and how she had to recover, not for his sake but for herself and, most importantly, for Janey. Finally, Cynthia urged him home, and he at last left the hospital as night fell. He rode back to the farmhouse in silence. His mind was numb and his body was drained of any energy. Luckily he was unfamiliar with the roads, their winding curves and smooth surfaces forcing him to concentrate on the drive and nothing else. He'd have to suspend the vigil he'd begun because tonight, Janey was his charge. He'd continue the vigil later, keeping watch until Annie was out of danger and in her own room, away from the morbid monitoring of the ICU. The doctor was right—there was someone who needed him so she could feel safe, secure, loved.

Gerta Connors, who had come to stay with Janey until Brian got back, was waiting at the front door. She'd heard his car pull up.

"How is Janey?" Brian asked, entering the house quietly.

"Sleeping—finally. The poor thing; she doesn't know if she's coming or going, what's night or day, what's up or down."

"That's another thing Janey and I have in common."

Gerta, one of Linden Corners' longtime residents and perhaps its kindest, opened her arms wide and embraced Brian, patting him on the back.

"Do you need me to stay?"

"No, that's not necessary."

Placing a comforting hand on his cheek, she said, "I'll be back at eight tomorrow, so you can go back to the hospital."

"Thanks."

Gerta left, and he went in to check on Janey, who was sound asleep, hugging tight her stuffed purple frog. She was protected, he thought, by the resilience of youth, its innocence and faith. She wasn't ready for the complexities of life.

He retreated to the kitchen and poured himself a glass of lemonade. He still wasn't drinking, still couldn't for health reasons, and these days, he didn't even think he missed it. Taking a sip, his mouth puckering from the tartness, he went outside into the beautiful clear night and wondered what he should be doing. Taking care of Janey was at the top of his list for sure. But he couldn't help but think that there was something else he should do. There must be, he reasoned, a way to help Annie recover.

He'd done nothing, still, about the windmill way out in the field. Cleaning up the awful mess was too daunting a prospect, one he just wasn't ready to face. He knew he had to face the inevitable, so he swallowed the resistance he felt and found himself, lemonade still in hand, walking toward the ruined old structure.

The windmill. How he'd been captivated by it when he was first passing through town, its majesty heightened by the lustrous green countryside. Now, as he closed in on the wreckage, illuminated by the glow of the moon, he found he could still easily imagine the untouched windmill's presence on the landscape. Maybe not all was lost.

The four sails had been knocked down and were lying in pieces on the ground. But the main structure, it wasn't all lost. The windows were all broken out, and boards were missing and pieces of the tower were scorched. Flames had eaten away much of the cap before being doused by the heavy rain. And broken pieces of siding were scattered everywhere, leaving Brian wondering if he could figure out which piece was important, which piece went where. Was it possible that the windmill could be repaired?

Could Brian bring the windmill back to life?

He finished his lemonade and set the glass down, and then he sat himself down in the grass and stared at the structure, just as he had the night before, but this time he had an idea.

He decided right then and there. He knew what needed to be done. He would rebuild the windmill. But just as suddenly, he realized how foolish a thought that really was. After all, what did he know of construction, much less restoration? Or windmills?

That night, as he drifted off to sleep, a wise old man's mantra came to him. "Always we must tilt at windmills," he had said, and seemed to be saying again in these ever-hopeful dreams. "But they turn and they turn, and you live."

*T*he phone woke him at seven o'clock. He grabbed it on the first ring.

"Hello."

"Brian, it's Cynthia."

"What's wrong?"

"Oh, Brian, you need to get here—now."

"What's going on?"

"I'm scared. They've taken Annie away for some tests—but they're not very forthcoming with information. Brian, Annie . . . she didn't look good. There was no color in her face. I've never seen her like that."

He felt his heart fall, felt tears threaten to flood his eyes. "I'll call Gerta and be there as soon as I can."

He hung up the phone and got out of bed. That's when he noticed Janey standing in the doorway, the cordless phone in her trembling hands. She'd heard the entire conversation. Brian's face went white as he realized the horrible implications. They'd tried so hard to keep Janey from harm, and they'd failed. She knew as much as they did, that the situation with Annie was more serious than any one of them wanted to let on, much less speak of.

The poor girl. He wanted to take her, hold her, comfort her, and tell *her that everything would be fine, that her mother would be fine. But he couldn't, and not only because he feared it might not be true but because she didn't give him a chance.*

"Janey . . ." he started to say.

She gave Brian no chance to catch her as she dropped the phone, its hard plastic making a loud clack on the hardwood floor, and tore out of the room, out of the house, and out of sight.

"Janey!" Brian called out from the hallway, but the only answer was the empty echo of a lonely house. No reply came, not then, and not an hour later after his exhaustive search.

Brian stood on the front porch calling out her name, his voice growing hoarse. He dropped to the wooden steps, cradled himself, fought back tears. He thought of Janey, her trembling lips and all that she'd heard. She shouldn't be alone, not now. Except she was, alone and lonely and afraid.

Brian was afraid, too, and silently sent a wish on the wind, hoping it was carried north, where it would be heard by a woman lying silently in a hospital bed. Annie had to reawaken, and Janey needed to see her. First, though, he had to find the little girl.

"Janey," he murmured to himself. "Where are you?"

For the first time since the accident, Brian realized the seriousness of the situation. Annie could die, and if she did, God, how would Janey survive another devastating loss? Who would be there for Janey?

PART TWO

APRIL

FOUR

You hear about the unparalleled beauty of the autumnal landscape in upstate New York and New England, and like thousands of New Yorkers, people make the trek to catch the fall foliage in all its splendor. But spring comes a close second in its allure, with trees blooming after the harsh winter weather and birds chirping in delight of the approaching warmth of summer. And today was a perfect spring day and a perfect day for driving. The road was mine and mine alone.

As my car crested the green hills somewhere along one of the Hudson River Valley's rural routes, an unexpected and wondrous image caught my eye, and temporarily I lost the way of the road. As my car's tires scrabbled against the gravel on the road's shoulder, I pulled the wheel to the left and corrected my aim down this tiny stretch of seemingly forgotten highway. But my eye wandered again, darting back and forth from object to road, until finally I caught a beautiful sight from the corner of my eye. I knew I had to back up, to see it up close. So I pulled over to the side of the road and got out of the car, where a clean burst of air filled my lungs. I sighed with contentment, a not unfamiliar feeling these days.

For the past six weeks I'd found myself relaxing and opening up. I would smile often and wide while traveling the countryside, caring little where the road went, just so long as I encountered more road and more still, smooth black pavement that urged me forward. Thoughts of my former life were behind me, dust along the hundreds of miles of road I'd already traversed. Days slipped by, then weeks, as road after road blurred, the landscape of wild growing grass and giant trees gently waving in the breeze now so familiar that it no longer caught my attention. But now, here before me, was truly something to see, something unique.

Rising up from the ground before me, shooting what seemed to be hundreds of feet into the air, was a solitary and majestic windmill, its four latticelike sails slowly turning in the light wind. Like the kind found dotting the landscape of foreign countries in a children's fairy tale, it was an arresting vision that awakened my imagination. I felt as though I'd been transported into a new time and place, where innocence and beauty are cherished. I had no idea why, but I had to see the windmill up close, and so my feet moved me forward, across the two-lane road and up into the high grass of the adjacent field.

The windmill was about two hundred feet from me, the only thing visible on this swath of land, its four sails like a Ferris wheel, touching near to the ground, only to spin upward to the waiting sky. It was set against an azure backdrop, making me feel as though I were staring into a giant postcard. The world I'd known just moments ago seemed to fade right around me, leaving me with the windmill and nothing else. Was this reality? How often do you see such a grand thing?

I started to move a bit closer, and that was when someone else joined me in my picture-perfect world. From over a distant hill came a small child, her long blond hair trailing behind her fast-moving body. Her arms were outstretched, as though she were embracing the wind, waiting for it to catch her and lift her and take her far, far away. Instead she took a tumble, and her tiny body started to roll uncontrollably down the hill. The windmill temporarily cut off my sight line, but then she reappeared, still rolling and rolling. The forces of motion diminished as she reached the bottom of the hill, and her body flopped to a stop. She lay flat against the ground, looking upward. She wasn't moving.

A short intake of breath caused me to freeze in my tracks. Then I came to my senses and ran to see if she needed help. The windmill loomed before me, and then I was beside it and the giant sails churned and I was struck by how unreal this entire scene seemed. Again I was reminded of a children's story, and I wondered if maybe I were some kind of prince, coming to the rescue of a fair maiden. By the time I reached the little girl, she was already using her elbows to prop herself up, and I noticed that her curious gaze fell directly on me.

"Hi," she said.

"Hi back. Are you okay?"

She scrunched up her nose at me. "Why wouldn't I be okay?"

"Because you fell?"

She let out a small giggle. "No, I didn't. I was just playing a game. The hill is very good for rolling. But it makes me dizzy, so I have to wait for the world to stop spinning before I get up. Once, I didn't wait and I fell back down, that time for real."

"I see," I said, grinning. She was a cute kid, with a smattering of freckles across her nose and a clear bright smile that gave the sun a run for its shine. She wore a pair of dungarees and a pink shirt, and there was a matching pink ribbon in her hair. Without much experience around kids, it was hard to tell her age, but I guessed it was around seven or eight. "Well," I continued, "as long as you're all right, I guess I should be moving on."

"Okay," she replied.

I gave her one last look before walking back through the silky green grass. A second later, she was right by my side, matching me step for step. I looked down at her and she looked up at me.

"You seem nice," she suddenly told me.

"Well, I *am* nice," I said, thrown off by this little girl's openness. It occurred to me that I shouldn't linger and I shouldn't encourage her, because, honestly, I was a stranger and she was an innocent little girl and this was the nineties, and people were suspicious.

"Where are your parents?" I asked.

"My mom's up at the house. Making lunch. I get impatient waiting for her to cook it. *Impatient,* that's Momma's word. So sometimes I go for a quick run to the windmill and back. It's fun." She cocked her head with curiosity. "My name's Janey."

"Janey?"

"My mom, she likes names that end with a *y.* I've heard her say it's her way of keeping me young, but I'm not going to be young forever. Someday I'll be Jane. That's my real name."

Janey was a real charmer. "I like *Janey,* too. It suits you."

"What's your name?"

"Brian."

"Briany," she said, and then giggled. "That sounds yucky."

"Yes, it does."

We had reached the windmill and I stopped, figuring this was probably a good place to break off our entertaining conversation. I had to get back to the car and my journey and she had to get back to lunch. Standing in the noonday sun, though, surrounded by the luscious greenery of the valley and the leafy trees and this wondrous windmill, I felt overcome with emotion. I stole another look up at the windmill. It was a simple wooden structure about forty feet tall, with a door that led inside and a series of windows on a second floor, which was surrounded by a catwalk. Atop the structure was a cap, which housed the spinning mechanism. Up close it was even more magnificent and words escaped me as I stood transfixed.

"You like the windmill?" Janey asked.

"It's . . . pretty amazing. Is it yours?"

She nodded her head proudly. "Sometimes I come down to play here. My mom does, too. The windmill is my mom's . . . umm . . . I forget, but it's a big word. She says it makes her feel better."

"I can see why. It's already made me feel better, and I didn't even know I needed cheering up. Well, Janey, it was very nice to meet you, and thank you for telling me about your windmill."

I shook her hand and was enchanted as she curtsied for added effect.

I turned to leave when I heard the little girl say, " 'Bye, Brian," making me sneak a peek back, where her tiny hand energetically waved in the wind. I returned her good-bye, and that's when I saw another figure appear over the hill. A woman, one whom I surmised was Janey's mother.

She quickened her pace, and a hysterical pitch caught in her voice as she repeatedly called out her daughter's name. That's when I realized she couldn't see Janey, whose little body was blocked by the windmill. Just me, a strange man on her property. I couldn't blame her for panicking. I thought it best to stand where I was, not run away. Startling her was bad enough; I didn't want to scare her, too. Janey, meanwhile, had decided this was a game, and she opened the door to the windmill and hid behind it.

The woman reached the windmill, emerging between two of the sails as they passed down a few feet above her head, and looked squarely at me. We were separated by no more than twenty feet.

"Where is she? What have you done—" The woman hurtled her accusation while trying to grab her breath and ended up stopping midsentence.

I pointed to the door, slightly ajar. A small face peered through the diamond-shaped window and then quickly dropped out of sight. I offered up an innocent shrug, like a child might do when caught red-handed, which only seemed to infuriate Janey's mom further.

"Don't move," she warned me, and I stuck my hands in the air like a criminal caught in the act, a poor attempt at lightening up the situation that went unappreciated. Then she opened the door to the windmill and stood her ground. "Janey, get out here this instant."

A mother's tone of voice can dictate the direction of any scene. Looking contrary, Janey emerged from her hideout. Truthfully, the girl hadn't done anything wrong, except for maybe scaring her mother, but she saved any explanation for later. Right now she knew to let the fear run its course.

"Are you okay, sweetie?" her mother asked, crouching on her knees. Yet she kept an eye on me, making sure I didn't move. I didn't.

"I'm fine, Momma. Just playing."

Her mother frowned. "I'm not sure I approve of this game . . . and who, may I ask, were you playing with?" She gave me a steely look that said that if she heard one wrong word, I was toast.

"I was playing with Brian—he's nice," Janey said, and there was a cute lilt to her voice that hinted at the curious and friendly girl I'd met just moments ago. Her mother seemed to hear it, too, and she lessened her grip on her daughter's arm.

"I didn't mean—" I started, only to be cut off.

"Who are you and what are you doing on my property?" she asked, walking toward me with cautious determination. I had to admit she seemed pretty gutsy, considering the circumstances. Intruders on her land weren't an everyday occurrence for her, no doubt, but here she was protecting not just her territory but also her child. Fear and anger overtook rational behavior. Good thing, as Janey had pointed out, that I was nice.

"It's an easy explanation," I said, and with her now just a few feet before me (with her hands planted firmly on her hips), I launched into my short, innocuous tale of pulling to the side of the road and wanting to see the windmill up close. "Truth was, I hadn't considered that it could be someone's property. I guess I thought it was county land or something. Anyway, that's when I saw your little girl take a tumble down the hill and I went to see that she was okay . . ."

Janey had come up beside her mother, grabbing hold of her arm. "That's why he's nice, Momma, 'cause he came to my rescue. Maybe what if I was hurt? Which I'm not," she quickly added, to stave off an attack of the worries. Janey and I exchanged smiles. Her mother failed to join in our exchange.

"Look, Mrs. . . ."

"Sullivan. Annie Sullivan," she said.

"No wonder she likes names ending with a *y* sound," I said to Janey, "because her name does."

Janey started to giggle, and I let out a short laugh, too. Annie looked at the two of us like we were co-conspirators, which in effect, we were. For someone not looking for trouble, I seemed to be doing a good job of inviting it now. I sensed a little blond-haired devil's influence.

"You learned an awful lot about my daughter in a short amount of time."

Again, I raised my hands in innocent protest. "I only asked her name. Janey volunteered the rest."

"And I didn't catch your name," she said.

"Yes, you did, Momma; he's Brian. And he's nice."

"Brian Duncan," I said, and this time I extended my hand to Annie. She accepted only because Janey pressed her to. Our hands touched, fingers suddenly interlocked by a firm grasp that seemed to hide unspoken words. She had a strong grip and held my hand for a moment. It gave me the chance to gauge her anger level. There was a slight gleam in her eyes that could have been a reflection of the sun. Maybe her fear was dissipating.

Annie Sullivan, anyone could see, and it happened to be my privilege to do so at the moment, was a beautiful woman. Her soft face was rounded and highlighted by bright cheeks, and her eyes were brown, filled with limitless expression. Her hair, shoulder length, was noticeably darker than her daughter's, a rich chestnut brown with hints of auburn highlights, depending on the slant of the light. She, too, wore dungarees, along with a blue print blouse that was untucked and splattered with what appeared to be paint.

"Well, Mr. Duncan, it appears I owe you an apology . . ."

"No, no—you were completely justified in your reaction. Heck, I'm just some strange guy who suddenly appeared on your land. You've been very understanding. I won't take up any more of your time." I bowed slightly to Annie, and then to Janey. "Good-bye, Janey. I have to leave and you need to eat your lunch."

She put a hand to her mouth in surprise. "I forgot! Thanks, Brian. 'Bye."

Annie instructed her daughter to go on ahead, that her sandwich was ready and the soup would have to be reheated. She'd join her in a moment. Then she turned back to me, shook my hand again, and thanked me for being so nice and thoughtful and caring.

"There aren't many people in the world you can trust these days," she said.

Annie was speaking my language.

"There are a couple of us left," I said, and our hands parted. She turned away and so did I, both of us going our separate ways.

To my surprise, she called out my name—not my last but my first.

"Yes?" I asked.

"You really like my windmill?"

The windmill. I'd nearly forgotten it in the face of such mortal beauty. For a split second, my eyes returned to the old mill before falling back on Annie's sun-touched face. I recalled the man from the jewelry store in New York, and his enigmatic phrase about tilting at windmills, how his lesson had come from nowhere, not unlike the windmill itself. And Annie, too, appearing from atop that faraway hill, plucked from some magical world and dropped into mine.

"I like your windmill very much. I've never seen something quite so majestic."

Her face lit up as though I'd complimented her, and she thanked me before we again turned our backs to each other. I was certain I could still see that smile, somewhat reluctant but spreading with an exponential warmth, which happened to mirror my own.

I returned to my car, and by the time I drove away, Annie Sullivan had disappeared from view. So, too, had the windmill.

But both images lingered long in my mind.

*　　　*　　　*

I'd driven east, then west, and also north and south, and many times I'd gone in no particular direction. No point of the compass had a hold on me, and my aimless journey continued, but to where and for what purpose, I still had no idea. The fun was in the finding and now, six weeks since I'd left my former life, I'd gotten the first sign that maybe I was heading in the right direction. The reason? That impossibly placed windmill, and the two utterly charming women who had instantly beguiled me.

I drove for only three more miles when I came to the nearest stretch of civilization, a little village by the name of Linden Corners. Population 724, established in 1887, or so said a wooden sign posted at the edge of the village. LINDEN CORNERS WELCOMES YOU, read another sign. I had the feeling that had I blinked, I'd have missed the whole town.

There are lots of places like this all over New York State, and in the Hudson River Valley, lots, too, that include the word *Corners* in their name, solidifying the already quaint feel so prevalent in this region. A favorite of city weekenders, the Hudson River Valley is rich with antique shops and B&Bs and fruit stands and lots of history, which is preserved in lovingly kept homes and museums. *Charm* is a word often used to describe this lush region, and Linden Corners was photographic proof of the word. Along with a variety of shops situated along the road, a hardware store, two antique dealers, an old-fashioned general store, and a trading post, Linden Corners boasted a lovely park that was lined with great elm trees budding with new life, and, at its center, a gazebo, white with black trim. Benches lined the park's perimeter, and there were people sitting, walking, all enjoying a perfectly sun-drenched spring day.

Passing through Linden Corners was happenstance, of course, as I could have taken any number of rural roads in my quest to cross out of New York and into Massachusetts. So the fact that I found myself drawn to the quiet charm of this hidden gem, beckoned first by its neighboring windmill, I wondered if something spiritual had pulled me in this direction. Seeking quiet contemplation, I decided here was as good a place as any to rest.

I imagined little Janey Sullivan sitting down for her midday meal, and my stomach grumbled. I'd already been on the road five hours today, having left Rochester around seven o'clock following a quick breakfast. The idea of a sandwich, maybe grabbing a bench in the village park to eat it, pushed itself to the forefront of my mind. Trouble was, this wasn't New York, where delis occupied every corner.

So I began to look for a suitable lunch spot and saw, a short distance away, a plastic sign overhanging a small building. It read MARTHA'S FIVE O'CLOCK DINER, an interesting name. Doubt crept into my thoughts, though, since there were just two other cars in the graveled lot. Hunger overrode my concerns, and I stepped out of the car and breathed in the fresh air.

My fears were unfounded. I liked the bright and sunny decor immediately and was overwhelmed by the most incredible smells coming from the kitchen. Old '50s music played on a jukebox, and a young woman behind the counter bopped along—until she caught sight of me. She gave me a welcome wave and offered me my choice, counter service or a booth. I noticed there was only one other customer, a lone guy sitting at the counter.

"The lunch rush is over, so it's your call," she said. Her nametag read SARA.

"Thanks, Sara. A booth will be fine."

"You've got your choice there, too."

Indeed I did. There were six empty booths along the far wall. I chose the one closest, with Sara following close on my heels, a pad and pen at the ready.

"Do you know what you'd like?" she asked.

"A menu?" I ventured.

"It's not very tasty," she said, to my surprise. "Would you like fries with that?" And then she laughed at her own joke. She called out to the kitchen. "Hey, Martha, I finally got to use the menu joke, the one you were going on about when I started." She turned back to me. "Six weeks, I've worked here, waiting to get my first good joke in."

And still waiting, I could have added but didn't.

From the kitchen door emerged a short, stout woman who was probably fifty years old at best, with short black hair and green eyes that reminded me of a cat's. "Sara, leave the nice man be. Honestly, that joke is older than my coffee."

The look on my face must have revealed a sudden fear, because both women howled with laughter, slapping each other on the shoulder. I offered up my best helpless look and they laughed again.

"You two are funny. You could take the routine on the road."

"We have. Where do you think we find the meat for our stew?" And again they were lost in a tempest of laughter. As amusing as they were, roadkill jokes on an empty stomach wouldn't bring out my personal laugh track.

The woman named Martha then held out her hand, I guess as a peace offering. "I'm Martha Martinson, proprietor, chef, frustrated stand-up comic."

"Hi," I said. "Brian Duncan. Just passing through."

"Faster than my oatmeal," she said, quickly adding an apology. "Sorry. I promise—no more food jokes. Sometimes I just can't control myself. It's just not often I get the chance to let loose, 'cause usually when strangers drop by, it's peak cooking time. No time for Martha's shenanigans. So, do you really want a menu? I can whip up anything you like."

"Half a grapefruit, a BLT on toasted wheat, and an iced tea."

"Coming up," Martha said with a smile, only to retreat then

to the kitchen, leaving Sara the waitress with me. She looked about twenty and wore a lot of makeup.

"As long as I'm waiting for my food, can I ask you a question?" I said.

She winked at me. I noticed the guy sitting at the counter was watching this entire exchange with bemusement. "I'm legal, if that's what you're wondering, and I sure hope you are. How long you planning on staying?"

"Sara!" came an admonishing sound from the kitchen.

Sara blushed, then leaned in and whispered, "Eagle Ears."

"You got that right!" replied Eagle Ears.

"Back to my original question," I ventured. "I was just curious—why is this place called the Five O'clock? It's an unusual name for a diner, don't you think?"

"Nope. It's simple really; just gotta know our routine around these parts. Most of the workers here are early risers—farmers, factory workers—and at that hour, they're hungry. So we've got a morning rush at five, and then the dinner rush twelve hours later. Oftentimes it's the same folks, too lazy to cook for themselves. So we call it the Five O'clock 'cause the other hours just don't matter."

"Hah!" came a voice from behind us. The man from the counter had ventured over to join us; guess conversations were fair play in this town and folks could stick their two cents in. He was probably closing in on fifty, but a weathered fifty, and was dressed in faded jeans.

"They call it the Five-O because five minutes after you eat the food, your body says, 'Uh-oh.'" He guffawed at his tasteless joke.

"Chuck, shut up and get out. Don't you have a store to run?"

Chuck started off, then turned back, looking squarely at me. "Don't get too comfortable here. Town like this will suck you dry. Look at me."

Truth be known, he looked like he could use a dry period. I waited until he left, and then turned my attention back to Sara. "Anyway, the Five-O? Five o'clock seems awfully early in the morning."

"The early bird gets the worm," Sara remarked.

"But we don't charge extra," came Martha's quick retort, along with a plate full of food that could have fed three people easily. The bacon was piled high under a thick slab of homemade bread.

"That sandwich come with heart surgery?" I asked.

They found that funny. I was kind of serious but let it go and began eating, tentatively at first but eventually with gusto. The food was delicious, the bacon crisp and laced with a hickory maple flavor that brought my tastebuds alive. Both women watched me eat from behind the counter, and neither tried to act discreet. When I was done, they cleared the plate away and Martha came by with a slice of a warm raspberry pie.

"On me—on account of the bad jokes. And don't let Chuck Ackroyd get you. His wife left him a while ago and he's been bitter ever since. We ignore him and so should you."

"Thanks," I said, realizing I couldn't eat another bite. Still, it would have been rude to refuse. Martha was so damned pleased with my appetite—and so hospitable—she joined me in the booth, sitting opposite me.

"So, Brian Duncan Just Passing Through, how long you staying?"

"With food this good, maybe years."

"Now that's a fine compliment. You come back tomorrow morning, I'll fix you scrambled eggs like you've never tasted."

"That would require an overnight stay."

"So? You in a hurry to get somewhere? Some woman waiting for you?"

At first I thought this was just harmless conversation, but

her expression told me otherwise. She was serious—about the eggs. Was I in a hurry? I had no set plans, no idea where I would be tomorrow, much less two hours from now. So I shook my head, no hurry.

"Then it's settled. Sara, call Richie over at the Solemn Nights and book a room for our new friend, Brian Duncan Just Passing Through."

"Well, wait . . . I was only—"

"Hush up, you. Some good cooking for a couple of days will do you good. Put a smile on your face—looks like you could use one."

I gave her a surprised look.

"I know a broken heart when I see one," she said. "Least I can do is keep the stomach full and content. That's truly how to make a man happy." And she smiled again, her penciled-in eyebrows raised as if daring me to contradict her.

So I paid my tab, left a healthy tip for the comic duo, and listened as Martha gave me directions to the motel. On my way out, she yelled, "See you bright and early. Five o'clock."

Even though the door had closed behind me, I could still hear their raucous laughter.

As I returned to my car, the events of the past couple hours ran through my mind. If the windmill had gotten me to Linden Corners, then Martha's old-fashioned cooking and hospitality encouraged me to stay, for a little while at least.

Linden Corners had a plan for me, and it was gently tearing at my defenses. I guess I was staying.

There was no better example of just how small Linden Corners was than when I pulled into the empty lot of the Solemn Nights Motel, a short half-mile outside of the village limits. The owner, a man who was very tall, very thin, very pale, stood in the door frame of the office, waving at me and smiling a grin full of crooked teeth. Obviously, not only had Sara called ahead but she'd also been generously forthcoming with details. I shut off the engine and shuffled out of the car once again, the third time in as many hours. Linden Corners seemed to have a lock on my actions. As I ventured up the stairs, the lanky fellow welcomed me to his inn.

"Won't find a better bargain for miles, Mr. Duncan."

"Looks very comfy."

"Oh, it's that and more," he said. "I'm Richie Ravens. I own the joint."

"Nice to be here," I said, taking in the lay of the land.

The Solemn Nights Motel was one oblong building with ten rooms, not unlike many roadside motels. But although some looked poorly kept, the Solemn Nights had a nice sheen and polish. It looked freshly painted, and there were small tables and chairs on the elongated deck set before each room. I was encouraged. Martha Martinson's unavoidable mothering influence, no doubt. Or maybe they treated all strangers this way. Or maybe yet, the windmill had indeed transported me back to a simpler time when people were nice and looked out for one another. Whatever, the Solemn Nights Motel lured me in. Even Richie Ravens, as odd as he appeared, proved agreeable.

He got me checked in, giving me a good rate for one night and a better one for two, and I found myself accepting the two-night deal without a second thought. What I planned to do for two days in this town hadn't yet occurred to me, but wasn't that what my trip was all about, going with the flow, taking situations as they came and exploring their possibilities? Richie talked a mile a minute during the entire check-in process, not really about anything in particular, mainly spouting off about the busy season, where he had to keep a waiting list.

"Weekends in the summer, forget about it. Booked solid. But it's slow these days, especially the weekdays, so I'm glad to have the company. How 'bout room nine? It's close to the ice machine."

I said that was fine, and we finished up our business and he handed me a key. I felt a momentary pang of regret leaving him alone, since he seemed to enjoy having someone to talk to. I was having separation anxiety from myself. This was the most I'd conversed with people since leaving New York, save for a few days spent at the end of March with my family in Philadelphia. (My parents, by the way, hadn't exactly looked on my plans with favor, but they did notice that my worry lines had dissipated, though I looked too thin from the hepatitis. Good with the bad, a mixed blessing, they claimed.)

The effects of my illness were mostly gone, too, but at times waves of fatigue washed over me. Now was one of those moments. So I grabbed my stuff from the car, opened up room 9, and plopped down on what turned out to be a surprisingly comfortable bed. I turned on the television, caught a bit of CNN, and fell asleep to the sound of a *Larry King Live* commercial. His guest was . . .

The next thing I knew, it was dark outside and a cool breeze was coming in through the open window. An alarm clock on the side table indicated it was 7:35 P.M. I'd been asleep four hours, and I felt refreshed. As such, I considered the evening's plans. Hanging around a motel room was not high on my list, so I left the room, hopped in the car—noticing that there were no others in the lot, not even Richie's—and drove back toward town.

I quickly discovered how it was possible this town got started at five in the morning—by nightfall, the streets were deserted and a quiet lull had settled in the air. My car was the lone one on the road, making me think that maybe it was later, like 2:00 A.M., and that the clock at the motel was wrong. The clock tower above the Hudson Valley Savings Bank, however, confirmed the time. As I drove on, I saw just one lively burst of life, at a local tavern called Connors' Corners, which looked like it was once someone's house, complete with a wraparound porch and a second floor. As if someone who used to have a lot of parties just gave up and started charging his friends, putting in neon BUDWEISER and SARANAC signs in the windows for ambiance. There were four other cars in the small lot, and mine joined them. I hopped aboard the porch, opened the screen door, and entered a dimly lit room that smelled just how it should—like a bar.

There were five other people inside, not counting the bartender, who was a tall older gentleman with a thick shock of white-gray hair and spectacles. He wore an apron and a smile, and he welcomed me with the hackneyed line, "What'll it be?"

For lack of something better to do, the other patrons watched as I ordered, making me self-conscious when I asked for just a plain seltzer. I skipped the wedge of lime. As soon as the words were out of my mouth, the patrons turned away, clearly uninterested. The bartender, however, seemed unfazed and poured the drink.

I took a seat, took a sip, and sampled my surroundings. Nothing much out of the ordinary. A long, smooth wooden bar, a series of stools keeping it company. Behind it, a row of colored bottles. Over it, a deer's head. There were a couple of tables with chairs scattered throughout the room, and in the corner was a large pool table, currently being ignored. So was the jukebox, the regulars opting instead for television, which had a ball game on ESPN. The boys of summer, playing at the height of springtime.

"Who's playing?" I asked.

"Mets. Winning of course," said the bartender. "So, how do you find the Solemn Nights?"

For some reason, I wasn't surprised he knew about me. Small-town life—the only thing that travels fast is gossip. A newcomer in town, even for just a day or so, caused a burning up of the phone lines. So I just replied that it was fine.

"George Connors," he said, introducing himself.

"Brian Duncan," I said.

"Just Passing Through."

Then I smiled. "Let me guess—the five-o'clock dinner spe-cial at the Five O'clock."

He nodded with approval. "You'll do just fine here. Except those in the know just refer to it as the Five-O."

I felt a pleasant sensation ripple down my spine. These uniquely friendly folk were doing their best to make life here comfortable for me—unusual, since just over eight hours ago I'd never heard of their town or met any of them. Suddenly, though, Linden Corners and the Five-O and the Solemn Nights and even Connors' Corners were more familiar to me than the nineteenth-floor offices of Beckford Warfield and my apartment on East 83rd Street. Now, Martha Martinson and Richie Ravens and George Connors acted like new best friends, easygoing and approachable. Faces from New York faded from memory, as though a great deal of time were slipping by.

So we chatted, George and I, in between pitches and hits and strikeouts, and the occasional distraction of another patron wanting a refill on a draft. George pulled the tap with the style of someone long practiced in the art of serving beer, and I said so, launching George on the history of Connors' Corners. Turned out that he was a third-generation bartender—lived his whole life in Linden Corners and took over running the bar twenty years earlier when his dad retired, only to die a year later from boredom, or so George claimed.

"Heck, I'm sixty-nine, believe it or not, nine years older than my dad when he gave me the place. Nowadays the wife is bugging me to retire, but I just can't do it. Maybe cutting back on hours someday, but until that day comes, I'm here until mid-night, every night except Sunday."

"Where's the fourth generation?" I asked.

"Humph. Good Lord saw fit to give me four beautiful daughters, none of whom showed any interest in pouring drinks and then watching folks pour 'em down their throats. But that's fine, since I've got grandchildren galore." He paused a moment, saw my empty seltzer glass, and asked if I wanted a refill.

"Sure."

"So, what's the problem?" His head nodded toward the booze, and my surprised reaction must have been pretty obvious. "Oh, there are no secrets in Linden Corners, so you might as well come clean."

"It's not what you think . . ." I started to explain.

"Not thinking anything," he said. "One thing I've learned in my years behind this counter—never assume too much about a man. And forget that 'you make an ass of you and me' baloney—only makes *me* the ass."

"Health. Six-month sabbatical from alcohol."

He nodded. "Liver stuff, huh? Gotta be careful there."

And that was that. He dropped the subject and directed his attention back to the Mets. They were still winning.

Time passed and a couple of people left; a couple new ones showed up. I sat alone and content, enjoying the congenial atmosphere, the sense of belonging that George had effortlessly instilled in me. Finally, around ten o'clock, the game ended (the Mets won) and I'd had my fill of seltzer. I got up to leave. I realized, though, that I was feeling a bit restless.

"You're a man in search of something to do," George said. "Beware my daddy's lesson in boredom." A smile brightened his craggy features. "You know, just occurred to me, this great idea. How'd you like to close up shop for me?"

"Excuse me?"

"Clean a few glasses, turn the lights off, and then lock the front door. It's real simple."

"But . . . you don't even know me."

"Call me a good judge of character, Brian. Look, the wife'll be pleased to see me early, and truth be known, I'm tuckered out tonight. Grandkids were visiting this past weekend and they ran me ragged. What do you say? I can't trust any of these fools"—he pointed to the three men who also sat at the bar— "'cause they'll help themselves to the tap. You—I can trust you, Brian Duncan."

And before I could answer yes or no, he tossed off his apron, came around the bar, and handed me a key.

"Midnight, kick these boys out." Then he told his regulars that Brian Duncan Just Passing Through would be tending bar the rest of the night and to be nice, to try not to rook him. He patted me on the shoulder. "You'll do just fine, son. All they drink is beer, three bucks a draft, no tabs. Good luck. Come by tomorrow to return the key; we'll see how you did."

"But George . . ."

I was still sitting on the bar stool, watching as George ignored my pleas on his way out the door and into the dark night. The screen door closed with a loud *thwack* that reverberated through the quiet bar. I spun around and found the patrons looking at me, all of them with empty or near-empty glasses.

"Refill, guys?" I said, attempting a smile and failing miserably.

They pushed their mugs forward expectantly, and suddenly, I was put to work. I was gainfully employed in Linden Corners.

FIVE

Before I knew it, two days had passed and still Linden Corners held me in its appealingly quaint grip. It was Thursday afternoon and I'd just returned from a trip up to Albany, where I'd done some shopping and enjoyed a quick lunch in the downtown area of New York's capital. Though not a renowned urban center like New York City, Albany showed itself to be a serious town with serious issues to contend with, and the sight of the state government in action, men and women dressed up in power suits, cell phones practically glued to their ears, made me long for the small-town pace of Linden Corners.

Truth be told, I'd been having a good time in Linden Corners and was eager to return. I'd taken Martha up on her suggestion, trying her scrambled eggs and easily finding much to rave about, though I confess I hadn't exactly arrived for the five-o'clock rush. I'd also filled in at Connors' Corners Wednesday night, not a spur-of-the-moment decision but something planned the night before, so George could have more than a couple hours off. In fact, he showed up only to open up at four in the afternoon, then left me alone for what turned out to be a very long eight-hour shift. Word had gotten around about the new guy, so folks showed up for a drink, a game of pool, and a little bit of small-town gossip, of which I was the big topic. Well, it ended up being a fun night, with Sara the waitress stopping by after work, glad to have me wait on her, all the while batting her eyelashes at me. Turned out she was twenty-two, but as the saying goes, Thanks but no thanks.

This morning I'd bypassed the major highway, opting for the backroads tour through the countryside all the way up to Albany, memorizing the route for the return trip. There were a couple places that had attracted my eye, including a roadside fruit stand a couple miles north of Linden Corners. It was coming up again, on my left, and I decided to check it out. Hanging around the motel, it was nice to have a snack handy, and given the lingering effects of the hepatitis, fruit was the right choice. There was a small wooden sign posted alongside the road, reminding drivers that the fruit stand was just over the next hill, and indeed it was, a series of four connected buildings, with wide wooden doors held open by white-painted stands overflowing with vegetables and fruit. With about a dozen cars in the lot and a couple more pulling in and out, it was clear this was no well-kept secret.

KNIGHT'S FRUITS, read a hand-painted sign on the building's roof.

I milled about with the other locals, picking out ripe red strawberries and grapes and cherries—some apples and oranges, too. Adding a plastic container of freshly squeezed orange juice to the basket, I decided I had plenty and headed to the checkout area. The woman behind the makeshift counter smiled pleasantly at me and asked if this was my first time at the market. She, too, had a friendly demeanor, with a smile full of white, gleaming teeth and a big pile of blond hair that curled naturally around her pretty face.

"First—maybe not last. We'll see."

"You must be Brian Duncan," she said. "I'm Cynthia Knight; my husband and I own this place. We live down the road from Annie Sullivan."

I couldn't hide my surprise, since I figured my encounter with Annie Sullivan had long gone off her radar. A mother with a seven-year-old girl had other things to think about. But still . . . the windmill flashed in my mind, and so did Janey, running through the field, her mother trying to catch her.

"Annie Sullivan told you about me?"

"Sort of. More like Janey."

"Ah," I said, handing over money for my purchases. We exchanged a bit more small talk, then I let her get on with the customers behind me, none of whom appeared upset or annoyed by the lack of movement in the line. Once it was their turn, Cynthia was all chatter with them, too. Good food, good service, good people. Could be Linden Corners' motto.

I was back at my car when I heard someone call out my name. I turned and saw little Janey Sullivan stepping out of the passenger side of a beat-up old pickup. She jumped down to the ground, waving wildly at me.

"It's Brian! Wow! It's Brian!"

Then, without looking, she darted out into the parking lot and started to run toward me. I sensed something was wrong, something dreadful, and out of the corner of my eye I saw a car backing up, the driver unaware of what—*who*—was behind her. Neither was Janey, meaning the two were headed for a collision. Annie wasn't even out of the truck yet, but she saw what was happening, and her mouth opened in terror.

"Janey!" she screamed out.

But that only made the situation worse, because Janey came to a sharp stop at the sound of her mother's frightened voice. I acted fast, dropping my sack of fruit to the ground as I raced forward, calling out to the driver to stop. To no avail—the radio was turned on loud, and besides, Janey was standing in the woman's blind spot.

I reached Janey just in time, scooping her up into my arms, which caused her to scream out. But it was not with alarm. Janey thought this was just an extension of the game we'd played the other day, and that's when it occurred to me that she wasn't even aware of what had almost happened. The car missed us both by about six inches, then drove off the lot and onto the highway. An oblivious driver like that had no business being on the road.

But at least Janey was safe.

I carried her over to the pickup, let down the back latch, and stood her on the flatbed. She jumped up and down with delight, as the other people in the parking lot watched with great relief. Seems Janey was the only one who missed all the excitement. A few folks came by, offering up kind words, thanking me for being in the right place at the right time.

One person who seemed not to share this gratitude was Annie Sullivan.

"What is it with you, mister?" she said to me.

Why was she angry at me and not at the idiot driver? "In

case you don't realize it, I just saved your daughter from being hit by that car."

"Well . . . it seems lately that every time I have reason to panic over my daughter, you're nearby."

"Maybe you shouldn't be panicking," I suggested, angry all of a sudden over her accusation. She appeared about to say something and then changed her mind. Instead, she pushed past me and looked up at her daughter, who was watching the two of us with confusion. "Honey, are you all right?"

"Yeah."

"Honey, how have I told you to answer?"

Janey rolled her eyes. "Yes. Yes, I'm fine. No 'yup' or 'yeah' or 'uh-huh.' "

"Wise guy," Annie said.

"I'm a wise girl," Janey said, trying to lighten the mood. "Why are you mad at Brian?"

Annie hesitated and stole a steely glance at me before replying. "Janey, I don't want you to ever run so carelessly again—in a busy parking lot, you should know better. And I know you think Brian is nice—and I'm sure he is—but he's a stranger, Janey, and what have I told you time and again? What did I tell you the other day, after the incident by the windmill?"

Janey's bright round eyes dimmed. "I'm sorry, Momma; I won't do it again."

"Okay, baby; it's okay. Let's just go inside and say hi to Cynthia and get you some strawberries." Annie held out her arms and Janey went to them, a tender embrace that showed just how close they were. A team once again, they headed toward the fruit market. Annie said nothing further to me.

As for Janey, she turned and smiled at me and said, "We're having strawberry shortcake for dessert. It's my favorite."

Then they disappeared inside the store, and I returned to my car, picking up the ripped bag of produce. Tossing it in the back,

I hopped in the car. As I was about to pull out, an older woman with gray hair wrapped in a tight bun placed her hands on the driver's door and peered in. Her face was familiar, but from where I couldn't remember.

"You did the right thing, Brian, and Annie's just overreacting." She nodded her head as she spoke. "I'm Gerta Connors—George's wife. We haven't officially met, but I saw you from the car window when George dropped by the tavern the other night."

"Oh—you're all George ever talks about, Mrs. Connors. It's very nice to meet you. And thanks for your supportive words just now. Don't blame Mrs. Sullivan; it's a natural reaction on her part, don't you think? She was more scared than anything. She didn't mean what she said about me, I'm sure."

"Probably you're right," she said, again with that insistent nodding. "Still, haven't seen Annie Sullivan so riled in . . . well, not for a long time." Then, in a quieter voice, Gerta said, "Annie's a widow, you know."

"No, I didn't realize that. I'm sorry to hear it."

"Coming up on two years, I think. Thank goodness for Janey—she's Annie's pride and joy, and I guess maybe today put a little scare into her. Poor dear. Well, I must hasten. I'm making a strawberry pie for George. If you're going to be at the Corner tonight, I'll bring you a slice. Do you like strawberry pie?"

"I don't think I've ever had it," I replied.

"Then you're in for a treat, especially with the Knights' berries. Cynthia's got the magic touch, her berries being so ripe and full of juice."

"You folks sure do know your passions," I said. "Thanks, Gerta; I'll be there."

"Passion, young man," she said, "is the energy of life."

I drove off then, with the promise of sweet pie in my near future.

*   *   *

"They call her the woman who loved the windmill," he said, taking a puff of his pipe and sucking in the sweet, smoky aroma. A cloudy mist circled above his head and then dissipated in the cool night air. It was Sunday night, and I'd been in Linden Corners for nearly a week. "Of course, that's not exactly the right nickname, 'cause it makes it sound like she doesn't care anymore for the windmill, and to say so would be a falsehood."

"So she's actually the woman who *loves* the windmill," I stated. "Present tense."

George Connors gave me a quick nod as he continued to rock in his chair. "Second only to that bundle of energy."

"Janey," I said.

Again, that quick, agreeable nod that seemed to run in the Connors family.

George and Gerta Connors were people of habit, good, up-standing citizens who regularly attended church, living life like good Christians, and that included opening up their home and their hearts to a stranger in search of something he couldn't quite name. Sunday was George's one day off; he'd decided years ago that in observance of the Lord's day, his corner tavern would lock its doors on Saturday night and remain closed all the next day, until four o'clock on Monday afternoon, when it was time again to go to work.

"On Sundays, there's other spirits at work," George told me.

I'd been helping out all week down at Connors' Corners, and I'd refused any sort of remuneration for my duties, which resulted in George's thinking me a damn fool and Gerta's taking a keen interest in my well-being. So when the invitation came for Sunday dinner, there was no refusing. Not that I would have, mind you. These were good folk with big hearts, and aside from some home cooking, company was probably what I needed most. With them, there was no hidden agenda, just a long-married couple whose kids had grown up and moved away and who were happy now to open their home to a soul in need.

It was dark now, after seven, and dinner was over by a couple of hours, the dishes all put away. (I'd insisted on cleaning up, despite Gerta's protests.) Gerta had gone to take a hot plate of food to a friend, a woman in her late seventies who lived alone. George explained this was part of Gerta's routine, giving him a few spare moments to himself on his one day off, a chance to enjoy his pipe without complaint. He and I retired to the porch, where we sat in wicker chairs and watched the sun fall and the stars emerge in the wide-open black sky above.

We'd talked for a while, then sat in silence enjoying the chirping of the crickets out in the field. George and Gerta lived in a small, two-story clapboard house, having moved in when they'd gotten married nearly fifty years earlier. Four girls had grown up here and gone and were now all married with children of their own. The Connors were proud grandparents to eleven kids; while dinner cooked, Gerta had proudly showed me photo albums filled with memories. Beyond the house was a small open field, a rusting swing set at the edge of the field the last reminder of the kids who'd once filled this house with laughter. Seeing the field had brought the windmill to my mind, and so began the conversation that would tell me so much about the woman named Annie Sullivan.

"Gerta tells me Annie's a widow," I said. "Can't be easy for her, raising a young daughter all alone."

"She does okay, Annie does. A good mother—and that Janey? A parent couldn't ask for a happier, more well-adjusted kid. Especially considering the tragedy she's had to know at such a young age." He hung his head low in obvious respect for the dead.

I was uncomfortable discussing Annie in this manner; it felt too much like idle gossip, and I said as much to George.

He puffed on his pipe, saw that it had gone out, and dug for his lighter. Once he had stoked the flame again and round puffs of smoke encircled him, he spoke again. "Well, Brian, I guess some might call it gossip, but you're going to learn all about Annie Sullivan anyway. Whether you learn it from me or Gerta or from someone else in town, or even Annie herself, it's not information that will evade you long."

"First of all, the idea of talking with Annie about the death of her husband doesn't strike me as likely. Or talking about anything else, for that matter. We've met twice—briefly, I might add—both times not under the best of circumstances. Assuming, George, that I'll even be in town for much longer."

"Oh, I think you're misreading our Annie Sullivan. She's a sweet girl—none sweeter in Linden Corners, if you ask me—but she's had a tough time of late, that's for certain. So if she comes off a bit brusque, it's not you she's reacting to. Just circumstance. Word is, Brian, her little girl can't stop talking about you. Calls you the Windmill Man."

"The Windmill Man?" I asked. "She barely knows me."

"I've seen four girls grow from little to big, and if there's one thing I learned, it's that kids make up their own minds, and they do it pretty quickly. Adults, we question people's motives, act all shy and reserved, and it's any wonder we make friends or meet loved ones, given our skittish behavior. Kids, though, they make friends like it's a magic act. Wave a wand and instant best friends. Janey's no different. Living up on that hill, she's pretty removed from town; people think it's not right. But she goes to school, makes easy friends, and, as far as I'm concerned, is a better judge of character than most adults. So if she says she likes you, better know it's genuine."

Having made an impression on Janey left me feeling special, honored. "And so how did you hear about the Windmill Man?"

"Gerta heard it from Cynthia Knight, who heard it right from the horse's mouth, as they say."

The network of small-town talk no longer surprised me, but

it sure did entertain me. "George, I've been in town six days, and already people are talking like I've lived here for years."

He nodded. "That's because you said the magic words."

"Magic words?"

All around us a quiet descended, shushing even the crickets, it seemed. In the sparse light of the porch, blackness just beyond, George rocked in his chair, a smile growing on his weathered face. "The reason you stopped in the first place, Brian, the windmill. You said you liked it, didn't you? Told Janey, told Annie. Believe me, you made an impression."

"And now the town is talking about the Windmill Man?"

"It's not the town that's important, Brian. It's the fact that the Woman Who Loved the Windmill mentioned you. Brian, Annie's not the same effervescent girl she once was. Why, when she came to Linden Corners, she was a wide-eyed beauty who fell in love with a town landmark, saved it, and in turn gave renewed life to this town. We're a grateful town, and so we look after her. After Dan died, she just closed up, kept to herself, and concentrated on raising Janey. And don't get me wrong—she's done a great job, like I've said. But a person can't just shut down emotionally; it's not healthy. You've got to live—not in the past but in the moment and for the future. You young kids don't always see it that way, 'cause wisdom comes with age." He paused, shaking his head. "I'll shut up. Now's not the time for lecturing."

"No, George, believe me—your words are greatly appreciated. More than you know."

"You sure about that?" he said, with a quizzical lift of his eyebrow.

I realized he hadn't been talking just about Annie. Though I'd spilled nothing of my own troubles, it had not taken much for George to see inside me, sensing the issues I'd yet to come to terms with.

"You're a shrewd man, George Connors."

We sat in companionable silence for a while, each alone with his thoughts. Mine turned toward this strange little town and how it had welcomed me with such wide open arms. It couldn't have been because I admitted to being drawn in by the windmill. A building doesn't have such power, and people don't obsess over such things, surely. And this added notion that there was a hidden connection between me and Annie Sullivan, well, that was plain malarkey, the confection of people with too much time on their hands. There was nothing to speak of between us, save for two not-so-wonderful encounters that only left Annie annoyed with me. So she'd spoken of me to her friends, probably in the context of being some weird freak who's taken a liking to her daughter. Then again, George couldn't have made up the Windmill Man part, and a small sense of joy crept into my heart. All this silly speculation, and over a windmill.

Yet its majestic image had not left my mind for any length of time since I'd come to Linden Corners. I'd seen it on my couple of trips out of town and more importantly, I'd seen it in my dreams.

"Tell me about the windmill, George; I want to know its history."

"Don't ask me. Go to the source."

"Annie Sullivan."

"She'll tell you all you want to know, and more."

I looked at him dubiously, and he smiled at me. "Stop thinking about things, Brian. Sometimes you need to just do. Speaking of which, there's something else I want to talk to you about."

"Oh?"

"Gerta lured you here with the promise of her good cooking, and don't get me wrong, the invite was an earnest one on her part. As for me, I've got a proposition for you, and—no, don't try to stop me. Don't interrupt, don't anything. Just hush up and you listen. You've done me a kind service this past week, helping out down at the Corner, giving an old man a chance to enjoy some moonlit nights with his wife—a rare opportunity, given the business I'm in. Summer's coming up, and Gerta and I were thinking of maybe visiting our girls for a couple of weeks, but to do so, I'd have to close the bar. We've done it before, so it's no big deal, really. But I thought as long as you were around, you might enjoy running the place. You're a natural behind the bar, the folks seem to like you, and you pour a mean drink. All essential requirements for the job. Whaddaya say, Brian Duncan Just Passing Through?"

"If I were to accept your offer, I'd have to change my name."

He guffawed, accidentally sucking in smoke. "See what I mean? You're not just quick on your feet, your mind's quick, too, and that's what'll keep the regulars coming back. And who knows? A nice-looking fella like yourself might bring in the younger crowd—those kids who think of Connors' Corners as a saloon for old drunks. Be a real summer draw."

His offer wasn't unexpected—and wasn't unappealing either. But it was scary, too, the prospect of staying in one place for the entire summer, committing what would essentially be the rest of my allotted time on the road. My plan all along was to be back in New York City after Labor Day and pick up where I left off, hopefully more emotionally sound and better prepared for my reentry into the world of corporate America. Would I be satisfied staying the summer in Linden Corners? Or was I destined to live the summer on the road, drive through New England as I'd planned, swim in the ocean, eat lobster, and grow tan from the sun's strong rays? Could mixing drinks and listening to small-town gossip keep my interest during the long, hot days of summer? An uncertainty grasped me, and I found there was no quick answer.

"You think on it, Brian, and get back to me," George said, his rocking chair casting moving shadows on the dimly lit porch.

"Don't misinterpret my silence, though."

"No judgments, Brian, and no pressure," he said. "Oh, and little pay."

"Gee, George, you really know how to sell it, don't you?"

He laughed as he got up from the chair, excused himself for a moment, and disappeared within the house.

Time was getting on toward nine that night. I was thinking Gerta was due back soon, and at that exact moment a pair of head-lights temporarily blinded me, as a car pulled into the driveway. Assuming it was Gerta, I got up to say hello, and that was when I noticed it wasn't Gerta's car. It was a pickup truck, beaten up and rusted through but somehow still able to run. A man in a ball cap stepped down from the cab and approached.

"Oh, it's you," he said to me.

It was Chuck Ackroyd, one of George's regular patrons down at Connors' Corners. He was dressed in jeans and a blue flannel shirt under a brown cowhide coat. I remembered him from the Five-O, when he'd warned me about the perils of small-town life. I'd also refilled his glass a couple times down at the bar but hadn't exactly engaged him in conversation. He struck me as the surly type, a lonely man with private troubles, letting them sim-mer inside while he fueled them with beer after beer.

"Evening," I said, coming to the edge of the porch.

"Is George here?"

"Yes," I said, inviting Chuck up on the porch. He bristled at my familiarity and walked past me, hopping up the short flight two steps at a time and then taking up residence in the seat I'd oc-cupied. I let it roll off.

George reappeared with a six-pack of beer in his hands and gave Chuck a welcoming hello. "You remember Brian, I'm sure."

"Of course. Your little helper."

His tone was patronizing, but George either didn't notice or pretended not to. Either way, we moved on, with George offering his friend a beer and Chuck quickly accepting.

"That'll be three bucks," I said.

George slapped his knee and laughed loudly. Chuck glared at me, and this time George did notice and did say something.

"Oh, Chuck, lighten up. Brian's a city kid. Thinks faster than he talks, and things just slip out. He's funny and smart and he's gonna be hanging around a while, so get used to it."

"Is that so?" Chuck said.

To contradict George would be insulting, so I confirmed his statement. To my surprise, I liked the sound of it. Made me feel like I belonged.

"Chuck's my most dependable patron," George told me. "Owns the hardware store down the street from the bar. I'm sure you've seen the sign. Biggest damn sign in town; ACKROYD'S HARDWARE EMPORIUM. Wonder why the sign needs to be so large? Well, people come for miles to stock up on necessities— have for years. Chuck's lived his whole life in Linden Corners, too—started the business, what, twenty years ago? You were, what, Chuck? Twenty-five?"

"Like I need to be reminded," Chuck said, running his hands across a bald patch on the back of his head.

"Hah—you kids. Worried about your hair. I went white at thirty. You see me full of gripes? Take life as it comes and hopefully learn to take it easy. Eh, Chuck? Brian, Chuck's been coming by every couple of Sundays for a couple drinks; we sit back and shoot the breeze. Started, oh, about two years ago, right, Chuck? Right after that storm knocked down my barn and you helped clear away the dead wood. Some storm that was, too. Worst I'd seen in—oh, who can remember these days? But bad? Brian, you should have seen it. Knocked down power lines and left us in the dark for days. Lots of damage, trees down, roofs caved in. The

local paper ran a spread of photos—a chilling record of that day."
He paused, thoughts winning out over words. Then he nodded, as
if agreeing with himself. "Come to think of it, it's a storm like
that that almost took down the windmill. It was in such bad need
of repair we all thought maybe it was best to tear it down. That's
when Annie stepped in, saved it. You never forget that kind of
thing. Nature's fury and humankind's beauty. Hard to beat."
George looked over at me. "Of course, Chuck here saw it as a time
of prosperity. Sold all the scrap from my barn and other places,
made a hefty profit. But that's okay, 'cause he got no pay from me
for hauling it off my land."

"Just good beer and good company," Chuck said, an edge to
his voice that indicated he didn't appreciate my knowing such details. He looked queerly at me because I wasn't drinking. Probably he was the type who didn't trust a man who didn't drink.
Heck, he was drinking, and I surely wasn't convinced that I could
trust him.

"Why didn't you rebuild the barn, George, if you've got
such a handy man coming by so often?" I asked, stretching out
comfortably along the porch railing. A gentle breeze blew past,
ruffling my hair.

"Too much effort," he said. "Also, had no use for it anymore.
This house, like the bar, is family-owned for three generations,
and back then, we did lots of farming and growing and the barn
served its purpose. If we rebuilt now, I just don't know what I'd
do with it. Easier to just have more space to watch the grandkids
run around. Yup, that storm sure did some damage. Suppose it
was nature leveling the playing field."

George continued to rock in his chair, puffing away on his pipe
like a wizened elder teaching us the legends of the past. Chuck and
I sat quietly, staring ahead into the dark night. Conversation waned
and I began to feel like a third wheel, intruding on the set routine
of two men who have shared a long history. I was figuring out the

best way to shove off when the opportunity presented itself. Gerta
had returned, apparently having gone shopping after taking the
neighbor her meal. I got up to help her, insisting that George and
Chuck remain seated. No objections there, and once I'd finished carrying in Gerta's packages, I announced my departure. Gerta, sweet
as pie, pecked my cheek with a motherly kiss and told me that anytime my stomach grumbled, I should head this way because there
was always room for another person at her table.

George opted to walk me to my car. "There's one thing I forgot to mention, Brian, you know, about my offer. Upstairs from
the bar, there's a three-room apartment that's been unoccupied for
a few months now. I had a renter, a young guy who ended up mar-
rying his childhood sweetheart and moving in with her and her
family. So it's furnished. Just needs some cleanup and the place
could be yours. We can talk about the terms later—about the job
and the apartment. And before you answer, take the night and
think about it. Stop by the bar tomorrow night and we'll talk—
over a nice, tall seltzer."

"George, you and Gerta have been so kind, I can't tell you,"
I confessed, meaning it. "I appreciate your hospitality and your
friendship."

"It's our pleasure," he said, giving my arm a reassuring
squeeze.

As I was leaving, Gerta reemerged from the house with a
foil-wrapped package. "You're not leaving without leftovers. I
know how you bachelors are, eating junk food the day long. Not
in my care you don't."

She foisted the package on me, only to say there was another.
Chuck jumped in to help with the load of food, and before I knew
it, he was helping himself to my dinner. We got to my car and
loaded the pans in the backseat. He slammed the door shut without warning me and almost caught my thumb. I gave him a surprised look.

"Enjoy the food," he said. "But when it disappears, I suggest you do the same. These are good people, and they don't need taking advantage of."

"That's not what I'm doing."

"Could have fooled me," he said.

I didn't like his attitude and couldn't care less how many beers were inside him. "Look, Chuck, the last thing I would do is hurt George and Gerta. They've been uncommonly kind to me and, it seems, to you. So why don't you and I just get along, perhaps for their sake?"

He didn't appreciate my good-guy approach and turned his back on me. Before I left, I called out to him as he made his way to the porch. "Have a good night."

He said nothing. Instead, I heard the snap of a beer can being opened.

Midnight rolled around. I was unable to sleep and frustrated by the notion of a sleepless night. It's not that the bed at the Solemn Nights was uncomfortable; rather, it was the opposite, with its downy pillow and firm mattress, and there were no noises to keep me awake. The few other tenants from this weekend had checked out this afternoon, once again leaving me and Richie Ravens the run of the place. No, sleep evaded me because I was distracted, by my thoughts and by George's proposition and by the idea of staying the summer in Linden Corners.

After thirty minutes of tossing and turning, I gave up, threw back the covers, and tossed on jeans, a sweatshirt, and my sneakers. Grabbing my keys, I headed outside. It was a cool night, down around fifty degrees, and the wind had picked up some. An earthy smell permeated the air; rain was on the way.

Already the windshield was wet with dew, and as I turned the engine, I flipped on the wipers. Then I drove off, flicking on the headlights to guide my way. With the radio off, I rode in silence, easing down the winding road slowly and surely. There were no other cars on the road, not past midnight on a Sunday night, not with the pressure of the start of the work week just hours away. I rolled the window down, felt the wind on my face, felt alive and free.

I looped the car around the county roads beyond Linden Corners, past the fruit stand and back again, then found myself heading west out of the village. Even though I'd started out on a random, uncertain path, my destination now was clear. I wondered, though, with the sky so blackened and the stars invisible from a dense covering of clouds, would I be able to see the windmill at this late hour? Had I possibly missed it?

But then there it was, caught in my headlights as I rounded a sharp curve. Since the wind had picked up, so had the windmill's sails, turning in a quicker rotation than I'd seen the other day, and I was pulled in by its power and energy. Realizing my best view was from atop this hill, I pulled to the side of the road, flicked on my car's hazard lights, and then stepped out of the car. I left the headlights on, focused directly on the windmill straight ahead.

I sat on the hood of the car, cross-legged, staring straight ahead. The cold attacked my body, the sweatshirt I had pulled on just not warm enough. I held myself tightly, arms wrapped around my legs, and sat in quiet contemplation, pondering the future.

I could never have imagined this moment, when I felt so alone with the world. This was a far cry from New York City, its bustling activity and pulsing lights, its overcrowded subways and teeming sidewalks. In New York City, you never stopped to really breathe in the air and think beyond the boundaries of the city. Here, though, in nature's backyard, you could almost taste the air and touch the sky. You were one *with* the world, instead of just one *in* the world, and a serenity I'd never experienced before washed over me. In this land that time forgot, my very future was upon me.

Maddie came to mind. She was a restless sleeper, and I imagined her now, wide awake in her apartment, waiting for the weekend to end, wanting the work week to start. She was never happier than on a Monday morning, ready to face the challenges of a new week. Maybe, though, she'd changed, like I had. Maybe life with Justin had given her a new appreciation for the downtime of weekends, where you could catch your breath and clear your mind and reenergize.

Did I miss my old life? It's hard to leave something you've known, a comfortable existence where risk meant taking a cab through Midtown at rush hour instead of the subway when you were already late for a meeting. Where ordering off the menu instead of from the specials board caused your waiter to raise an eyebrow. But I'd taken the biggest risk of my life by walking away from the well-defined and predictable challenges the city had offered. Truthfully, I had no regrets about my decision, not now.

Just then a drop of rain landed on my head, and then another. Big, single droplets that dotted my sweatshirt. Any moment the sky would open up and soak the dry land with much-needed rain. An unexpected swish of wind passed me by and suddenly I was reminded of George's story of the furious storm, wondered if that was what we were in for. I stole a brief glance at the windmill and saw that its sails still spun, despite the rain. And like the windmill, I wasn't going anywhere. I wasn't leaving. No storm would chase me away.

And I realized I wouldn't be leaving Linden Corners. No, I was going to stay, accept George's offer, and spend my summer in a town that had generously and openly welcomed me into its fold. When doubt and change and risk arose, I would meet them all head-on, challenging—even embracing—them.

And there I sat in the pouring rain, tall on the hood of my car, my arms outstretched like the sails of the windmill. I was filled with the promise of a new day, a new life—a future.

SIX

After two days of rain and gray skies, the sun finally burst through the clouds on Wednesday morning, and by ten o'clock the sky was alive, a vibrant blue. It was a beautiful spring day in the making. White wisps of cloud floated by, a steady breeze the only remnant of the storm. Forty-eight hours had passed since I'd made my decision to stay in Linden Corners, twenty-four since I'd informed George, and just over twelve since I'd made the apartment upstairs from

Connors' Corners my permanent temporary home. The rate was decidedly better than at the Solemn Nights, and after one night of restful sleep, I'd concluded that this tiny place was more comfortable and certainly more livable. For lack of a better way to say it, I was home.

But I left that home on Wednesday morning with the idea of spreading my wings, seeing more of Columbia County, exploring what the Hudson River Valley had to offer its newest resident. With my Grand Am freshly washed and gleaming in the sunlight, I began to head out of town—before I met with a distraction almost immediately. Darla's Trading Post and Marla's Groceries were neighboring stores that shared the same building, and in front of it were several items on display that were meant to entice folks to pull over. One of the items was a spinning rack, filled with postcards.

I pulled the car into the unpaved lot and shut off the engine.

A woman was sitting outside the stores on a wooden bench that was chained to the building. Squinting through thick-lensed glasses, she stared at me, trying to figure out if she knew me or not. *Not* would have been the answer had she asked, but she didn't. Just kept staring. She was probably my age, with a pear-shaped body and brown hair that fell halfway down her back.

"Help you with something?" she asked me. "Something caught your eye, the way you suddenly stopped here. Maybe the lamp?"

There were a few items set out on a folding table, one of them a lava lamp. The sticker quoted a price of twenty-five dollars.

"Doesn't quite go with my decor," I replied, and she bristled with annoyance, clearly not happy that her amazing sales pitch didn't work. Heck, a store like the trading post, I could be its only customer today, and so any savvy entrepreneur would make the best of the situation. *Savvy* wasn't the word that came to mind to describe her, though.

I moved beyond the table to the rack of postcards.

"You like the postcards?" she asked.

"Yes. How much?"

"Gotta ask Marla," she said.

Oh, of course, the Gregory twins, Darla and Marla. I guessed that the one I'd been speaking to was Darla. George had filled me in the other night about various members of the Linden Corners business community, and the story that stuck with me the most was the one about the twins who went into business together. Darla owned the Trading Post, which was really just a collection of old junk and unwanted items that were resold for whatever price they might fetch. A handy store, George informed me, for setting up a new apartment on the cheap. Marla, on the other hand, owned the grocery store, which carried the staples of life— milk, eggs, cheese, cold cuts, soda, the like. In Linden Corners, this was the only convenience store I'd seen, so no doubt it did a fair business.

The story went that the Gregory twins had separately ex- pressed interest in taking over both stores, though neither could afford it alone. So they pooled their limited resources, each picked a store to run, and the rest was history. They'd grown up apart, one with the mother, one with the father, and reunited in high school—and started dressing alike and talking alike, just to get back at their parents. The story went that despite this battle plan, they never really bonded as most twins do, but habit had set in, and they were still together.

Just then, Marla appeared in the doorway of the grocery store, no doubt having heard her name.

"Hi," she said, her voice friendly, more like that of other Linden Corners folk and less like her sister's. But her look was ex- actly the same as Darla's, the long hair, the pear-shaped body, the thick glasses. Identical twins. There was only one way to tell them apart—their demeanor. "I'm Marla Gregory; that's my sister, Darla."

I introduced myself, and they nodded, acknowledging they'd heard of me, from Martha Martinson.

"At the Five-O," I said.

Marla nodded approvingly. Darla frowned.

For a couple minutes, I spun the rack while Marla chirped in with recommendations, and I ended up with three postcards that featured certain parts of the Hudson River Valley, including one aerial view of the river that was truly spectacular. Darla watched with contempt as her sister happily pointed to others.

"Oh, this one down here is nice, more local than the river," she said, indicating a card on the bottom rack. I crouched down to check it out and found, to my surprise, that it was a postcard of the windmill, one of just three left. The first had bent corners, but the other two were perfect and I grabbed them both, added them to the others, and brought them to Marla.

"Five postcards—that'll be a dollar thirty-five," she said. "Come on in so I can ring you up."

I joined Marla in the grocery store, where I added a Coke to my purchase.

"You know you've got two of the same here?" she asked me.

"I know; that's fine."

She gazed up at me through her thick glasses. "You like windmills?"

"I like *that* windmill."

"Beautiful thing, isn't it? Can't tell you how many people stop in for a cold drink, tell me they had to stop 'cause of that windmill. Only one in the valley, so it's unique, you know? These cards were done a few years back, so you're getting the last of them."

I noticed that Darla had gotten up, listening to our exchange from the edge of the store. She hadn't stepped inside. "If you ask me, that windmill's just a creaky old thing that doesn't serve any purpose."

"What purpose should it serve?" I asked, my tone somehow defensive.

"Well, heck, the thing don't work—hasn't for years." She paused, as though waiting for me to challenge her. I wouldn't take the bait. She wasn't going to win this argument.

"Darla, leave the nice man alone, will you? Couldn't sell him that lava lamp, don't take it out on him. Or on the windmill." To me she added, "Darla doesn't always appreciate the beauty in life."

Darla seemed to take that as a challenge. "Uh, Mr. . . . you know what, don't leave yet. I think I've got something for you after all in my store."

"That's really not necessary . . ."

But apparently she thought it was, and she left me with Marla, who was rolling her eyes at her sister's attempt to win my favor. Competition was tough between ordinary siblings; these two had raised it to an art form.

A couple of minutes went by before she came back, still not stepping into her sister's store, her hands hidden behind her back, a satisfied grin on her face. She thrust out her prize with great dramatic flair, and I stepped back in surprise. "Oh . . ." I said, staring at her found treasure. "What is it?"

"Silly, it's a windmill! You said you liked them."

I suppose I had, and I suppose it was. This was a child's toy, made of a series of colorful pieces of foil, curled outward and then woven together at the center. Darla held it by a long stick. "You hold it to the wind and the wheel turns. Just like a windmill. Sure, it's not like that fancy windmill over the hill, but it's your very own."

"I think I'm a little old for it, don't you think?"

She wasn't going to be satisfied until she'd made the sale.

"There must be some little girl in your life you'd like to give it to. What do you say, Windmill Man—five dollars?"

Darla's use of the name *Windmill Man* took me by total surprise. This was silly, really, all this talk of the windmill and my association with it. Before coming to Linden Corners, I'd never even given windmills any thought, and apparently it was fast becoming an obsession I had little control over.

"Three dollars," I found myself saying, and then heard Darla's loud voice accepting the deal, like an overeager auctioneer. Marla stood there, obviously not pleased to have had her sale undermined by Darla's preying on my sympathies. She jumped in with her own offer.

"You want, I'll give you a pen and you can fill out your postcards now, and for a small fee I'll take care of mailing them. I got stamps."

"That's very kind of you, Marla," I said, much to her pleasure.

Ten minutes passed as I filled out two of the postcards, one to my family back in Philadelphia and one to John Oliver back in New York. Since I'd been gone, I'd sent him several postcards, from Niagara Falls, from Toronto, from other sights along the way, keeping my friend informed of my whereabouts without having to call. He got one of the windmill postcards; the other, I kept for myself.

I finished my business with the Gregory twins and left them to their bickering about who had made more money on their individual sales (Marla had, but only because of her clever mail scam). As I headed out of town, I drank the Coke I'd bought. Three miles later, I turned the Grand Am off onto a narrow, two-lane stretch of road. On either side of me were wide-open fields and the occasional driveway leading to a house that couldn't be seen from the road. I was driving slowly, enjoying my surroundings and not really in a rush to get anyplace in particular. It was this aimless wandering that had led me to Linden Corners, and I saw no reason to alter my habits.

A sharp incline was up ahead, and I pressed hard on the accelerator for more power. Atop the hill, I saw a mailbox on my left, noticed the name SULLIVAN painted on it, and wondered if this was Annie and Janey's driveway. I remembered the child's windmill Darla had made me buy, and I thought it would be a nice gift for Janey—and perhaps a peace offering to Annie.

So without much further thought, I turned the car off the road and up the driveway, riding the bumpy dirt path until I emerged from under a gathering of low-hanging trees. Before me stood a large farmhouse, a pointed turret perched atop the second floor and a wraparound porch hugging the main structure. Painted white with sky blue trim, the house was beautifully and lovingly restored.

I pulled in beside the truck that was there, got out of my car, grabbed the toy windmill, and then wondered exactly what it was I was doing here. Annie Sullivan had made clear her opinion of me in the parking lot of the fruit stand. In front of witnesses, she called me a stranger, the nearest thing to a curse word in Linden Corners. And here I was, dropping by for an unannounced visit based on a whim. And a windmill.

I pushed all nervousness aside and hopped up the couple of steps to the porch, then rang the bell. A deep chime sounded throughout the house, and I heard the scrape of a chair against the floor. Someone was coming.

That someone was Annie, of course, looking not unlike I'd first seen her, wearing clothes that were splattered with paint. The expression on her face was similar, too, a mixture of annoyance and curiosity, at least as far as I could see through the screen door. Annie stared at me without saying a word. I'd come by and rung the bell. Now what? Now what, indeed.

With sudden inspiration and a bit of a flourish, I pulled the toy windmill out. I said nothing, and didn't need to, as a passing breeze caught the windmill's spokes, making them spin and spin. Perfect timing, I had to admit.

Annie's taut expression suddenly softened, and she smiled with obvious and unexpected delight.

"What am I going to do with you?" she asked, annoyance giving way to a tinge of a grin.

Her question was rhetorical, I assumed, because she failed to offer up an answer, and so did I, opting instead for a placating shrug. Since our acquaintance had gotten off on the wrong foot, I figured the less said, the better. So I stood in silence, waiting for her to make the next move. Closing the door on me probably came to mind. Instead, I found myself hearing an invitation for coffee.

Having just had a Coke, I wasn't thirsty. "I'd love some coffee," I said.

Annie opened the screen door and led me through a tastefully decorated hallway, past a cherrywood grandfather clock and an assortment of knickknacks on the wall, and we emerged into a country-style kitchen that spoke of warmth and family, with rich baking smells and the aroma of fresh-brewed coffee filling the air. She offered me a chair, but I opted for leaning against the island in the middle of the room, and accepted a steaming cup of black coffee. Coffee's taste can often be a disappointment to me, especially after its rich smell, but here, I was rewarded with a superior cup, and I told her so.

"Thanks. I'm addicted. All day long, cup after cup. It's any wonder I sleep."

We both drank, and an awkward silence fell over us.

"Where's Janey?" I asked.

"School. Second grade—it's hard to believe it."

"Oh," I said. "Of course she's in school. I forget, sometimes, what time of year it is."

"It's spring," she reminded me, "and so last week was spring break—she had the days to herself."

"What, no Daytona Beach for her?"

"She's seven," she informed me, but she knew I'd been kidding. Still, we'd exhausted this particular avenue of conversation, and again, we were left with silence. We sipped our coffee simultaneously, exchanged mutual grins, and immediately went back to the safety of sipping.

"So . . . you're being nice to me," I said after a while.

She paused before setting the cup down. She wore a conciliatory expression. "Yes, well, I suppose I owe you an apology."

"No, no—I was just kidding you . . ."

"Really, Brian, you've been nothing but kind—caring, too, and, I have to say, quick on your reflexes. My actions the other day over at the fruit stand were horrible, the way I lashed out at you. I drove home cursing myself—silently, of course. Can't be too careful around a seven-year-old."

"Must be a fun age."

"*Fun* is one word," she said, with a hint of sarcasm. "*Impressionable* is another."

"A real handful, huh?"

"You tell me—you've seen her in action," Annie said, setting down her coffee mug. It had a windmill design, I noted, just like mine.

"May I ask you a question, Brian Duncan? Without your thinking me rude?"

"That's a loaded question—but sure. You've intrigued me."

"Who are you?"

I might have taken offense at such a blunt question, except her tone wasn't accusatory. Rather, she was genuinely curious about me; here I was, this stranger who had come from nowhere and managed to become a fixture in her daughter's life.

"Just some guy who happened to be passing through," I said, using the description Martha had bestowed on me. "A man who got lured in by the simple life. This place, Linden Corners, has quite a pull on strangers, or at least it has on me."

"How long have you been here?"

"Barely a week," I said. "I'd never even heard of Linden Corners until I drove through it that day we, uh, met. I was on my way from one place and headed for another, and I guess timing was on my side. I stopped for lunch at the Five-O, and next thing I know, I'm taking a room at the Solemn Nights and working at Connors' Corners as a relief bartender—a job I don't exactly have much experience with." I shrugged. "Kind of odd, if you think about it. And to tell you the truth, it's your fault."

"Mine?"

"Well, Janey's."

"Janey's?"

"Well, actually, the windmill's."

The corners of her mouth widened at the mention of the windmill, giving her face a pleasant glow. "How exactly did my windmill influence you?"

How indeed? I told her I couldn't say, that it was more of a feeling, really. There I was just innocently driving down a road, no idea which road I was on or where I was going, just . . . driving, and next thing I know there's this amazing sight before me, this windmill, and I described the sensation that washed over me, of slipping through time to a world unlike any I'd known before. All the while, she listened with great intent, taking in my enthusiasm and nodding when I spoke of the windmill's elusive and magical hold.

When I finished, Annie said to me, "Are you in a hurry?"

"These days, I'm never in a hurry," I replied.

"Would you like to see my windmill?"

"I've seen the windmill," I said.

"Let me rephrase it, then," she said. "Would you like to go

up inside my windmill? Come on—it'll be fun. I haven't shown it in a long time, and it's high time I did."

"You keep calling it *your* windmill," I said, "and you speak of it with such passion, Annie. Such energy. It must be true what I've heard—you really are the woman who loves the windmill."

"That's a silly old name," she said, though clearly she was pleased to have heard it again, "and it was given to me by a man so sweet and wonderful and caring, he gave me two amazing gifts. The windmill and—"

"And Janey," I said. "You sound like you miss your husband very much." I paused, seeing the smile on her face waver slightly, and a feeling of remorse swept over me. "Oh, Annie, I'm sorry if I've intruded. . . . Can't seem to get away from doing that, huh? So, well, maybe it's time I left. There's this thing I had planned . . ."

"Brian, please—you haven't upset me, if that's what you're worried about. It's just . . . well, let's say we drop the subject. Forget whatever you had planned—which I don't believe for a minute—and let me show you my windmill."

So I accepted her offer, and without further delay she took me out the back door and into the fresh morning air. Above us, the sun was almost at high noon, and its rays cast a long, languid shine all around us, reflecting off the expansive lawn and exposing hidden golden flecks in Annie's chestnut-colored hair. As we walked, Annie spoke about the day, talking about how the rain had delayed her hopping on the mower and slicing through the long grass.

"Maybe tomorrow," she said.

"Are you sure I'm not keeping you from your work?" I asked. "It's a big lawn and probably takes you a while. Plus, you look like you were in the middle of something." I indicated her shirt, the paint splatters.

"Oh, that . . . well, I suppose you'll see for yourself," she answered, but said nothing further on the subject.

To get to the windmills we had to walk across the lawn, past the barn and a sandbox and a swing set that looked handmade, thick pieces of dark wood held together with strong metal fixtures. Once beyond the confines of the house and yard, we steadily climbed a small hill that, from our perspective, meshed with the distant horizon at its top. At its top, though, we had a magnificent view of the valley, its velvety lawns and small forests of trees, its homes and barns and silos. The countryside revealed a world lush and welcoming. And in the center of it all, in a deepening valley, unlike any other object in our vision, stood the windmill. Lonely and majestic, its sails turned slowly, nearly at rest in the cool calm of this glorious spring day.

"Wow," I said, the sound more like a breath escaping me than an actual word. The sight was like the postcard I'd purchased only an hour ago, but this was three-dimensional and larger than life and more visually striking than could possibly be imagined. I stole a glance at Annie standing beside me, and you could not have painted her expression, for her face betrayed a series of moods and sensations that went deep below the surface, to a place that only her own heart truly knew.

"Come on," she said with sudden urgency, and grabbed my hand and pulled me forward.

We ran together, two strangers linked not just by flesh but by a shared interest that had miraculously revealed itself to us. Our feet seemed to move above the ground of their own will until we'd reached the windmill. In this time and place, we were one.

Standing underneath the grand mill, I watched as its huge sails passed within inches of my face, first one, then a second, a third, and finally the fourth one, each emitting a soft breeze, like intimate little kisses. I'd been this close to the windmill before, once, with Janey, but there and then I'd been filled with an awkwardness and apprehension, a sense that I didn't belong. Now, though, it felt like I was meant to be here, like I belonged.

"Tell me all about it," I said, and she agreed to. And that was when I noticed that our hands were still locked together in a firm grip, sending tingling electric shocks all along my spine. And this was not the windmill's doing, not this time.

My lesson started with logistics as I learned first about the various parts of the windmill. That the main structure was called the tower, and the part above that which controlled the sails was called the cap, and that the cap spun separately from the rest of the structure, enabling it to move with the fluid motion of the wind. It was the cap that the sails were affixed to, and inside the tower was a strong metal beam that was imbedded deep in the ground. At last Annie took me inside, and it was here she began to tell me the story of how the windmill came to be.

"The tale doesn't begin with the windmill; it can't. Because the windmill was born from circumstance, out of necessity. And although there were those who cheered its construction, there were detractors, too, those who saw the windmill as a piece of the past. And remember, back then it was a time of progress, of industrial revolution and for forsaking farming methods thought to be outdated. But for Donovan Van Diver, who built the windmill in 1912, this was not a concern to him. No, for him and his family, the windmill was fashioned out of sheer practicality. He built it right on this spot, and here it has stood for nearly ninety years.

"This region was heavily populated with Dutch settlers," she said, "and they brought with them their unique and wonderful customs and beliefs, and their own beautiful architecture. This windmill is notable among the many Dutch buildings and structures that still stand throughout the Hudson Valley and Columbia County.

"*Donovan Van Diver,* you may be thinking, is an unusual

name, a mix of two cultures and heritages, and you'd be right in your thinking. The Van Diver family settled in this region in the mid-1800s, immigrants who had landed at Portsmouth, New Hampshire, and who had gradually made their way inland. With its closeness to the mighty Hudson, as well as the lush green valleys, they knew this was perfect farmland. Along the way, Donovan's father, Derek Van Diver, met Kate Sullivan—in Boston—and they fell in love. They moved here, and eventually Derek and Kate took over the farm from his parents, who died, oh, maybe ten years after arriving in America. The farm was prosperous for years, mostly grains. Some dairy, too. As the story goes, though, there was a persistent problem of the land becoming soaked, water-logged, and it wasn't until Derek and Kate's eldest child, their son Donovan—named for Kate's grandfather—grew up that a solution presented itself. Donovan, no more than twenty years old, was a young man fascinated by history, and so he thought to look to his Dutch ancestry and traditions, and in doing so, learned about the uses of windmills. And he proposed building one himself.

"So one summer day, Derek and his son Donovan and many of the farmhands set themselves to work, to the task of erecting a windmill, like many of their forebears had done back in their homeland, where windmills had been in use for a couple centuries. Whether for grinding grains or pumping water, the windmills harnessed the power of the wind. They also added a grandeur and elegance to the landscape, and the windmills became world renowned not just for their practical uses but also for their architectural beauty."

"That they are," I said, "unique, grand, elegant."

"Far more so than the 'new' style of windmill, the American windmill," she said, going on to describe the streamlined modern windmills, the simple spinning wheels atop tall posts that tended to dominate America's heartland. They might have been more ef-

ficient, easier to build, and easier to repair, given the tendency of
fierce tornadoes to rip through that open expanse of country. But
for Annie, the American windmill just didn't compare to her
Dutch version.

All the while Annie was speaking, I sat enraptured, not just
by her tale but also by the emotion in her voice. She spoke
strongly, unwavering in her passion for the windmill, and by
transference, for life itself. Considering that two months earlier
I'd been lost in the quagmire of urban living, so consumed with
achieving and excelling and just being, never stopping to appreciate the simpler things in life, the fact that I was now in the company of such elegance, the woman and the windmill both, had me
in a state near euphoria. Sitting inside the windmill's tower, hearing stories of the past, the people, of their trials and tribulations,
their hopes and dreams, their losses and legacy, I could almost en-
vision myself building my own windmill.

"Tell me," I said, as the story of Donovan Van Diver came to
a close, "how Annie Sullivan came to know the windmill."

For the first time, she hesitated and bowed her head in silence, as though she'd lost her place on the page. I couldn't see her
face, but I detected a flash of sorrow as it moved across her features. When she finally looked back up, her eyes were moist and
they stared not *at* me but *through* me, to the world beyond the
window. The sun had slipped behind a cloud, and the turning
sails of the windmill were casting giant shadows on the ground,
like ghosts from the past.

Annie curled up within herself, wrapping her arms around
her legs. "When you're just a kid, like Janey, every day is an innocent adventure. You play and you learn and you live, one day to
the next, basically unaware that it's a journey, a path you're traveling, and that it will take you to wonderful and dark places both.
And you are blissfully unaware of the twists and turns life will
take. As you grow older, that realization kicks in and the arro-

gance of adolescence takes over, where you think you can carve that path yourself, cut right through the overgrowth and walk unchallenged through a clearing, straight on in the direction of your choice. Then, at some point, the innocence slips away, the arrogance is trampled, and you're left with what? The bitterness of adulthood? The conclusion that everything you envisioned for yourself is lost? You can't cling to your plans, because they come with no guarantee."

This wasn't philosophy she was spouting but experience. My heart melted at the desolation she must have been feeling, and I felt at fault. I'd pushed beyond the memories and into the pain, taken her out of the past—the safety of history—and thrust her into her present. Even after two years, she still bore the pain of her husband's death. By asking about the time she'd come to love the windmill, I'd asked her to examine memories that she'd tried to bury.

"Annie, I'm . . . God, all I ever seem to do around you is apologize."

"No, Brian, it's me who should be sorry. . . . It's just, you know, you can fall in love with a silly thing like a windmill because it's safe and easy. With its solid, unconditional love, you know nothing can take it away from you. For ninety years, the windmill has lived on, sometimes frail, sometimes strong, but it's always been there. For me, it's the one thing I can count on."

I felt a lump lodge in my throat. "Finding something you can count on, you're very lucky." I paused, uncertain what more I could say. "Look, Annie, it's none of my business, and I can't presume to empathize with your loss, but you also can't give up," I said, my heart heavy with emotion for her, sad for her and mad at myself, for asking too much, pushing too far, and taking her someplace she still wasn't ready to go—forward.

She wiped away a trickling tear, and said, "That's what Cynthia's been telling me: 'You can't hide, Annie, not from life.' "

I swallowed that lump, those words digging deep into my own heart. "Cynthia's a smart woman, but she also has to realize that sometimes you need to close down for a while, you need time to heal, and that sometimes it takes longer than you think, longer than others want it to take."

Annie's gaze was on me, and when she spoke, it was like a whisper. "You're not speaking just about me, are you?"

Afraid to speak, afraid my voice would betray me, I merely shook my head. There was a connection between us now, a shared and silent intimacy that had cropped up in the face of our pain, and by admitting it to the other, we had taken an uneasy first step toward each other. We sat together, not having to say a word, and it felt warm and comfortable and special. And then it was gone, a vulnerability picked up by the wind and taken from us.

"How about we save the story of me and the windmill for a rainy day?" she asked me, her mood brightening. "Let me show you something really spectacular."

"I can't wait," came my eager reply.

So we left our wounds at the open window, where the wind could catch them and blow them away, and Annie took me up the winding metal staircase to the second floor, which was narrower because of the windmill's shape, and into a still sizable room. It looked to me like this was Annie's secret getaway, her sanctuary.

"Well, that explains the paint splatters," I said, looking at an easel, and beside it, a table overflowing with paints and brushes and assorted cleaners. There was a canvas on the easel, but it was covered with a white sheet, and Annie said it was staying there.

"I'm not ready to show it," she said.

"No pressure," I said, "but I'd love to see some of your work."

She was smiling and obviously felt pride in her painting.

"I'm no professional. It's just a hobby, but . . ." There was a small closet against the far wall, and she opened the set of doors to reveal a series of canvases. She invited me over, and I crouched down near her as she flipped through painting after painting. There were ten in all, all natural landscapes, all beautifully wrought, with rich, vibrant colors and an amazing knack for detail. Trees in spring, awash with buds. A brook in summer, bubbling along. And, of course, the windmill, three paintings in all, each more remarkable than the other.

"Oh, Annie, they're really quite beautiful," I said, taking hold of the last painting and bringing it out into the light. Annie had captured a lovely summer sunset, an iridescent sky set behind the glorious windmill, and playfully running across the lawn was a little girl not unlike Janey.

"Like I said, it's just a hobby," she said. "And it's very soothing. I can't tell you the number of days I've spent inside my windmill, days when Janey's been at school, days she just sat and played beside me. That day . . . that sunset—it really happened. I took a photograph, and I knew it needed to be painted."

She let me pore over the paintings a while longer and then finally coaxed me away and closed the closet doors. She told me to follow her.

There were three windows on the second floor of the windmill, each facing a different direction, but as she led me over to them, I noticed they were more than just windows. They were doors.

"This is my favorite part," she said, and opened one of the doors.

I'd seen from the ground that the windmill had a railing encircling it, but I hadn't realized completely that you could actually walk outside it, indeed walk around the entire perimeter of the windmill. But you could, and we did, Annie once again taking hold of my hand and leading me forward. We were probably twenty feet above the ground, not terribly high, but from this perspective there was a sense of being higher than the clouds, able to reach out and touch the sky and float on the air and bask in the sun. Annie led me around and around, and we circled the windmill in near dizziness. Finally she brought us to a stop, just behind the turning sails, to where I could look above and almost touch the thick metal pole that held the sails so firmly.

And there Annie and I remained, two people who had both known sorrow but who now found joy in the unlikeliest of places, atop a lonely and majestic windmill. We stood with our hands clasped and our hearts full, the two of us strangers no more. Time could have stopped, save for the gently turning sails of the windmill.

SECOND INTERLUDE

Gerta, as promised, arrived at eight o'clock, ready to hustle Brian out and on his way to the hospital while she cooked breakfast for Janey. But that wasn't the calm picture that awaited her at the Sullivan farmhouse. Instead, a frantic Brian appeared at the front door.

"I can't find Janey."

Which was followed by an explanation of what had happened that morning, Cynthia's phone call, Annie's

*being taken for "tests," Janey's accidentally overhearing it all. She'd run
away and Brian couldn't find her.*

"Where have you looked?"

"Everywhere."

"The windmill?"

"First place I looked."

"The barn?"

"Locked, so she couldn't have made off on her bicycle."

*The only other place Brian had been able to think of, a place where
Janey might go to connect with her mother's presence, was the place he had
dubbed "Annie's Bluff," but that was a hike, not easily found on foot, especially not by a seven-year-old, even a determined one.*

*"I don't know what to do, Gerta. Help Cynthia at the hospital
or . . . keep looking for Janey. If only I could talk to her, ease the pain she's
feeling, the confusion, answer her questions. Hell, if only Janey would just
show herself, at this point I'd sneak her into the hospital to see Annie."*

*"She'll be back. She's scared and eventually she'll realize she needs
someone—she needs you. Right now, you're all that sweet thing has."*

*They decided to split up, with Gerta taking the outdoors and Brian
taking the indoors, and it was on his fourth trip upstairs that he heard a
rustling sound. It seemed to be coming from above, from the attic. He circled back from Annie's room, where the clock—in the shape of a windmill—announced the time with nine revolutions of its sails. How Annie
treasured that clock; how comforting he suddenly found it. That was the
thing about clocks and watches, there were always more seconds and minutes and hours, more time to come, more time to achieve the things you had
yet to accomplish. There was still time to hope.*

*The time, though, had come to find Janey, and he dashed up the
stairs to the attic, and that's where he finally found the tousle-haired girl,
nearly lost in a sea of cardboard boxes, their contents littering the floor of
the attic. Janey looked up at him and wiped her dripping nose.*

"You okay?" he asked her.

She said nothing, just held her stuffed purple frog, held it tight.

When Brian moved closer, she scampered back a few feet but found herself backed up against a cardboard box. Brian was close enough to her now to see that her eyes were red, swollen. Nearly two hours had passed since he'd last seen her, and his heart broke at the thought she'd been alone all that time.

"Janey, talk to me, please."

She still wouldn't talk, but at least she didn't move away from him. Progress, he thought. She's opening up.

"Janey, I'm sorry. For . . . everything. For your not being able to see your mom, for not telling you the truth . . . but Janey, let me help you. It's the only way I can help your mom right now—by helping you."

She sniffled. Then, in a flash, she rushed into Brian's waiting arms, burying her face against his chest as sobs wracked her small body. Now wasn't the time for words, so he just held her, tightly, vowing then and there to never let her go, not as long as she needed him, even if it meant forever. Life was delicate, but youth was fragile and needed to be handled with care and love. Brian found himself smiling, realizing how lucky he was to have this little girl in his life, how full she'd made it in such a short time.

Finally, Brian spoke. "Hey, what are you doing up here, anyway?"

She brushed away tears, staring up at him. "I came to find something."

"And did you find it?"

She shook her head. "Not yet."

"Can I help?"

"You don't know where they are."

Brian looked at the mess on the floor. "Seems neither do you. So maybe four eyes are better than two."

She resigned herself to his help. "Okay, start digging."

Brian eased in closer to her, studied the contents of the box now opened before them. It was full of photographs that had yet to be placed in albums and rolled-up canvases painted by an obviously talented yet untrained hand. They were Annie's illustrations from years ago. Raw but filled with bright colors, reds and yellows and oranges. Sunny, like the woman herself.

"If you tell me what we're looking for, maybe we'll be done sooner."

"Plans," she said.

"Plans? What kind of plans?"

"For the windmill, silly. Momma kept them, from the last time she rebuilt it. If we find them, we can make it turn again. And then Momma will be better, I just know it."

Brian couldn't help it, not here and not now, seeing how brave and hopeful and, yes, innocent she was. The tears rolled down his cheeks. They intensified as Janey tried to comfort him, hugging him tight and telling him that she knew her idea was the perfect solution. Finally he was nodding his head, agreeing with her.

"I had the same idea, sweetie," he said. "I want to rebuild the windmill, too. But I don't know how."

"I do—the plans!"

"Then let's find them."

The two of them—a team now—continued to search the many boxes, poring through mementos and photographs, culling the stacks of material, going deep into the attic until, at last, they'd found what they'd been searching for.

"That's the box!" Janey exclaimed.

Brian removed the thick duct tape and took off the box top, exposing a treasure trove of items. What he wanted, Janey said, was at the bottom, and it took a few seconds for him to dig down, careful not to damage the other family mementos that filled the box.

It was amazing to Brian that the Sullivans had kept so much of their family history. This included a lot of information about the windmill and, in particular, the architectural plans, which he found at the bottom of the box, rolled up and crinkled, the rubber band long since snapped. Brian took hold of them, scurried over to better light, and unraveled the plans so he could see them. A series of drawings and numbers, it might as well have been Greek to him.

"*Can we do it?*" Janey asked, her mood brightening, a dramatic difference from only moments ago.

Truthfully, he had no idea. "*Yeah, we can.*"

"*So, it's a good plan?*"

"*Yes, Janey, a brilliant plan.*" And that's when he had his own brilliant plan, or at least that's how he saw it. There was no denying what needed to be done.

"*Janey, time to get dressed. You need to visit someone.*"

He knew it would be breaking the rules, but he didn't care. At nearly eleven o'clock on that second morning after the accident, after Brian and Janey had together found the windmill's plans, the two of them arrived in the parking lot of the hospital.

"*Wow, it's big!*" Janey exclaimed, dancing with anticipation.

"*You promised me, remember—*"

"*—to stay quiet.*"

"*If you want to see your mom, yeah.*"

He got her all the way to the fourth floor with no problem, then got her to the waiting area of the ICU, where he found Cynthia and Bradley, her husband, both looking severely exhausted from their tour of duty. When they saw Janey, though, they both perked up. Cynthia ran to embrace her.

Brian checked in with Bradley.

"*How's Annie?*"

"*She's back in her room, apparently out of danger. Dr. Savage told us time would tell.*"

"*That's all?*" Brian asked. "*Is Annie awake?*"

Cynthia shook her head.

"*Hence my secret weapon.*"

"*They won't let her in.*"

"*Who says they have to see her?*"

A plan was hatched, with Cynthia and Bradley distracting the nursing staff while Brian quickly led Janey into her mother's room, covering her mouth as he did so as a precautionary measure.

"Momma!" Janey whispered as soon as the curtain was drawn.

Annie was asleep, as she had been for two days now, not a promising sign, Brian knew, but he also knew that her body needed the rest. The tube was still attached, breathing for her, and he explained this as delicately as he could to Janey. Gently, Janey held her mother's hand, squeezed it.

"You rest, Momma, and I'll come and visit and tell you about what Brian and me are doing. . . . Oh, Momma, it's a wonderful surprise—"

"Ssshh," Brian said.

She gave him a stern look. "I'm not gonna say what it is—that would spoil the surprise."

Admonished, Brian smiled.

Janey was a strong child who'd weathered bad storms before and who had come shining through them like a burst of sunlight through a cloud. She had an amazing resilience that was easily transferred to those around her—Brian, Cynthia, Bradley, and, no doubt, Annie, too.

Suddenly, there was a flicker of life from the bed, the twitch of an eyelash, and Janey's eyes opened wide with anticipation. Brian held the little girl's other hand, and suddenly the three of them were connected. A link of life. And then Annie was awake. The first sight she saw was her daughter.

"Hi, Momma," Janey simply said.

Annie managed a slight smile, but it was enough to thrill Janey.

"Momma, Brian's here—he brought you a present. It's one you have already, but he thought you'd like it here."

Brian stepped forward and withdrew from a plastic bag the windmill clock from her bedside at home.

"Thought you'd like to see an old friend."

A minute later, he had the clock plugged in, and he set the time to nearly noon, so that in only three minutes the sails of the windmill would turn a dozen times.

Janey giggled. Brian's heart swelled. And Annie, a smile on her face, drifted back into a more peaceful slumber.

Brian knew he'd done the right thing, bringing Janey here. The doctors could give Annie medicine, they could guess and speculate and hope, but there was one thing they couldn't accomplish. There were regions of the heart even doctors couldn't reach. Only little girls could find their way there.

Janey. She was their hope; she was their future. She was Annie's lifeline.

From the corner of the room, Brian watched as Janey snuggled in close to her mother and fell asleep, too, probably the first real rest she'd had in days. The sight was natural; they nearly glowed with life.

PART THREE

MAY-JUNE

SEVEN

So you're still there?"

"I'm still here."

"How long's it been?"

"Uh . . . five weeks? Something like that."

"I thought it had been a while since I'd gotten a new postcard," he said. "Getting restless?"

"More like comfortable."

"Brian Duncan, farmer. Who would have thought it?"

"John," I said, my tone indicating I was getting tired of this banter, "I'm not a farmer. I just happen to be temporarily living in a small town that's known for its farming—among other things. And note the key word there—*temporarily*. Someday, probably soon, I'll be continuing my trip. I was thinking Maine might be nice for the late summer."

"Not back to the city?"

"No, John; I'm not ready. I said six months and I'm sticking to it."

"Okay, okay—don't get so defensive. I was just wondering."

It was late May, nearly Memorial Day, and I'd been in Linden Corners since the middle of April. During the past several weeks, the town's gentle nature and pace continued to win more of my favor. Though I'd set no definite deadline for my departure, even I was surprised that I wasn't yet ready to leave.

I was still tending bar. In fact, George had upped my hours and my pay, and I had steadily learned the various tricks of the trade, which weren't that difficult, as it turned out. There was little or no demand for mixed drinks, and no demand for exotic drinks, with most of the service coming directly from the beer tap. I had learned how to change a keg, which was the most strenuous aspect of the job. More often than not, I stood around, talking with the locals and soaking up the flavor of the town.

It was coming up on four o'clock in the afternoon, opening time, and I had work to do. There were pretzels to be set out and a jukebox to start, so I had to wrap up this call with John Oliver. That would force him to get to the point of his call.

"Look, John, I know you can sit around all day and chat, since this call is on your company's bill, but me, I've got a bar to set up and customers who depend on me. And we don't exactly have a cordless phone at the Corner, so I can't walk and talk and work. So, better to spill it now. What's up?"

He hesitated, confirming my suspicion that he'd had a reason for calling.

"John, just spit it out."

"You know, I hate being put in the middle. . . ."

"John . . ."

"Okay, all right. Maddie wants to contact you."

I dropped the pint glass I'd been holding. It slipped right from my hand and fell to the hardwood floor and shattered into too many pieces to count. It wan't that I hadn't thought about Maddie; I had. But the idea that she wanted to talk to me shocked me.

"You drop something?" John asked.

Yeah—my heart.

"Just a glass. You took me by surprise is all."

"Sorry—but there didn't seem any easy way to broach the subject," he said. "She's been pressuring me for a couple weeks now, and I kept putting her off, hoping it—she—would just go away."

"No such luck?"

"Nothing to bet with, that's for sure," he said.

I asked for more details. He'd run into Maddie in, of all places, Sequoia, the restaurant where I'd eaten with Maddie and Justin and the people from the Voltaire Health Group. The place that had spiked my oysters with a nasty case of hepatitis, which had led me on the road to a new life. Maddie had been there with some woman John didn't recognize.

"Didn't get a name either."

But Maddie had asked about me. *He's doing great,* John had said, not wanting to reveal too much, and that had been that. Until two days passed and Maddie called him at work and asked for my phone number.

My senses suddenly came to life as I thought about the city

I'd left behind. I could smell the fast-paced energy of New York City, taste the high style (and price) of dining out. But I was also flooded with memories of Maddie's sweet scent and silky touch, the alluring tilt of her head when she posed a question, the occasional slip of her Southern accent, the way she moved and spoke and breathed. All of these images came rushing back to me, nearly overwhelming me. Luckily my surroundings drew me back. Suddenly, all I saw were unwashed pint glasses and all I could smell was beer.

"No," I finally said. "I don't want to see her or talk to her. John, things are going too well right now; I'm at peace. And I'm having fun. Hey, it's the carefree life and it's what I want right now. I'm not ready for another ride on the emotional roller coaster."

"Well, think about it."

"I have."

"Sleep on it," he said.

"John, you're supposed to be my friend. Why do you sound as though you've pitched a tent inside her camp?"

"I'm not taking sides, Brian, I just think . . . no, I'd better not . . ."

"Say it," I said strongly.

"Brian, it's time to come back to the real world. You've lived the fantasy, you've run away and found a new life, but it's not yours. It's someone else's, like a summer share with strangers. But it's over. Maddie was the best thing to ever happen to you, and she wants you back. She wants to talk about it."

"It? Does she know what 'it' is?"

"Brian, just talk to her."

An emphatic "no" escaped my lips, and then I instructed him not to give Maddie any information regarding my whereabouts. Still, he pressed me further, as only a good friend can do, but I wasn't going to stand for it. I told him I had to go.

"Just answer me one thing," John said. "Is there someone else in the picture?"

"Is that you asking, John, or are you asking on Maddie's behalf?" I asked, now totally and thoroughly pissed off. "Hey, John, check out the definition of *loyalty,* then call me back sometime."

And I slammed down the phone.

The intrusion of New York City into my easy existence in Linden Corners was jarring, and I didn't want to deal with it. So I turned on the jukebox, turned up the volume, and spent the next half hour burying myself in work. Then it was time to open. The regulars started arriving and I began pouring drinks. The music played and we talked and joked and enjoyed one another's company. The hours passed and I forgot all about John's phone call.

George and Gerta were away this week, off visiting one of their daughters and her family, leaving me the run of the place. I'd managed to make friends with a number of the regulars, none of whom had any interest in the fact that I was some city slicker, and so the conversation leaned toward topics like the wife who complained about this and that, or the boyfriend-girlfriend troubles of the younger set, or the whining nature of kids today, which suited me fine. The one man who failed to join the conversation was Chuck Ackroyd, who hadn't, from the moment we'd met, made a secret of his dislike for me. I had a sense he saw my presence as a threat to his friendship with George, and nothing I did could change his mind. Not even a free beer.

"This one's on me, Chuck," I said, refilling his glass before he'd even asked. It was a gesture in the right direction—at least that's how I saw it.

"Aren't you taking advantage of George's good nature by giving away his product?"

I was tempted then to make him pay for the beer; instead, I walked away and started a conversation with someone else.

That was when the door opened, and someone I never ex-

pected to see inside Connors' Corners entered. It was Annie Sullivan, looking freshly scrubbed and full of energy. She sidled up to
the bar and flashed me a happy grin.

"What'll it be, stranger?" I asked.

"Do you recommend the wine?"

"Looking for a new paint thinner?" I joked.

She laughed, and said, "In that case, how about a diet
Coke?"

Since our afternoon at the windmill, Annie and I had seen
each other only a couple times in town, and once, I'd been invited
over for dinner. And that was because Janey'd been mad that she
had missed me that one day. But Annie had been busy since she
had taken a part-time job at a nearby antique store three mornings a week.

"How's the antique business?" I asked.

"It's nice getting back to work after . . . well, too long, you
know. But it's not going to last—only until summer comes and
Janey's home again with me."

"Speaking of Janey, where is she that you can come and hang
out in a bar—and on a school night?"

"Cynthia's watching her. I had a couple quick errands to
run."

"Is stopping at the local tavern one of those errands?"

"Well, I came to see you."

"Me?"

"On Janey's behalf. I come bearing an invitation—to a picnic. Memorial Day is coming up, as you're no doubt aware, and
the town has an annual picnic, and it's lots of fun, and—oh my,
I'm starting to sound like Janey, talking like this. But, heck, if a
child's enthusiasm rubs off on you, consider it a blessing in a cyn-
ical world. So, what do you say? Cynthia and her husband,
Bradley, will be joining us, and Janey wanted you to be there, because, as she says, 'He's nice.' "

"How about you?"

"Yes, I agree with Janey. You're nice."

"No. I mean, are you inviting me to the picnic as well?"

Even in the dim light of the bar, I could see her blush, not the red flush of embarrassment, just a faint hint of nervousness. Annie tried to laugh it off.

"It's not a date, Brian Duncan, if that's what you're thinking."

"Good. Then I'd be happy to join all of you," I said, surprising her with my response. "And thank you. There are signs about the picnic all over town and I was wondering what I'd do with myself. The idea of being the one stranger in a town full of friends was daunting to say the least."

"Consider yourself a stranger no more. Heck, you've got the run of George Connors' tavern—the first non-Connor to do so ever, far as I know." She drank deeply from her diet Coke, setting the glass down when she'd finished. "Well, I've got to run; there are still a couple more errands on my list. But we'll see you— Monday, about noon? Come to the farmhouse—Janey wants us all to arrive together."

I promised I'd be there, and then Annie was out the door as fast as she'd come in, leaving me oddly thrilled by her presence, comforted by her invitation. If John's call had caused me to question my motives for lingering in Linden Corners, I was now reassured that the decision to stay in the land of the windmill was a good one.

I picked up Annie's empty glass from the bar, and Chuck Ackroyd wandered over. He looked as though there was something on his mind.

"If I were you, I'd avoid that woman, Annie Sullivan."

"Oh?"

"Couldn't help but overhear that little invitation to the picnic," he said.

"Not that it's any of your business, but since you've made it so, out with it. What's your problem with Annie Sullivan?"

"She's trouble, is all."

"And from what I see, you should know from trouble, Chuck."

His face scrunched up, like he hadn't fully understood my meaning, that he'd just been insulted. He slapped three bucks down on the bar and told me that that should cover the cost of his beer.

"Used to like this place," he said. "Can't say I feel the same now."

And with that, Chuck Ackroyd left.

He couldn't dampen my mood, though, not with the Memorial Day picnic to look forward to, and the chance to spend it in the company of such good people as Annie and Janey Sullivan.

Linden Corners was the picture of the classic American village, all decked out for one of the nation's most patriotic holidays. It was a remembrance of the dead and also a celebration of the unofficial start of summer. And no one could have asked for a nicer day, with temperatures in the seventies and a sun riding high in a sky painted with a few white clouds that held no threat of rain.

It was eleven o'clock on that Memorial Day Monday, and as I drove through town, I saw that the gazebo in the park was awash in red, white, and blue, and a banner stretched across Main Street from the bank to the fire station, welcoming Columbia County residents and visitors alike to the twenty-fourth annual Linden Corners Memorial Day celebration. Later that afternoon there would be a parade and a town-sponsored barbecue held at the fire station, and there would be sports and activities for children and adults alike. And all the families would gather on the town green.

Marla's and Darla's shops were open and would probably do

a brisk business, selling cold drinks and holiday knickknacks. The Five-O was closed, and Martha had put a sign in the front door that encouraged folks to enjoy the barbecue and that she'd see them there. Most other businesses were closed for the day, even Connors' Corners, but George, back in town, confessed he'd probably break down and open up later, after the fireworks.

It was festive enough to have been Independence Day, but as I'd learned, a neighboring town held the celebratory honors for that holiday, so Linden Corners went overboard on Memorial Day.

Already the village square was filling up with people. Cars and trucks filled the lots, and even the county sheriff's office had sent a deputy to keep the traffic flowing. I'd never seen Linden Corners so filled with energy and with life, with folks simply enjoying one another's company.

I passed through town and rode high into the hills and up to the lane that led to the Sullivan driveway. Janey was waiting for me on the porch and came running over as soon as the car came to a stop. She was a special kid, always smiling whenever I saw her and always able to get me smiling, too, no matter what kind of mood was occupying my mind.

"We're going to have so much fun today," she informed me, and I said I hoped so, which got her going, filling me in on everything and anything that had to do with the day's events. At seven years of age, she was a veteran.

Annie emerged from the house dressed in a pair of white slacks and a blue blouse, a navy sweater casually tossed around her shoulders. She looked beautiful, I thought. With her chestnut-colored hair and that faint hint of blush to her cheeks, she was an all-American beauty, made even more lovely by the sight of Janey at her side, apple-cheeked and grinning.

Me, I wore casual slacks and a red shirt, long sleeves rolled to my elbows. I was ready to relax in a serious way, and that meant playing with an energetic seven-year-old.

"She's been talking about this day all weekend," Annie said.

"And I've been thinking about it," I confessed, looking down at Janey. "Thank you very much for inviting me to your picnic."

So that was how the day began, a mother and her young daughter adopting for the day one lost soul, the three pooling their resources to become a makeshift family on a day tailor-made for one. From all appearances, Memorial Day in Linden Corners was going to be a spectacular success, and we were intent on being part of it. Annie gathered a picnic basket, assigned me the task of carrying the heavy cooler, and issued Janey a reminder to take her toy-filled knapsack. We packed everything into the back of Annie's truck, left my car in her driveway, and made our way back to town where we parked behind Connors' Corners (in my driveway, actually). A double-trip for me, but Janey had wanted us to arrive in the village together. Then we made our way to the village park and found Cynthia and Bradley Knight already spreading out a large, oversized blanket, what Bradley called our home base for the day.

The Knights were a couple in their thirties, Cynthia being the proprietor of the fruit stand at the edge of town and Bradley being a lawyer up in Albany. Bradley was a formal kind of guy, sleeves rolled all the way down, all the buttons buttoned, not a hair out of place. I'd been told not to call him Brad. But he was good natured, too, with white-blond hair and dimples when he smiled that easily won over folks who thought of lawyers as good for nothing. Cynthia was just plain wonderful, a great friend of Annie's and an easy person to talk with. You could tell at first sight that Cynthia and Bradley were very much in love with each other but hadn't yet gotten around to having kids. They'd been married only three years.

Annie, Cynthia, and Bradley welcomed me into their tight-knit fold and we spent an enjoyable afternoon in the park, watching the parade—the school band, the local church groups, the county Little Leaguers—and devouring a delicious lunch of sandwiches from Annie and fried chicken from Cynthia and, of course, lots of fresh ripe fruits. Janey sat atop my shoulders and waved cheerfully at the passing marchers, happy to be above the spectators and calling out to Annie to "look how high I am." We played hide-and-seek and Frisbee and an assortment of other games, until I was just plain tuckered out. I dropped to the blanket with relief. Janey went and played with a school friend whose parents were set up nearby the gazebo, leaving us four adults a moment's peace. Bradley and Cynthia decided to take a walk around the park, and that in turn left Annie and me alone on the blanket, stomachs full from lunch, and, speaking for myself, with a heart full of joy.

"I can't tell you, Annie, how much I'm enjoying myself."

"You're a good sport, is what you are. I knew Janey would run you ragged. She's having fun doing it and I can't tell you how much I appreciate that. Hard to explain it, Brian, but she's taken a real shine to you. And she hardly ever does with . . . well, people she doesn't know."

"So I'm not a stranger anymore?" I asked.

She kiddingly punched my arm. "Strange, yes. But seriously, I can't thank you enough for spending so much time with her. I fear sometimes that she's lonely. You know, what with her father dying so soon . . ."

Her voice trailed off, perhaps because she realized she'd begun to open up. This was the first time she'd spoken of her late husband in my presence, first time I'd heard her say that he'd died. His death was still a mystery to me, and Annie's mentioning it was a sign either that she was beginning to deal with it or that she had just become more comfortable with me. I hoped both were true.

"How about a walk?" I suggested.

"Caught your breath already?"

I was staring directly at her when I said, "No, my breath is still taken away."

She shied away from the compliment but got up anyway, and I joined her. We took up a nice, leisurely pace while keeping a careful distance from one another. Unlike our day at the windmill, where our fingers had touched and our hands had curled around each other's, there was no hint of that intimacy now. There was an energy between us that, though it didn't bring us closer together, seemed to keep us from straying even further apart. The feeling was undeniably comforting and also completely unnerving. Our being together wasn't a date, we weren't two people testing out romantic waters; no, we were just two lonely and confused people finding tentative friendship in the wake of sorrow.

But finally, after an awkward silence, Annie began to open up to me, and I to her.

"Do you mind my asking about your husband?" I asked.

"I don't often speak about him, and when I do, it's usually because Janey's asked me a question about her dad. She misses him, even though sometimes I wonder how much she really remembers him." Annie paused, no doubt fighting the emotions that were ripping through her. "Janey was only five when Dan died, and in the beginning she asked me lots of questions—when is Daddy coming home, stuff like that—because she didn't understand. I still wonder how much she gets, and I still wonder if she's the luckier one. Not a day goes by that I don't think of Dan and the love we shared and the life we dreamed of. My saving grace is Janey, who looks so much like Dan it's frightening. Her smile, her eyes, even her disposition, so sunny and outgoing, it's Dan to a T."

"From where I stand, Janey's got a lot of you inside her, too," I said. "Like the way you blush when someone hands you a compliment . . . yeah, just like that."

She pushed me away, off the narrow path we were traveling. "You're mocking me."

I stopped for a moment, feigning hurt at her accusation. "Me? Mock?" And when she faced me, my hand instinctively reached up and felt her cheek, so warm and so soft. My hand lingered, and we gazed into each other's eyes like sudden, star-crossed lovers. Seconds later, the moment was gone, my hand withdrawn. Annie and I resumed walking.

"How about you, Brian Duncan Just Passing Through," she said, avoiding what had just happened between us, "what's your story? Shouldn't you have a career or a wife or a girlfriend or— oops."

My face, always the betrayer, had done it again, revealing my inner wounds like a banner. "No, no, it's only fair, since I started it. And my story is not so sad—more self-indulgent than anything else. The long and the short of it is this: I had a girlfriend who was practically my fiancée who also happened to be my work colleague and then one day she decided she'd rather sleep with the boss and get a hell of a promotion than be honest with me."

"My God, Brian, you make it sound so clinical."

"Detachment frees up your mind," I stated.

"But closes down the heart."

"Can you say you're any different?" I asked, not intending to sound so accusing. But that was exactly the way Annie heard it, and I quickly apologized. "Forget I said that, okay, because I'd hate to spoil this day."

Her face softened and we were once again on solid ground. In the waning afternoon sunlight, we finished our walk and returned to find Cynthia and Bradley playing cards with Janey.

"We're playing Go Fish, and I'm winning," Janey stated proudly.

"Such a shark—interested in lawyering?" Bradley said, tossing down his hand while the rest of us laughed.

Dinner was just around the corner, both literally and figuratively, since the firehouse would start serving at six o'clock. There, we had a bountiful choice of hot dogs and hamburgers, sweet sausage and blackened chicken, with salads and salt potatoes, which we carried back to our blanket and feasted on with great relish. Next came the desserts, with Cynthia unwrapping a dozen different pies, which it turned out were for anyone who wanted a slice. Seems dessert was a community event, with everyone bringing too many sweet treats, enough for the entire town to be able to sample bits and pieces from neighboring blankets. It was our chance to say hello to the folks we knew, and that included George and Gerta, who joined us for coffee and lingered with us to watch the fireworks display.

At nine sharp, with nightfall upon us and stars scattered throughout a dimly lit sky, the fireworks began, thunderous bursts of brightly colored lights, reds and greens and blues and oranges, a vast and explosive rainbow. Janey and the other children watched with fascination, inspiring the adults to "ooh" and "aah," too. At last, the grand finale was fired off, and after burst after burst of rich, explosive color, the smoke fizzled and the noise ended and a silence fell on the entire town. There was instant and spontaneous applause.

The evening over, families began packing up their things, leaving the park with warm new memories of another Linden Corners Memorial Day. Janey had fallen asleep almost immediately, and Cynthia and Bradley offered to take her home and get her settled in for the night. Annie, they said, should stay out, enjoy the cool night and the pleasant company, and I guess that latter part referred to me. She didn't fight it too long, and soon the Knights were off for the night, and Annie and I, once we'd returned the cooler and picnic basket to her truck, were again alone.

"How about a drink?" I asked.

"Thought George decided not to open up tonight after all."

"He's not," I said, "but not only do I have an in with the

owner, I also have a key." And I dangled the single key in the air.

She told me to lead on, and five minutes later we were settled on two stools, a glass of wine and a seltzer before us, talking about the events of the day. Our conversation wasn't forced; our company wasn't awkward. To keep potential patrons from thinking we were open, I kept the lights to a minimum, including leaving the porch light off. It kept most people away, but there was one visitor whose persistent knocking finally became a nuisance.

It was Chuck Ackroyd.

"Closed," I said through the locked door.

Still, he banged on the glass, harder it seemed, until I thought it was going to break. I unhooked the chain and opened the door slightly and tried to tell him to go away. His breath hit me first; he probably had more booze in him than I had behind the bar. And before I could send him off, he saw Annie sitting alone at the bar.

"What di' I tell you," he said, his words horribly slurred. "Kee' 'way from her; she's nuttin' but trouble. Caused me nuttin' but pain—is all 'er fault."

"Look, Chuck, whatever your troubles, I'm sure Annie's got nothing to do with them, so why don't you go on home, sleep off the effects of the keg you've obviously consumed, and maybe tomorrow you'll see things in the proper light."

Being nice to a belligerent drunk, I found, was a complete waste of time. Chuck pushed hard against the open door and made his way over to Annie. She gave me a concerned look, afraid of his ramblings and what they might lead him to do. So I grabbed him from behind and he came at me, swinging hard and fast, but not fast enough, because I managed to duck his punch. He spun too hard and fell to the floor, no doubt dizzy and nauseated.

From the floor, he pointed an accusatory finger at Annie, and again reiterated his belief that his troubles, whatever they were, had been her fault.

I helped him to his feet, walked his unsteady limbs to the door, and shoved him outside and onto the porch, where he lost his balance and tumbled down the couple of stairs to the sidewalk. He lay flat on the ground, not moving, and I hoped he'd passed out. Maybe in the morning, he'd think twice about his actions—that is, if he could even remember them.

I returned to Annie and apologized for Chuck's behavior.

"It's not your fault," she said. "He's . . . he's just bitter from his divorce. His wife left him a while back. He hasn't taken it well, and I guess on days like today—family time—the booze is his escape."

"Why would he blame you?"

"Beats me," she said, perhaps too quickly. But whatever the reason, it was put aside when Annie asked me if I'd like to dance.

"Uh . . . sure. Let me put on some music."

I put a coin in the jukebox and picked a song by Faith Hill called "This Kiss," and soon the bar was filled with the hummable country tune. Annie approved of my choice. The two of us began a slow and steady dance, our feet grazing the hardwood floor, our fingers linked. Holding her so close, I could smell her hair and see the definitions of her soft skin. A feeling of magic came over me as we gazed into each other's eyes. I felt drawn to her, though I was nervous and tentative, and I think she felt the same way. And as the song crescendoed and our bodies moved in closer, there was no stopping our next move.

Our faces close, noses practically touching, I felt my lips brush hers, a hesitant kiss from me and a hesitant return kiss from her. Still, neither of us pulled away, and our lips lingered, pressing tighter. Softly, she opened her mouth and our tongues lightly brushed. How long we held that kiss, I couldn't say—perhaps the song's lyrics had inspired us—but when we did finally part, we realized the song was over and we were dancing to the sound of silence.

"Oh," she said.

"Yeah, oh," I said.

"It's late," she said.

"Should I take you home?" I asked.

"I can drive myself," she said.

"My car is parked at your house," I said.

"Oh," she said.

"Yeah, oh," I said.

Another moment passed before we parted, and the next thing I knew, it was as though our kiss had never happened. Annie was now formal and businesslike as she began to clean up our empty glasses; I busied myself by turning off the jukebox. She felt awkward and so did I.

We left the bar and she drove through the dark streets of the village and into the even darker countryside to her farmhouse. There, standing in the driveway with my car door open, the little dome light adding a slight glow to the night, Annie and I stared one last time at each other.

"Thanks, Brian, for making today such a special day . . . for Janey."

"Thank you for inviting me. . . . Thank Janey, will you?"

"I will. Well, good night."

"Good night."

Annie turned from me, swallowed up by the dark night as though she didn't truly exist. I wondered, for a moment, if I had really even kissed her. But as I drove back to my apartment, I could smell Annie's sweet perfume and still taste the touch of her lips. It seemed to me that my hardened heart had unexpectedly begun to soften.

*   *   *

It was past midnight when I finally got home, but I doubted I would sleep that night. Not with that shy and hesitant kiss weighing so heavily on my mind. A complication? Yes. Unwanted? Maybe. Regretful? Absolutely not. But scary nonetheless. I needed a distraction and flicked on the television. The news was on, an hour later than usual, and I figured the night's movie must have run long or something. It turned out that maybe the gods were working overtime, because whatever had delayed the broadcast, I was definitely meant to see it. Not the top national or international news, not the extended weather forecast or even news of the night's scores. No, it was a short, buried piece about midway through the program, about a new drug that had not been approved by the FDA. I heard the name *Voltaire* and my head snapped up. I tuned in.

The anchor had tossed the story to a reporter, who was standing in front of the FDA building in Washington.

"Rick, the news out of the Food and Drug Administration about the new drug Tensure is nothing more than shocking. In development for many years, the drug, designed to aid in treating hypertension, was today denied approval by the FDA, over claims that some of its test findings were either inaccurate or, as one source alleged, altered. Little else is known about this disturbing development. Voltaire Pharmaceuticals, a division of the Voltaire Health Group, makers of Tensure, could not be reached for comment and has yet to issue a statement."

They moved on to the next story and I flipped off the television. I sat there in the near dark, silent and alone, absolutely blown away by the news. The Beckford Warfield Group, Justin and Maddie in particular, had a public relations nightmare on their hands, especially if Voltaire had falsified the research on the new drug. Heads would roll at Voltaire, and Justin's might, too. And Maddie—right then, I felt the pit of my stomach drop out, and all the food I'd consumed during the picnic made my stomach lurch in protest. *My God,* I thought, *what a mess.*

I'd thought Linden Corners was far enough away to shield me from the life I'd lived in the city. But escape, it seemed, was just a frame of mind. New York City, with Maddie and Justin and the troubles of the past, had just insinuated itself into my new and humble little life.

The results, I feared, could be disastrous.

EIGHT

The month of May slipped away, and June arrived, with summer. The sun rode high in the sky and temperatures gradually rose with each passing day. I now had memories of my own of those crisp spring days that are unique to Linden Corners. Foremost among them was the kiss Annie and I shared on the cedar floor of Connors' Corners. Weeks later and in the light of day, that kiss seemed almost like a dream. We had not spoken of it since. In fact, Annie and I had barely seen each other.

My days were filled with explorations of the valley, sometimes by car, often by way of a bicycle that George loaned me, claiming to have bought it years ago "during the wild and impetuous days of my youth." Evenings I spent mostly helping George run the bar, as well as—all too often, it seemed—finding myself seated at the Connors' dinner table. It was like they'd adopted me, and I guess there was no harm in that, since it presented a solution that solved a loneliness problem for three souls.

I slept less, a sure sign that I had healed from the hepatitis that had downed me a lifetime ago. So, despite my late hours at the tavern, I found myself rising earlier and earlier the longer I stayed in this gentle farming community. As though I had to milk the cows and tend the herd, I rose with the sun and enjoyed morning bike rides along the empty, dew-laced roads, waving at my neighbors and newfound friends as they went about their daily rituals and I, mine.

It was a late June morning when I found myself along Route 23, and before I could even think about it, the windmill emerged over the hill, catching my eye and filling my heart with that inexplicable but now familiar sense of pleasure. The windmill was my good-luck token, a constantly spinning talisman that drew me in with its power and its force and the lure of its magic. It drove my direction, as I turned the corner and headed not for the village center and my little apartment but up Crestview Road and on to Annie Sullivan's farmhouse.

Just a half mile up, I noticed a small yellow school bus stopped at the Sullivan driveway. Janey and Annie were skipping down the gravel path, Janey's sweet face lit up with a big grin. She had a knapsack on her back, which I thought might topple her, but she balanced herself well and in no time had clambered aboard the bus. She didn't see me, and the bus trundled along to pick up the next kid.

Once the bus cleared the driveway, there was nothing, except my bike, between me and Annie. Against the backdrop of the valley's green swaths of grass, I was hard to miss.

"You're still here?" she asked.

"Do you mean I'm still here, as in in front of your driveway at seven-thirty in the morning or I'm still here, as in still in town?"

She didn't answer but on her face was a look of sudden contemplation. It wasn't as though we hadn't seen each other since our secret kiss. We had, but we hadn't been alone, and that was the big difference. Now it was not just a two-lane stretch of highway separating us but also a sea of uncertain emotion. She was thinking something—what, I couldn't say.

Then I heard her ask me, "Got plans today?"

"Excuse me?"

"You heard me. Do you have plans for the day?"

Yes, I had heard her, but her words had surprised me, and sometimes you like to hear things a second time, to make sure your ears really work.

"Uh, none, really. I usually don't make any plans. Makes the day that much more interesting—unpredictable."

"Must be nice," she said, sounding slightly envious. "Tell you what, Mr. Lazy Pants—come back at ten o'clock and bring your bike with you."

"Can I ask why?"

She thought about that before answering. "Actually, no, you can't ask. But you can answer this: Do you like peaches?"

"Peaches?"

"Yes, Brian, peaches."

"I like peaches," I said stupidly.

"Good. And you know, Brian, you may want to clean your

ears a little more regularly. You never know what you might miss."

"I'll get right on it. So I may not be ready by ten."

"Fine. I'll expect you at ten after. Five minutes extra per ear." At that, she waved a temporary good-bye and turned back up her driveway. She didn't skip, but I noticed a distinct spring in her step anyway. Heck, there was one in mine, too, and I was on a bike, heading back toward town to prepare for something that involved bicycles and peaches. And a woman I had kissed but with whom I hadn't had the guts to speak of it.

Twenty minutes later, sweat dripping from my pores, I grabbed a slow, satisfying shower, wondering the entire time what Annie could possibly have in store for me. Maybe she had had something planned all along and was going to call me. Or maybe my presence was convenient, and she asked me along out of courtesy. And was this what I really wanted, the blossoming of another romance, if that's indeed what it was? The two of us clearly were both afraid and shy and tentative about whatever was happening between us, both still carrying fresh scars from past relationships. Those deep wounds made us uncertain about how to proceed with our lives.

I had to ask myself some questions: Had I run from New York City and all that Maddie had meant only to fall into the arms of another woman? Was this what I'd been searching for, or the direction that the gods were pointing me toward? Yes, I was intended for someone, and that someone was intended for me, but perhaps New York hadn't been where I'd find that person; perhaps I'd have to go forth and find her. Happiness was possible; you just had to take a chance, leap in, and fight for what felt right. Because taking chances meant living life, and without chance, there was nothing but emptiness and darkness and solitude.

All this during a fifteen-minute shower, and the best conclusion I could come up with was to take shorter showers. But heck,

I'd needed to clean my ears. Dried, shaved, and dressed, I went across to the Five-O and had myself a light breakfast. Before too long, it was closing in on ten. I was ready for anything.

Apparently I'd listened well, or so Annie informed me as I pulled my bicycle into her driveway at precisely 10:10, coming up beside her pickup, where I noticed she'd already stashed her own green ten-speed, along with her easel and paints and a burlap-covered canvas. And in the front of the cab was a wicker picnic basket. There was a devilish grin on Annie's face, a look that told me she liked knowing where we were going when I did not. She had me at a complete disadvantage. Maybe not complete, because I was going as a willing participant, wherever we happened to be going. It was her secret, soon to be shared with an eager listener.

She ushered me into the passenger side of the truck, waiting as I strapped myself in. I joked about how now I really couldn't escape. She responded by slamming the door and then locking it. I was her captive, and a willing one at that.

"Just sit and relax and stop asking so many questions. No wonder you and Janey get along so well—you both have the same patience level."

"I don't have a patience level," I remarked.

"Exactly my point."

As she peeled the truck out of the driveway, her sudden laughter filled the cab; no doubt she was thrilled about our secret excursion. I told her how much I'd like to join her in her glee, and so finally she revealed where we were going.

"Not counting the windmill, it's my favorite place in the whole valley—right along the river."

Second only to the windmill, I thought. This must be someplace special.

We drove for about a half hour, down narrow roads that wound their way through the hills and dips of the valley. We drove through small towns that were as beautiful as Linden Corners yet slightly different, too, and I commented how it was as though we were stuck on some endless loop of road. Finally, Annie turned off the paved road onto a dirt one, and the tires threw up clouds of dust in our wake as the truck climbed higher and higher. We emerged through a bushy layering of leafy trees and came to an abrupt stop on the top of a ridge.

"Is this a parking place?" I asked, noticing there were no other cars around. Or people, for that matter.

"It is now," she said. "Come on—help me unload the bikes."

I did as instructed, and we mounted our bikes, she taking the lead. Down below, the river stretched languidly, and above us, the sky seemed endless.

"Well?" she asked.

"Show me more," I urged.

And she did. For the next two hours, we wended our way both by bike and by foot through the hidden regions of the Hudson Valley, enjoying the waves of wind on our faces, basking in the sun's rays, led on by the languorous rhythm of the river. All the while we were laughing and smiling and not thinking beyond the next turn of the path. If any awkwardness had developed between us after our unspoken kiss, it was washed away now by our mutual appreciation for this time and place, alone with the world and ourselves but pleased, too, to be sharing it with a newfound friend.

Where the path had taken us, I couldn't say, but Annie was in complete control and she magically guided us back to the truck, where we put away the bikes and grabbed her supplies from the back and the picnic basket from the front. She led me to a rocky bluff, high above the river, where I proceeded to spread a blanket on the ground. Inside the picnic basket was a bottle of seltzer; the fizzy water was refreshing after the long ride.

So it was there, up on our very own Mount Olympus, where we ate Annie's version of ambrosia, fried chicken and macaroni salad, and for dessert, peach pie.

"You folks sure do know your pies," I said. "Where I grew up, the choices were limited to apple, cherry, or mincemeat, whatever that was. Here in Linden Corners, you've got your strawberry and your peach and whatever else you and Gerta and Martha can get your hands on."

"Pie is serious business in Linden Corners. There's little debate about that. And you see why I asked if you liked peaches."

"If I didn't this morning, I do now," I said, taking another slice from the tin.

We finished our feast, and Annie poured a glass of white wine into a plastic tumbler and then settled comfortably on the blanket, staring out at the river's soothing waters.

"I started coming here for the view," she said, "and ended up coming back for the tranquillity. You know, when you leave a place behind and it lives only in your mind and your memories, it begins to take on a life of its own, and the potential exists for you to make too much of it. To increase its importance. But sitting here, seeing this, Brian, it's like meeting an old friend and picking up right where you left off." She paused, then looked over at me. "Sounds silly, doesn't it?"

I shook my head. "Not at all. But I don't understand one thing—you speak of this location as though you haven't been here in years. It's only a short ride from the farmhouse."

"I used to come here a lot, it's true, before . . ."

"Your husband died?"

She nodded. "Yeah, but before Dan and I married, too. Actually, up here is where I went to think after he proposed to me. I was twenty and I'd just finished my junior year of college over at Bennington, and I was having financial troubles and was thinking about taking a year off. My aunt, before she passed away, lived in the valley, over in Malden Bridge, and so I went to stay with her, maybe get a job somewhere. I found this big rock one day as I rode around, and it gave me space to think, no pressure from anyone or anything, just me and the sky and the river. So I guess you can think of this place as my thinking pad."

"Annie's Bluff," I said.

She grew silent, and I thought I detected tears in her eyes. "Brian, that's really sweet. I never gave this place a name, never thought to. It was just a place to come to. But now . . . now, I'll always remember it as Annie's Bluff, and I'll always remember who named it."

"Shucks, ma'am," I said, trying to stave off a growing sense of embarrassment. "So, did Dan propose to you up here?"

"No, Dan never came here. Sure, he knew I had this secret place, but he never pressured me to share it with him. Two people can share so much of each other, but not everything. You can't help but keep a part of yourself hidden away; it's human nature."

"Then how come you're showing it to me?"

"Frankly, I wasn't sure I could come back here, by myself or with someone else; I wasn't sure I was brave enough. Brian, those were such happy, glorious, wonderful days, with my life stretched out before me, my choices limitless. So much, though, has changed. I was afraid maybe this place had, too." Then she hesitated. "Thanks—for coming with me." She paused, took a drink from her tumbler. "You probably think I'm nuts or something, the way I dragged you here, not telling you anything about where we were going."

"I've had fun."

"Had?"

"Having. I'm *having* lots of fun," I assured her. "So, you never did tell me—how did the windmill come into the picture?"

"Didn't I say I'd save that for a rainy day?" she asked.

I looked up at the bright blue sky and pretended to catch a raindrop in my palm. "We'll have to improvise."

"Okay—the windmill," she said, thinking. "Let's see . . . where to begin? Well, like you, I'd never heard of Linden Corners, and why would I? It's just one of dozens of small villages in the river valley. But I had heard about the windmill when my aunt mentioned it one day. She showed me an article in the paper about its maybe being torn down. 'What a shame,' she said. Me, I stared at the photograph of the windmill, and for days, my curiosity was piqued; I couldn't get the image out of my mind. I decided I had to see it before it was destroyed. So I drove to Linden Corners and found the windmill, and oh, Brian, as run down as it was, the sight of those giant sails, gently turning with the shifts in the air, I was transfixed."

"I know the feeling."

"There was a county meeting a few days later, where they were to discuss a referendum to tear it down. I went. I couldn't believe it—I spoke up against these leaders, me, a nineteen-year-old girl who'd lived in the region all of two months. What I discovered was that I wasn't alone in wanting to save the windmill, and I became fast friends with some of the locals, among them Gerta Connors. She's the one who took me to the farmhouse, and that's where I met Dan."

Her story came to an abrupt close, as though she'd been reading a chapter from a book and it had come to an end and she was afraid to turn the page. She gazed down on the river and somehow found her strength. "Dan was a conflicted man, desperately trying to hold on to his family's farm but also be his own independent and modern man, trying to help his elderly parents as much as he could. But he was twenty-five and had a job himself, working, ironically, for the state legislature in Albany. As for the windmill, I guess he didn't give it any thought one way or the other. You see, the Sullivans were going to sell that piece of land back to the county, and the money would help keep the rest of the farm going."

"So what happened?"

"The beauty of small-town America. Turns out the bank's loan manager's wife had sided with the preservationists, and so she convinced her husband to give the Sullivans an extension on their loan. And then I and some others volunteered our time and energy and some money, too, and we restored the windmill."

"And in the process, you and Dan Sullivan . . ."

She cut me off with a quick nod of her head. "Yeah."

A momentary silence enveloped us, somehow drawing us closer. Hers was a wonderful, inspiring story of determination, and I told her so. "And so that was how you became known as the woman who loved the windmill."

"More like 'saved.' Except in Linden Corners, we speak from the heart."

"This Linden Corners, it's a special place. A throwback to a time when being neighbors meant being friends," I said. "I can't help but feel spoiled by it. This is a world far beyond the one I knew, a city pulsing with a life of its own, while here I am surrounded by nature's riches—the trees, the river, the sky, not to mention the beautiful woman at my side."

The compliment simply slipped out. I hadn't had time to think about it; I just said the words, and there they were, right on the table (or blanket, as it were), my acknowledgment of Annie's beauty. And she didn't press me on it; she seemed to favor simply letting it sink in and warm her insides. My words produced a glow that emanated from her smile. She then changed the subject altogether and my words evaporated into the air.

"Brian, tell me why you left New York City."

"Wow—where'd that come from?"

"Actually, from Gerta."

"George's wife?"

"Brian, do you know any other women named Gerta?"

"Good point."

"And good try at deflecting the question. Eventually you're going to have to tell someone—whether it's me or George or somebody else. We're a curious people, we Linden Corners folk, and when we welcome a new friend, we like to know all about them. And so far, as wonderful as you've been to all of us—"

"And all of you to me."

"Stop trying to change the subject," she said again, her tone playful but stern at the same time. She didn't want to offend me, but she still wanted her question answered.

"Okay, okay, you win," I said, trying to compose my thoughts, letting my mind drift down the river to where it might find the world I'd left just a few short months ago. "Well, I gave you the shorthand version previously, but I guess that wasn't enough. The story starts and ends in New York City, where for close to fourteen years I worked and lived and even loved, and then one day it all came crashing down. And I decided, then and there, with little regard for all I'd established and also with little regret, to pack up my stuff and split."

"And that's it?"

"That's it."

She poured herself more wine and then offered me a sip. "Just a little?"

I shook my head. "Can't. You know."

"Right. Hepatitis. Brian, you sure that's not just another form of escape, a crutch that enables you to hobble along in this new existence of yours? It's a reminder of what you left behind, and maybe somehow it strengthens your resolve."

"You missed your calling, Dr. Sullivan," I said.

There was no getting around the issue anymore, around the

reason for my being in Linden Corners and the events that led up to it, so I continued my story by backing up to my move to New York City all those years ago.

"I'd been in college, had been dating my high school sweetheart for five years. We were both graduating. We were all set to plan our life together when one day she just ended it, saying that she felt like she was still in high school and that as long as we were together, she'd feel that way. She needed to grow, and there was no way she'd grow with me attached to her."

"Attached?" Annie asked.

"Like an anchor, weighing her down."

"Ouch."

"My friend John Oliver had just moved to New York City and I went to visit him for a weekend and ended up staying, getting a job and living the life of a single twentysomething in the big city. Lots of parties, bad dates, low pay, and long working hours, but it was fun and filled with an undeniable excitement. When Justin Warfield and his public relations firm came courting, the years of struggling began to pay off. I took this amazing job, met this incredible woman—who also happened to work there—and suddenly I was in my early thirties on the fast track for the kind of nice, family-oriented life I'd always dreamed of. Everything, the saying goes, was going great.

"Then I got sick," I told Annie, "and everything snowballed, culminating in Maddie's betraying me. That was the catalyst that drove me from the city."

"So this Maddie, what did she say about sleeping with your boss?"

I shook my head. "I didn't ask her about it."

"So you never gave her a chance to explain herself?"

"What was there to explain? She was sleeping with the boss, and apparently she was good enough at it to get herself a promotion."

"That's rather a simplistic take on the matter, don't you think? Very black and white. Do you think you might have been hasty? Not giving her a chance to talk and maybe fill in some of the gray areas?"

"Annie, what would it have changed? Nothing. The end result would have been the same."

"For the two of you, maybe, in terms of sharing a future together. But Brian, you threw your life away, all that you had worked for. Why? Because of a broken heart?"

"Not broken," I said, "wounded. And I guess I needed time away to allow it to heal."

"So you don't call what you did running away?"

I laughed, a short, sharp bark that took her by surprise. "A common theory. That's what my friend John called it, too, and each time I talk with him, he reminds me of it. He wants me to come home."

"And?"

"And I think I'm enjoying myself here."

"You know what I think?"

"I think you're going to tell me."

"That's right—I am. You, Brian Duncan Just Passing Through, are hiding out."

"And what's wrong with that?"

"What's wrong with it? Brian, it's not living. You think having all this free time during the day and then spending what would otherwise be lonely nights tending bar satisfying? From the way you describe it, you had a pretty successful career. You're smart and talented, and now look at you, wasting it all."

"To spend time with you," I said. Actually, the words had popped first into my mind, but before I knew it, they were out of my mouth and hovering in the air between us.

She looked away, toward the river, not saying anything, probably afraid to or uncertain of what to say.

I decided to fill the void. "Annie, if I were really running away from my problems, I'd still be on the road, moving from town to town like I did for the first six weeks after leaving New York. I'd be dropping postcards to my friends and family, telling them what a great time I was having, all the while wallowing in my misery and feeling sorry for myself. But that's not what happened, not when I passed through this valley. I like Linden Corners; I like being able to take it easy after so many years of working so hard. Call me spoiled, but even I know it can't last. I can't keep draining my savings and I certainly can't live on what George is paying me at the tavern. For the summer, though—for now—I'm content."

"Is that what I am, then, a summer distraction?"

"Truthfully, Annie, I'm not sure what you are. Meeting someone like you—no, not someone *like* you—meeting *you,* that's not anything I planned on. But I do enjoy the time we spend together, and I like playing with Janey and being invited to your holiday picnics and your special places, like here, up on this bluff. . . ."

Annie hugged herself close, her arms around her knees. As though she were cold. But she wasn't, not with the afternoon sun creating a warm circle of light around us. No, it was a defensive move. Clearly, our innocent picnic was venturing into uncharted territory, and for both of us, it was dangerous territory, too.

"Brian?" she asked, still not looking at me.

"Yes?"

"I'm . . . I'm not ready."

"Sshh," I whispered. "Neither am I."

She turned to me, and in her eyes I saw the pent-up loss and sorrow, as though they wanted to leave her, seep through her tear ducts and drop into the river far below. I found myself wanting to kiss away those tears, so I leaned in, watched as her eyes closed, and pressed my lips to her eyelids, first one and then the other, tasting salty tears as they trickled down her cheeks.

I pulled away, and our eyes met. And then we kissed again, our lips meeting and touching and our tongues searching and longing. For a time, on a fresh summer's day, two souls who had known sadness and betrayal found solace and friendship atop a rocky bluff while below, the mighty river surged on, and above, the wispy clouds drifted by. Nature was alive all around us, en-livening us.

"What are you like when you *are* ready?" I asked as we parted. "Wow."

Annie couldn't help it—she let out a giggle that reminded me so much of Janey, of her sweetness and her innocence.

"Must have been the wine," she said.

"Or things more intoxicating," I said, staring deep into her eyes.

And then the moment between us passed, and Annie and I gathered up the remains of lunch and headed back to the truck with the picnic basket. But thankfully, our afternoon was not yet over. I helped her carry her easel back to the bluff, and there she set up her makeshift studio and began to work her magic on the canvas, while I sat and alternately watched her and watched the river, and even-tually I drifted off into a sun-induced slumber, and the hours slipped away.

Later, when she dropped me and my bicycle off in front of Connors' Corners, I asked her if she'd take me back there someday.

"I . . . that's not an easy question to answer, Brian," Annie admitted to me. "School is ending soon and Janey's going to be home with me, which means my hands will be full, full time. So . . . well, let's just remember today. We'll see each other, I'm sure. Linden Corners, it's real small."

I tried my hardest not to look away when I said, "Sure. No problem."

And as abruptly as our day had begun, so did it end. Annie drove off to meet up with Janey's school bus, and I went upstairs and sat alone on my bed, staring at the ceiling and feeling the constant thrumming of my heart.

Life holds so many precious moments that if you're fortunate to recognize them for what they are, they become keepsake treasures of the mind and heart, something to keep close, so when you're down or lost you can call them up, like files on a computer, to get you through the darkness. I was grateful for that day on Annie's Bluff, especially in light of the unexpected tragedy that was to sweep through Linden Corners in a literal heartbeat.

For three days, I heeded Annie's words and remembered our day together in my dreams; I saw moving pictures that were splashed with rich, vibrant color, images that returned to me whenever I was alone or in the dark or facing a sudden case of doubt about our burgeoning relationship. If indeed that was what our friendship was becoming.

Wednesday passed, and Thursday, and suddenly it was Friday night, opening weekend of the summer solstice and payday for many of the folks who lived and worked in town. So it was going to be a night for celebration, or so George had warned me the night before.

He arrived earlier than usual, three o'clock, and I was upstairs in my room when I heard him tooling around the bar. I went down to see about helping him set up. He had put every glass on top of the sleek bar and was busy washing them, one by one, then setting them on a series of cloth dish towels until they dried.

"Hey, want some help?" I asked.

"No, no—I'm enjoying myself very much. It's a tradition started by my grandpa, oh, long, long ago. You see, today is sort of a mini-holiday. We call it First Friday, and the bar never sees a busier night all year. As a young lad, I'd come every year and start washing all the glasses and sweeping the floor, and even shining up the brass in later years, and I gotta tell you, Brian, it feels good doing it all again. Real good."

"Well, surely I can help with something."

He put me to the task of checking the kegs and bringing up some cases of bottled beer and stocking and storing them so they'd be nice and chilled for the long night. As we worked, George whistled and hummed and said very little, and I didn't engage him in conversation but merely let him go about his happy business, heartened to see a man still take such pride in his life's work.

Before too long, it was four in the afternoon and George went over and turned the lock on the front door. Soon the cars and trucks started pulling up. Folks entered the bar and ordered up the first round, and that got the night off on the right foot, a night of time-honored tradition, kept out of respect for folks who lived nearly one hundred years ago. As happy hour segued into early evening, the crowd grew, until there were probably forty people in the tavern, a large turnout, George said with pride, and went busily back to his station behind the bar. Happy-hour prices, he instructed me, were in effect all night.

At seven-thirty, Gerta showed up with a couple plates of dinner, one for George and one for me, and she hung around for about an hour, alternately cleaning glasses and telling George to take a break and take it easy, but he barely listened, so involved was he in his business. Finally Gerta bade her good-byes and the whole bar waved back, and then the party continued.

The jukebox played and folks danced, and I saw the pool table get more action than I'd ever seen, with quarters lining the rim, a bunch of patrons eager to play eight ball. Conversation flowed as much as the beer, with the topic changing more often than the keg—though that, too, needed to be changed, and I lugged a couple fresh ones from the basement at about nine o'clock.

Me, I didn't notice the hours passing, since there was no time to watch the clock, and aside from taking part in little bits of chatter here and there, I'd been working steadily alongside George, enjoying watching a true tavernkeeper at his peak. He showed me a thing or two about keeping the patrons satisfied.

At ten, he urged me to take a break. "Ten minutes, Brian. Go ahead; I'll be just fine."

I wanted to refuse, but before I could, he pushed me away from the bar and then closed the counter that separated the bartenders from the customers. True, I hadn't worked this hard since George had offered me the job, and I decided a quiet break would reenergize me. I went outside, past a small group that had assembled on the porch for a breath of fresh air, and sat myself down on the steps.

Someone wasted little time in joining me. I turned and saw Chuck Ackroyd, a bottle in his hand and a sneer on his face.

"Whatever you've come to say, Chuck, I'd appreciate it if you'd keep it to yourself."

"You know what I was doing this time last year?" he asked me. He obviously wasn't waiting for an answer, because he told me. "Working behind that bar. Yup, George always said First Friday was his busiest night, and in the past couple of years, he'd call me up, ask for my help. And I gave it; didn't ask for any money, either."

"Uh-huh," I said, not wanting to antagonize him any further. His message was clear, even if his beer-sodden mind wasn't.

"Now you come along and George doesn't need me." He drank from his beer, a long, loud gulp. "Didn't even call me to say he wouldn't be needing me. Nope, not even a phone call."

"I'm sorry for that, Chuck. But look, I'm not trying to bust a friendship at all. You and I seem to have gotten off on the wrong foot, but any antagonism between us has come from you, not me.

So why don't you do us both a favor—stop looking for trouble where it doesn't exist. I'm not a threat to your friendship with George. I'm the hired help."

He laughed over that one, sputtering beer as he did. "Sure thing, Mr. City Boy, if you say so."

I had a feeling he wasn't done, and I don't mean with the beer.

"You still seeing that Sullivan chick?"

I could have punched him, but instead I played it cool. "Annie and I are friends; that's it."

"Everything fits into a neat little box with you, doesn't it? To George, you're the hired help. To Annie Sullivan, you're the friend. What about me—you got me in one of your little boxes?"

"Hopefully, one with the lid closed."

"Yeah, that's it, Mr. City Boy, play the smart ass with me. You know, you say Annie's just a friend, but I've seen you two, like that night . . . heck, Memorial Day. Had the bar all to yourselves. Tell me something—do you always kiss your friends?"

"Chuck, I'm ending this conversation now. I'm going to go back inside and help George, and the next time you and I see each other, we'll forget we had this unfortunate little chat. Sound advice, don't you think?"

I was getting up to leave when he said words that stopped me in my tracks.

"It's Annie's fault my wife left me."

"Excuse me?"

"She couldn't keep her man satisfied, if you know what I mean. Dan Sullivan, that prick, wasn't happy at home, so he went wandering and found what he wanted with my wife. She took off, and it's all Annie's fault."

I wondered if there was any validity to this story, and then discounted it. Consider the source.

"Look, Chuck, if your wife left you, the reason is probably a lot closer to home than the Sullivan farmhouse."

"Superior assholes, all of you," he said. "Started with Dan, and now you."

"You know, Chuck, maybe it's not that others have a superior attitude. Maybe it's just that you have an inferiority complex. If you want your life to improve, start assigning the blame where it belongs and then move on."

Then I was gone from the porch, away from his belligerent accusations, resuming my place beside George for what turned out to be the remainder of the long night, a four-hour stretch that saw George stop only once to pee. No break, and definitely no leaving until the clock struck two.

Which it finally did, and the last group of folks filed out and crossed the street, where Martha had opened up the Five-O for the special occasion, serving earlier-than-usual breakfasts and lots of hot, steaming coffee, a responsible end to one of the most joyous parties I'd ever been in the thick of.

George turned the lock on the door and wiped his brow with a washrag. "Wow," he said. "That was one big, spectacular blowout. The best First Friday yet. Oh, Pop and Grandpa, they're looking down proud from the heavens—and probably raising a few in honor of tonight. Makes me a happy man. And Brian, I couldn't have done this without you, that's for sure."

"Thanks, George. I had fun."

"Saw you looking around once or twice," he said. "Looking for a certain someone?"

"You mean Annie? No, I figured she was home with Janey, especially when I saw Cynthia and Bradley come by around eight. Besides, I don't see First Friday as Annie's scene."

"Oh, I remember another Annie, and her first First Friday with us. It was just after she saved the windmill from being torn down, and we had a special kind of celebration that night, surely. In fact, I think that was the night she and Dan—well, started going together." His eyes panned the bar, soaking up memories of the atmosphere. "Yup, this bar has seen lots of times, good ones mostly, and I was witness to them, night after night."

"Beer after beer."

"That's for certain."

"George, can I ask you a question?"

"Anything, my boy."

"Annie and Dan—were they happy?"

"You been listening to Chuck?"

"Maybe."

"Look, Brian, you're a nice man, and Annie, she's a nice lady. Defines the word *nice,* really. And whatever has happened in the past is just that, the past. You've had your troubles; so has she. But somehow you two found each other, and even though I don't presume to know exactly the nature of your relationship, I do know you've helped her emerge from a two-year funk. That's Cynthia's word, mind you, and she passed it along to Gerta and so I'm passing it on to you."

"She's helped me, too."

"Good. Then that's all that should matter. The future, Brian, keep looking to it. Think of Annie's windmill—you ever see its sails go backward?"

He didn't say another word and neither did I. The two of us spent the next hour energetically cleaning up the lingering effects of my first and, as it turned out, George's last, First Friday.

I was coming up the stairs from the basement after bringing down an empty keg, and I found George sitting on his stool behind the bar, slightly slumped over. On the bar was a pint of beer, freshly poured. It waited for the next customer. George had poured his final glass. As I sat down at the bar, tears fell uncontrollably from my eyes, and, despite doctor's orders, I drank that beer until nothing remained but the love with which it had been poured.

NINE

The words came easily from the heart.

"You live your life well, you live it long, and then God shines down on a certain day and you enter his kingdom," said Father Eldreth Burton, the resident pastor of St. Matthew's Roman Catholic Church, as he stood graveside while administering comfort to family and friends, all of whom had come together to say final good-byes to one of their own, one of the best. That Monday morning was alive with the energy of life. Birds flew overhead, moving images against a lustrous canvas of blue sky, their gentle song lifting our hearts, and the sun's powerful rays warmed us on this most solemn occasion. No one could have asked for a more beautiful summer's day.

After a mass in which eulogies were delivered with verve and spirit, and truth and laughter, too, the mourners ventured beyond the simple white clapboard building to the town's historic cemetery, where generations of loyal townsfolk were long buried but in no way forgotten. Forever, they were a part of the town's tapestry. It was there, on land touched by history, beside his beloved grandfather and father, that George Connors was laid to rest.

I was surrounded by folks who had been born in Linden Corners, and this might have left me feeling like a stranger. Who was I, really, this Brian Duncan Just Passing Through, to be overcome with sadness equal to that of those who had known George for years or decades or a lifetime? Maybe it was being the last person he spoke with, maybe it was finding him slumped over behind the bar, but George had moved me, touched me, welcomed me into his world with that simple phrase, "What'll it be?" In such a short stretch of time, George had made a lasting impression on me, as though I'd known him all my life, a surrogate father who instilled in me confidence and knowledge and self-worth, qualities I'd lost sight of back in New York City.

Having to be the one to tell Gerta had filled me with tremendous sorrow and extreme trepidation. I knew for certain I couldn't tell her over the phone. I did, however, call the local doctor, Marcus Burton—the pastor's retired brother, to attend to George and deal with the necessary details, and once that was done, I wound my way down dark, empty streets until coming to the Connors' home of nearly fifty years. Gerta was waiting for me on the porch, sitting quietly in her rocker, her wedding photographs cradled in her arms.

"I felt him leave me," she told me.

I sat with her there, and for two hours, as the dawn broke over the horizon, I listened with rapt attention as Gerta unfolded story after story of a life shared, stories laced with the magic of love, stories that filled me with a a sense of warmth that bordered on envy as I realized how lucky Gerta and George had been to find one another. These stories carried both Gerta and myself through a busy weekend of funeral preparations, which intensified hourly as his family arrived from various corners of the state, including his four daughters with their spouses and numerous children— the tangible legacy of George's love.

The same folks I'd spent the weekend with were now assembled before the grave, gathering strength from their numbers. In addition to his four daughters—Lindsey, Melanie, Nora, Viki— there were eleven grandchildren, nice-looking kids who stood proud and attentive, supporting their moms and dads and their grandmother. Gerta was brave, stalwart, keeping her tears at bay, needing to in order to get through this ritual. Here, now, she was her family's leader, its voice.

Keeping Gerta close in his sights was Chuck Ackroyd, decidedly sober and with his head bowed. He'd done a fair amount of things to alienate too many folks in town, yet George had remained steadfast in his friendship, and now, with George gone, Chuck's tenuous link with the town was frayed even more. Gerta, though, I noticed, took comfort in knowing that he was just one step behind her.

Me, I was among the townspeople, a large contingent of folks who had known George for years, many of whom had been part of the First Friday celebration, all of whom remarked on how well George had seemed; everyone was shocked by his death. Everyone who ran a business in town was there, too; Martha, the twins, Richie Ravens from the Solemn Nights. And at my side, offering me more comfort than I'd expected, was Annie, and with her, Janey. Though she was only seven, Janey knew from death and showed just how grown up she could be, standing in her dark skirt and blouse, her blond hair reflecting the sun's yellow glow.

Father Burton guided us through the interment, offering prayers and a loving benediction. Tradition dictated the remainder of the service, with each of George's daughters tossing a handful of earth on the casket as it was lowered into the ground. They remained, talking quietly with Father Burton while the rest of us started to drift off, back to our lives and homes with the hope that today's celebration of life in the face of the death would help us all live just a little bit better.

Annie and Janey and I started down the grassy hill of the cemetery; we didn't get very far before I heard my name. It was Gerta, being led down the hill by her eldest daughter, Nora.

"I wanted to speak with you," Gerta said as she approached. "You see, Brian, we haven't talked about the Corner yet."

"Oh, Mom, isn't it too soon?"

I had to agree with Nora. "Gerta, maybe this can wait . . . you know, until you've had some time to think—"

"Oh, hush now. Everyone's treating me with kid gloves, and I've gotta tell you, I'm stronger than all of you give me credit for. George and I, we talked a lot about what our lives would be like without the other. And I do miss my George so very much, more than words can ever say, but you've got to let me deal with that in my own time, my private time. See, though, I'm a practical woman, always have been, and I don't want to see George's work forgotten."

"I realize that," I said, "and surely George made provisions for the Corner for after he . . ."

"Brian, you can say it in front of me. George died." She put a soft hand to my cheek. "I'll never forget the comfort you showed me that early morning, listening to me tell my stories. Tell my life. And George, well, he was a good man, kind to all, but I never did see him take such a fast liking to another person like he did with you—excepting of course with me. One look, that's all it took." She smiled. "But if you want to wait a couple of days before making a decision, we can postpone."

"Maybe it's best—"

Once again, she cut me off; I guess it was her prerogative. She turned instead to Annie, who was listening in, and said, "Talk with Brian, dear; see if you can't convince him that what George would have wanted most was to see the Corner continue."

"I'll do my best."

Janey piped up. "I'll help, too."

"Thank you, sweet angel," Gerta said. "That will be a big help."

Then, before Nora could lead her mother back down the hill and to their car, Gerta's eyes twinkled as she stared at me and Annie and Janey.

"You know what you three look like?" she asked.

I shook my head.

"A family."

Then she gave me a warm embrace, her hands patting my back with maternal assurance. I caught Chuck Ackroyd's gaze as he watched from nearby the grave site, and it wasn't one of sympathy. He stalked away. There was no sense explaining the situation; he saw my friendship with Gerta as competitive, and that was that. Grief knows no boundaries, and like us all, Chuck would have to deal with George's death in his own time, his own way.

Our makeshift family—a description ignored by Annie— headed out of the cemetery and onto the sidewalks of the village, toward Main Street, where Annie had parked her truck. Once we were at the truck, Janey hopped in and Annie went around to the driver's side. She stopped and regarded me with uncertainty.

"Brian . . . thanks, you know, for joining us today."

"We were there for each other," I said.

"Death is never easy, especially for the young."

"And not so young," I added.

She smiled ruefully. "Yeah."

"Momma, don't say 'yeah,' " Janey said from inside the truck.

"Maybe she's not so young, either," Annie remarked with a tentative smile.

We said our good-byes then, and they drove back to the farmhouse; I went upstairs to the three-room apartment above a bar that I called home. For now, at least—for who knew how long? I couldn't sit still, couldn't stop imagining the sound of George tooling around downstairs, getting ready for another day behind the bar, and so I grabbed my car keys and headed down the stairs. I was just about ready to drive to parts unknown when the ringing of the phone stopped me. With one hand on the doorknob, I hesitated long enough for the phone to ring a second time. One the third ring, I went for the receiver.

"Hey, Don Quixote, what say you from the merry land of windmills?"

"Turning as always," I said. "How's it going, John?"

"Same old," he said, which meant that even on a Monday morning, he was bored by his job and already placing long-distance personal calls. I had to figure I was one of many he'd made or was planning to make. He was in a chatty mood, and for fifteen minutes we talked. Actually, he talked and I listened to things going on in his life—there was a new woman he'd met but with whom he'd yet to do the "dirty deed." If that was what he was still calling it and if the woman had any sense, John would be doing only the "solo deed." Still, it was nice hearing a friendly voice—nice, too, that I had to add little to the conversation to keep it going, a fact John became aware of late in our call.

"Everything all right with you, Bri?"

All through the call, I'd debated whether to share my thoughts with him, and I relented, figuring it was better to get it off my chest. And so I told him about Friday night, the blowout party at the bar and how seeing George in prime form was the evening's highlight, and then I hit John with the news of George's death.

"It's funny, John, the way George went about his job that night—it was like he knew it was his last chance. His wife said the same thing, how all day long George seemed to be savoring each step, each motion. Imagine it, John—here we are already in our mid-thirties and we're still searching. Here were two people who, by our age, had been married more than ten years and had kids and were enjoying life full throttle."

"Hey, I'm living—and loving it."

"Yeah—alone, unless you can convince your new girl-friend . . ."

"Hey."

"Seriously, John, doesn't it sometimes feel like you're just going through the motions?"

"If she's not as pretty as I'd thought," he said, then laughed heartily.

His juvenile sense of humor actually managed to cheer me up some. "Look, John, I gotta go. There's . . . well, I've got some thinking to do."

"You coming home soon?"

Was I? Good question. "Well, I guess that's one of the things on my mind. Gerta—that's George's widow—she kind of intimated that she wants me to take over running the bar. Like, on a permanent basis. I just don't know . . ."

"You know what I think?"

"Yes, actually, I do, John. You think I've run long enough and it's time to leave this half-horse town and get back to city life."

"See? Even you know. And you could probably have your old job back, too, what with the trouble going on over there. The shit's really hit the fan with Voltaire, and from what I've heard, well, it blew up in Warfiend's face big time. Last time I saw Maddie, she looked really haggard. I think Warfiend's been giving her hell about the losses they're taking."

"Yeah, well, I'm sure that's not all he's giving her," I said. "Look, John, thanks for the update. And, you know, for listening . . ."

"As always, my man, as always. And come home, dammit— I miss my bud."

"I'll think about it."

He said good-bye and I said good-bye, and next, I heard a dial tone and realized I was still holding the receiver. Replacing it, I retrieved my car keys from the edge of the bar and started on my way out again. The phone, usually so quiet during the days rang again.

"Connors' Corners," I said into the phone, my voice hollow in the quiet of the bar.

"Hi. I was wondering if you'd be open later today."

Anger overtook my better judgment and I almost hurled a handful of obscenities at the insensitive sap. In the end, I merely replaced the receiver onto its cradle.

"No," I said aloud to the empty tavern, "the bar is closed today."

And then I left, gently closing the door behind me.

I drove on endless stretches of road, paying no attention to signs, turning on a whim, my direction as aimless as my life. I didn't keep track of time. I'd missed lunch, and somehow the day slipped away from me. As the light began to silently die in the sky, I found I had left the upper Hudson Valley region and was below Poughkeepsie and halfway to New York City. Suddenly I was faced with a terrorizing choice: drive south and pick up where I had left off or drive north and return to my home in Linden Corners. *Home,* I mused, was no longer a comforting word, since where mine lay I couldn't say.

Where I ended up that night, as it turned out, was ultimately fairly close to Linden Corners. I finally drove back to the windmill, just as I had so many nights ago, when the rain fell and the answers I sought seemed to be given. Tonight, as I pulled to the side of the road and climbed atop my car's hood, I noticed hundreds—maybe thousands—of little lights, pinpoints in the sky that illuminated the world below. I sat and contemplated my life and my future, all the while thinking about George and the other folks in Linden Corners, and the choice now facing me.

The windmill, as always, inspired me, but I reminded myself that as magical as the windmill seemed, it was not all-knowing, a psychic portal into another world. No, whatever I needed to understand about myself and my life, it needed to come from within, and if the windmill served any purpose, it was a reminder not to give up on my dreams, to keep myself open to opportunity.

And then opportunity knocked . . . or at least it turned on the light.

The small window on the second floor of the windmill was suddenly filled by a square patch of yellow light. Someone was home, and at nearly nine o'clock that night, I had to assume it was Annie. Still, would she leave Janey all alone in the house? Maybe Janey was with her. Or maybe it was someone else. Whoever it was, was about to have company.

I crossed the field, my sneakers wet with the night's dew, and I thought about how the grass could use a cutting. I trekked onward and was soon in front of the mighty windmill, its sails slightly illuminated by the upstairs light.

I stepped up to the door of the mill and simply knocked. One quick rap that echoed loud in the quiet air. There was no response from inside, but then I heard the door on the second floor open and light spilled out, creating shadows on the ground. Annie stepped out onto the catwalk.

"Who's there?" she asked.

"Just your friendly neighborhood windmill repairman," I said, stepping back from the tower to wave up at her. I saw nervous features soften as she waved back.

"Come on up," she said.

I took her up on the offer, opening the door and winding my way up the circular stairs until I reached her studio. I liked that Annie had these not-so-secret hideaways, places to escape to but places that weren't all that difficult to find, either.

"Hi," she said from atop her stool, where she sat in front of a canvas, the front of which I couldn't see. She set down her paintbrush.

As I came around, I saw that she'd already covered whatever it was she was painting.

"Can I see?" I asked.

She shook her head. "Maybe when it's done," she informed me, and then she asked me what I was doing out so late.

"It's just after nine."

"That's late for Linden Corners, remember?"

"I guess I'm on New York City time—same time zone, different concept," I said. "Besides, I haven't slept well since . . . well, all weekend, and now probably all week."

"George?"

I nodded. "I barely knew him, Annie, but . . ."

"Feel like you knew him all your life?"

"Yeah," I said, afraid that in this dimly lit atmosphere, our conversation might lean toward the morose. So I inquired about Janey and found she was staying overnight at a friend's house.

"She needed some kids her own age to play with, and two of her school friends were having a sleepover and they called and invited Janey, too. After the funeral today, I thought it best for her to get out and have some fun. Sometimes she has to take on adult weights, and I worry. This will be good for her."

"Good for you, too," I said. "Even moms need breaks."

"Tonight, I'm a mother by way of telephone and a simple craftsperson, a painter."

"A pretty painter," I said.

My compliment embarrassed her and she lowered her head. "Me? I'm a mess."

She was wearing a paint-splattered smock, had on no makeup, and her hair was slightly awry. "Okay, you're the prettiest mess in the room."

"Thanks," she said with a grin. "Really, Brian, what brings you out tonight?"

"Truthfully? I needed some time to think, and your windmill seems to help me, believe it or not. Look who I'm talking to—of course you believe it. I've come before, parked on the side of the road, sat atop my car, and just watched as the windmill turned and turned. It tends to clear my head."

"On the hood, roof, or trunk?"

"Huh?"

"Where do you sit?"

"Oh, usually the hood."

"Brian's Bluff," she said with a sweet smile.

Her words drew out my own smile. "Yeah, we each need our own sanctuary. Although, Annie, after this weekend . . . with George dying and thinking of Gerta living her life without him . . . I've got to be honest with you: I'm tired of bluffing."

Her brown eyes widened, liquid pools of chocolate that filled me with a craving—not just for them but for all of her, and I leaned in to her quivering lips and planted my lips on them. The kiss was as tender as our first, though it lingered much longer. I pulled her in close, wrapped my arms around her, and drew her off the stool, all the while continuing our kiss. When our bodies finally drew apart, we found that our eyes stayed locked on each other's.

I touched her face, her soft cheek, her red lips, which pressed down gently on my fingers. Still, we didn't look away from each other.

"Brian . . ."

"Sshh, don't . . ."

She pulled back slightly and went to her canvas, lifting the cloth covering to reveal a partially finished painting of Connors' Corners. "I was afraid you might be leaving, and well, I thought you might want something to remember the time you spent here. Am I right, Brian? Are you planning to leave?"

I held my breath a moment, scared to answer, my eyes dancing between the painting and Annie.

"Give me a reason to stay, Annie."

My message was clear and she responded quickly, without any hesitation. Annie came to me, and I embraced her again, more fiercely this time, holding her close and tight while our mouths searched and found and hungered and our bodies pressed tightly together, as though sealing a bond we'd simultaneously agreed to.

My legs wavered suddenly and I grew light-headed. Annie's body flowed with mine to the floor, where we lost ourselves in the passionate heat of the moment, kissing, touching, feeling, our bodies expressing all of the pent-up emotions that were suddenly released. I rolled over, Annie on top of me, and my elbow hit the floor.

"Wait," she said, and though I didn't want to let her go, she got up and came back with a sleeping bag in her hands and an explanation on her lips. "Sometimes Janey and I spend the night up here, especially hot summer nights."

"Tonight's a hot summer night," I said.

Annie laughed and turned off the light inside the mill, leaving only our shadows that moved against the wall. She lured me into the sleeping bag and we kissed again. This time I moved my mouth down her neck to her throat, thrilling at her taste, while she slid her fingers through the hair at the nape of my neck.

I peeled off her artist's smock, my fingers moving from button to button, undoing her denim blouse until I revealed her lacy-white bra and the soft, flat curve of her stomach. She slipped out of the shirt and guided my fingers to the snap of her bra, and in an instant, the lace fell away to reveal her voluptuous round breasts. I took them in my hands, the dark nipples first in my fingers, then in my mouth, suckling and nuzzling with urgency and passion. She drew my mouth back up to hers, and our tongues played a dance. Her fingers began their own journey of discovery, pulling my shirttails free and unbuttoning my shirt. She slipped it off my shoulders, and I felt her fingers slide over my chest, her hair graze my nipples.

She lay me down on my back, opening the snap of my jeans with one easy motion. Then she slid her hand further down, touching, squeezing, driving me wild with uncontrollable passion. We could wait no more. I tore off the last of Annie's clothes and then my own, and soon there was nothing left to expose but our inner hearts, and we did so soon enough, as I moved over and entered her with a gentle, easy, and ongoing push, never taking my lips from hers, never taking my eyes from her. As the sweetness of our love intensified and I moved faster, she moved with me. Our two bodies moved as one, both of us panting and groaning and thrusting, our mouths searching and suckling, our bodies arching and wracking together until we lost ourselves in a long, explosive moment of sheer, ecstatic bliss.

The power of our passion overwhelmed me, and I released myself into her. She arched to meet me as if to take in every last drop of my love, every piece of my heart. And then we collapsed into each other's arms, panting and flushed, unwilling to loosen our embrace.

So we lay there, my arm around her shoulders, holding her close and tight, she so soft and so quiet. We gazed at each other and smiled and kissed each other with utter tenderness. It was a kiss that spoke volumes, and I felt as though someone had recharged me, had given me new life and new hope. My skin was electric and alive.

We lay there, for how long I couldn't say and I didn't care; time, like the rest of the world, had faded away. We lay there communicating only by touch. Because in truth, we were each alone with our own thoughts.

I spoke first.

"I was afraid," I whispered in the dark, "that I would never be able to love again, and now—"

Annie interrupted me. "Brian, you show your love every day, the way you felt about George, the way you're able to make Janey smile. You feel, maybe too well, and you love . . . well, that you do well, too. Just because you shut it down for a time doesn't mean you don't have a heart."

I kissed the top of her head, nuzzled the nape of her neck, and whispered into her ears a quiet thanks. Annie rose from the floor, and I was suddenly filled with the awful sense that I'd somehow belittled the power of her words and had pushed her away. But she came back shortly, and in her hands was a tube of acrylic paint. I gave her a curious look, but she just shushed me.

"Maybe you need proof," she said, and then she squeezed a small blob of paint onto her finger. Even in this translucent darkness, I could tell the color was red, a rich and vibrant hue.

She took her finger and began to paint simple strokes on the center of my chest. I couldn't figure out what she was doing. But I watched every move, every stroke of her hand, until she was done and pronounced me finished and complete and able to love.

Annie had painted a heart on my chest.

"I feel like the Tin Man," I said.

"And so you are," Annie told me, "just like him. He thought he needed a heart, too, and look how wrong he was."

I kissed her passionately then, as though both my hearts were pumping new life into me. Our passion mounted and stirred. I felt her opening up to me again, and this time she guided me inside her. Our lovemaking this second miraculous time was more fierce, more hungry. Time slipped away from us until we were both dripping with sweat and smiling with satisfaction. It wasn't until we'd fallen back against the floor panting that I noticed that my red heart had bled, leaving in the flesh between Annie's breasts a shadowy hint of a heart all her own, or at the very least a vibrant part of mine.

Our skin was lit by moonlight and warmed by the energy of our lovemaking. We moved to the open door and stood on the windmill's catwalk in the shadow of the sails, wrapped together in the sleeping bag. Quietly, we watched the stars twinkle above us.

I felt her tremble, and then noticed tears on her cheeks. I swallowed a lump at my throat and spoke.

"I can't compete with a ghost," I said.

Her hand ran smooth against my arm. "Oh, Brian . . . oh, you mean the tears." A small laugh escaped her mouth. "You don't know much about women, do you?"

"I guess not. Why are you sad?"

"I'm far from sad—just the opposite," she said, smiling up at me. "I'm glad that you're here with me, cradling me in your arms. I wouldn't trade this moment for any other, past or future. This kind of security, comfort, is so rare."

"It doesn't have to be," I said, tightening my hold on her.

"For either of us," she said. "Look, Brian, I don't want

this . . . us . . . to start off on the wrong foot. You've already told
me about Maddie, her betrayal, and about your high school
sweetheart who stole your dreams. . . . Now it's my turn . . . to tell
you about Dan." She paused, turned to me, and kissed me reassuringly. "Dan was a wonderful man, a good father, but he was frustrated, too, by the limitations of his life. He wanted so much; in
fact, he wanted everything. Lots of kids, his parent's farm to be
prosperous, his wife to succeed, and his job to be the defining aspect of his manhood. He lived for his job, working up at the state
capitol, pushing paper but dreaming large. He thought of running for some kind of government post, and he talked to me at
length about it. But you know what, Brian? He was lacking
something—true drive. Sure, he had his dreams, but he didn't
have the passion to make those dreams come true.

"For the first three years of our marriage, everything was
great. We were happy. Then Janey came along, and our happiness
intensified, or so I thought and so Dan thought. What Janey really did was fill a widening gap between me and Dan, because he
didn't have the life he wanted and I couldn't give it to him. So one
night, he went searching for some answers."

"Annie, if this is too painful, too much to bear in light of
what's transpired tonight, I can wait."

"I've started. I have to end it, too," she said, resuming her
story.

Some of which I'd already heard from Chuck Ackroyd. Dan
Sullivan sought escape in the arms of another woman, one Vicki
Ackroyd, a fellow government employee who, in the mind of her
small-town husband, was attracted to Dan's ambitions, or at least
his talk of them. "Two very separate things," Annie reminded me.

"The affair went along for probably two years before Vicki
began pressuring Dan to declare his candidacy against an incum-
bent assemblyman. He wouldn't do it, didn't think he could de-
feat him. In hindsight, Vicki was probably very good for Dan, be-

cause she told it as she saw it. If Dan wanted to get ahead, he had to take some risks. If losing an election was one step backward, actually running was two steps forward. So really he would have gained something either way."

"You seem to know a lot about what Vicki Ackroyd thought," I added.

"She shared her thoughts with me, before she left Chuck and Linden Corners for good. For Washington, actually. Seems Dan was getting ready to join her, and he was ready to tell me he wanted to end our marriage. I'd been suspicious, but how could I confront him? I needed him, and so did Janey—and tearing apart this family wasn't in my plans. See, what Dan failed to realize was that we all have certain dreams, but they don't all come true. He couldn't see beyond his own fear. Anyway, the night he was going to tell me the truth, Dan never reached home. His car crashed into a tree. He died instantly."

"Was it . . . ?"

Quickly she shook her head. "An accident, that's all. Or maybe the hand of fate, I suppose. See, Brian, we're always running from something. Dan, from a life he felt betrayed by. Me? I haven't wanted to admit the truth for some time, and aside from Cynthia and Gerta, I have not really discussed it. Janey knew her father as a good and decent man, and I prefer it remain that way. I'm not even sure what memories Janey has of her father. Nothing thrilled Janey more than spending time with Dan, accompanying him on his errands or watching him work, or listening while he read her bedtime stories. Yes, Dan had his faults, but deep down, he was a caring man. Maybe life cheated him, too."

She paused, and her eyelids flickered in the dim light of night. "So maybe I'm running from a truth, and if so, that's my cross to bear. What about you, Brian?"

I was touched by the ease in which she'd revealed herself and I found myself equally willing to talk.

"*Running away.* I've heard that phrase a lot these past months, and lately I've taken it more seriously, trying to figure out if that's really what I've done. And you know what I've concluded, right here and right now? Everyone's been telling me that refusing to deal with Maddie's betrayal, skipping out on all that I'd built for myself, that those were the actions of a man running from life. I think they're wrong. I stuck to my principles, ran with my gut—and look where it got me. It brought me here to Linden Corners and to you. To me, that's a sign of a man running toward something. Toward something very wonderful indeed."

We were done talking for the night, and we went back inside the windmill, where Annie lit some candles she kept for emergency purposes. "We lose power a lot during thunderstorm season," she explained. And so we made love by candlelight until they burned down and the sun rose. Then we shared a humongous breakfast before Annie went to pick up Janey. I went home and showered, lingering long under the hot spray as I replayed the night's events over and over, until I thought my heart would burst.

Sleep came easily, and I dreamed well, of renewed life, of renewed love, and of a new kind of commitment. My subconscious knew the truth; it knew that no time soon was I leaving this little town. Linden Corners was in my blood, and so was a woman named Annie.

TEN

Can you really throw your life away and find not just success but meaning in your new one? I was living proof that yes, you could, and all it took was a woman with incalculable charm and a girl with an incurable smile, and a spinning windmill that fueled the passion we all felt.

My friend John wasn't so convinced, despite the conversation we'd been having for the past thirty minutes. If stubbornness were a drug, John would be an addict. And if he were a record, he'd be a broken one.

"So when are you coming home?" he finally asked. "Your six months of seclusion are almost up, and, well, I've got to make plans myself. The apartment, for one. It's still yours and I'm only a sublet—and an illegal one at that. How long can we fool the landlord? Hey, how long can you fool yourself that this Linden Corners isn't going to betray you, too?"

"If you knew this place, John, you wouldn't even think such a ridiculous thing."

"I knew Maddie, too, and worse, so did you."

I wasn't going to have this conversation again and told him so. Instead, I brought the talk back to the apartment, telling him to stay comfortable and that I'd keep him updated on my plans. In the meantime, I had things to do.

"What kind of things? You don't work during the day and I do, but I'm not the one wrapping up this call."

I laughed. "Talk to you later, John."

"Moo," he replied.

The city boy was convinced I'd gone farmer.

I was at Annie's house, and neither she nor Janey were home. I had promised to take care of some plumbing problems and I'd spent much of the morning looking at pipes and poring over instruction manuals. Frustrated, I'd thought, why not call a professional plumber, like I'd have done in the city, and well, that kind of thinking led me to pick up the phone, not to call a plumber but to hear a friendly voice from the city. And so I called John.

Now, instead of going back to the plumbing, I sat down on the porch swing. It was a lustrous day, early summer warm, the kind of weather that makes you feel glad to be outdoors.

Since that magical night a week ago when Annie and I had made love, the days had passed with shining beauty, and I had a sense that nothing could go wrong. Indeed, nothing had, aside from the bathroom sink. With Janey in school during the day and my working at night, Annie and I had those sun-dipped mornings to ourselves, and we spent every one of them together, enjoying our blossoming romance. But come nightfall, I went to the Corner and then back to my apartment to sleep. I had yet to spend an entire night at Annie's, and for now, we both felt that that was best. Neither of us wanted to overwhelm Janey or lead her on with the promises of a future that had, so far, gone unspoken between us.

We were tentative, too, in revealing too much of our passion to others, if only for our fragile hearts' sake. We'd both been burned; we both still needed time to recover. We gave each other a lot of room and found ourselves able to share our painful experiences with each other. Our days were spent companionably, interrupted only by powerful bursts of passion, when we would steal ourselves away and make love for hours. One day we even ran the fruit stand on the outskirts of town, so Cynthia could have a day off with Bradley. It was there, working side by side, stacking fruits and vegetables, helping customers, trading gossip (and tempering any about us), that I finally realized that I no longer thought about New York City. No, all I could see was Annie, her bright smile and the way the sun caught the auburn highlights of her hair, the joy she instilled deep within me. I could imagine no other life.

Now into our second week of being together, our routine was achieving a comfort level. One day, Annie had dashed off to the antique shop early, leaving me to my chores. I was staying at the house until Janey returned from school, so I decided there was no better place to wait than under the welcoming shading of the farmhouse porch.

I found myself dozing beneath the sun-dappled sky, the wind on my face, the breeze in my hair. The night before at the Corner had been a busy one, and I'd stayed up late cleaning the bar. I gave in to sleep and had a wonderful dream where I was not just a visitor in this village but a full-blown resident, a native. In my dream, Annie and I had met years ago and Janey was our daughter and this was our farmhouse, and out beyond the dewy hill was the windmill we'd built, a place that fed us our lives, happy day after happy day. And at nights, I'd help out George Connors, who was still alive and pouring drinks, and I'd work by his side, learning not just the bar trade but also the real lessons to be learned from life. And in my dream, the mailbox at the foot of the driveway said THE DUNCANS, and atop the tavern was one simple word that embodied its very spirit. It said, GEORGE'S.

That's when I woke to find inspiration staring at me in the face.

"You okay?" Janey asked.

I rubbed my eyes, once, a second time, as though doing so would blend the fantasy in my mind with the reality before me.

"Yeah."

"Don't say—"

"I know, Janey. Sorry. Yes, I'm fine."

She giggled.

"How was school?"

"It was school."

So worldly, and at such a tender age. But the worldliness was because she was smart, and that counted for something; she was one kid who actually listened to her parent and paid attention to her schoolwork.

"Your eyelids were all jumpy—did you have a nightmare?"

"Actually, it was a dream, and it was a nice one. And that dream gave me a great idea. And you can help with it, if you want."

She dropped her knapsack, a heavy thud against the wooden porch. "I love ideas. And I love helping."

"Good. Let me grab a couple Cokes and then we'll get on our way. Go ahead and hop in the car."

"Where are we going?"

"You'll see."

"Ooh, a surprise. Those are the best."

That was all it took, and while I left Annie a note and fetched our cold drinks, Janey did as I'd instructed. Before long the Grand Am was heading down the driveway, out onto the main road, and toward downtown Linden Corners. The ice-cold colas were refreshing on this hot day.

For a midweek afternoon, business was noticeably slow. Marla and Darla sat in their lawn chairs, watching the passing traffic. The Five-O looked deserted, and I guess that was par for the course for that time of day; it wasn't named the Three-O, after all. Martha was probably already in the kitchen, though, working up dinner specials in anticipation of the evening rush. But I passed the Five-O and pulled into a nearly empty parking lot.

"What are we doing at the hardware store?" Janey asked.

"I need some hardware—what else?"

"Okay," said my agreeable companion.

We entered the store, the jangling bells over our heads announcing our arrival. A blond checkout clerk looked up and waved a hello and welcome before turning back to her customer at the counter. Janey smiled and returned the wave and I smiled and returned the hello. Friendly neighbors were what Linden Corners was all about, right?

Then Chuck Ackroyd stepped into my sight line and my smile disappeared.

"What are you doing here?" he grumbled.

"I need some lumber," I said.

"Uh-huh."

I took that to mean "follow me," since Chuck started toward the back of the store, where a large LUMBER sign hung above the aisle. So I followed, Janey's hand in my mine, she skipping by my side. We entered a separate room that smelled of fresh-cut wood, shavings littering the floor. Janey sneezed and giggled and pushed some sawdust with her sneaker. I took a look at Chuck and decided it would be best to be quick about my task. Luckily, Chuck was all business, and we talked and debated and measured until finally he guided me toward the right size wood and he wrote down the order.

"I also need some paint, a couple of paintbrushes. That ought to do it."

He guided me out of the lumber room and toward the paints and I picked out a gallon of gray, and smaller sizes of red and gold, and then grabbed a couple brushes and a tin of turpentine.

"I can have your wood cut to size and ready by tomorrow afternoon. You wanna pick it up?" he said as he walked us to the checkout at the front. The young woman who'd been so friendly earlier began adding up my bill.

I thought of my car and its lack of trunk space and asked Chuck about delivery service.

"Costs extra. Twenty-five-buck delivery charge."

"I guess I'll pick it up." I could always borrow Annie's truck.

Just then Janey tugged at my shirt, and I looked over at her, only to see her pointing at a sign behind the cash register. It said, matter of factly, FREE DELIVERY FOR PURCHASES OVER $100. I gazed at my receipt; I'd spent ninety-eight dollars and forty-three cents.

"Janey, do you like to paint?" I asked.

"Sure. Who doesn't?"

I looked at Chuck. "Toss in another brush."

Ka-ching.

"I'll see you tomorrow afternoon—about this time," Chuck said.

"Thanks. Bring it to Annie's farmhouse."

He grimaced but said nothing. I was ready to leave anyway, having spent more than enough time with my least favorite resident of Linden Corners. Janey, though, having picked out a paintbrush for herself, decided she had some unfinished business of her own.

"Excuse me, Mr. Ackroyd?" she said.

"Yeah?"

She shot me a knowing look; his language was far too casual.

"Why don't you like Brian?"

"I . . . I . . . " he tried, apparently flustered by Janey's forth-rightness. "Hey, kid, mind your own business, huh?"

"You're mean," she replied, and then (after all, she was only seven) stuck her tongue out at the sour-faced adult. I had to stifle a laugh, and I took hold of Janey's hand and led her from the store and back out into the sunlight. Once we were back in the car, I did start to laugh.

"Oh, Janey," I said, "What would I do without you?"

Instead of the usual sunny reply, my question was met with silence. Concerned that I had somehow hurt her feelings, I gazed over at her and saw her smile had nearly become a pout. This was completely out of character.

"Hey, what's wrong?"

Janey didn't reply. She just stared out the window and con-tinued to do so for the entire ride home. My mind was swirling with questions, with ways of interpreting her silence. I'd never seen this side of Janey, and I felt ill equipped to deal with the change.

Finally, we arrived back at the farmhouse. Janey had scooped up her knapsack from the porch, and she turned to me. I saw tears in her eyes.

"Janey, please, what's wrong? What did I do?"

"Nothing," she said, "not yet."

"What is it you think I'm going to do?"

"Leave."

"Leave? What do you mean? . . . I won't leave you, Janey. Why would you ever think that?"

She didn't answer. Instead, she ran toward me and threw herself into my arms, where she proceeded to let the tears fall, incredible sobs that wracked her little body and made me hold her tight—until I knew that not only could I not leave her but I could barely stand to let her go. But I did, eventually, as she unclasped her arms from around my neck. She wiped some tears away from her reddened cheeks.

"I love you, Brian."

She bounded into the house, leaving me there with my own tears streaming down my face, wondering how a simple trip to the hardware store had brought on this heartfelt, puzzling moment between us.

The answers came later. I'd closed up the Corner for the night and found myself bypassing my upstairs apartment and heading back out to Annie's. A light was on in her living room when I drove up, and I flicked off the headlights. I quietly took the steps to the porch, where I was met by the nicest sight I'd seen all night—Annie herself. She had been late in coming back from the antique shop and so Cynthia had agreed to watch Janey when I had to go open the Corner. Before I left, I called Annie and told her I'd like to come back, that I needed to speak to her.

"Hi," I said.

"Hi," she said, opening up the screen door and stepping out onto the porch. Our lips touched, and we embraced each other and kissed again. In the glow of moonlight, I saw worry in her eyes and I reached up to touch her face to feel the worry and share it, or maybe even take it away.

"What's wrong?" I asked.

"Did something happen today?"

"Janey."

"So something did happen."

"That's why I wanted to see you—tonight, before too much time passed. Come here; sit."

We sat on the wooden swing that hung from the roof and settled in. Then she faced me and I faced her, and briefly, we smiled at each other.

"Janey asked me if I was planning to leave," I said.

"Leave? You mean . . ."

"Leave her. Leave here. I don't really know. She took me by surprise, Annie, and it kind of scared me. Janey's so full of life, always laughing and smiling and so open with others. Today, though, I saw a very different side to her. We'd just come from the hardware store, where we were buying—"

I stopped mid-sentence, since I knew I'd already hit on something, but I couldn't quite understand what it was. Annie, her face a trembling mask, was fighting back tears and a wave of déjà vu overcame me, remembering how Janey had fallen so quiet and how I didn't know what to do except embrace her. So I leaned over and now took Annie in my arms, still wondering what I had triggered.

"Annie, what did I do wrong?"

"Don't worry," she said, breaking free from the embrace and facing me once again. "It's nothing you did. It's nothing you could have known, and frankly, it's . . . well, wow—that's one incredible child I have." She paused, collecting her thoughts before putting them into words. "Brian, one of Janey's favorite things as a child was riding in the car beside her father. She worshipped Dan, followed him around, and cried when he would leave for work. But on the weekends—she knew when those were because Daddy didn't wear a tie and that meant he was going to be around all day. Often she would accompany him on his errands. I guess she remembers more about him than I expected. You see, the last place she ever went with Dan . . ."

"The hardware store?"

Annie slowly nodded. "I remember the day so vividly because it was only two days before Dan's accident. He'd been working on a project in the barn and needed some supplies, and so he headed down to Chuck's store, and of course he took Janey with him. She was only five, but somehow that memory must have stuck with her. Today brought it back—brought all of it back. Not just the trip, but the fact that it was the last one she took with her father."

"And today it triggered the memory?"

"Mostly the memory that he never returned."

"And now she's afraid that will happen again?" I asked.

Emotions were rippling throughout me, some reaching just beneath the skin, prickling my nerves and tugging at my heart-strings and washing over me until I wasn't sure what to feel, what to know, certainly not what to do. Worried that I'd opened un-healed wounds in this little girl, I was waiting for Annie's scold-ing, but all she did, and how telling it was, was hold my hand and say nothing. In that tender touch and beautiful silence, I knew that Annie didn't blame me. That she trusted me, with herself and with Janey.

Finally, the silence was broken by my own voice, cracking from the lack of moisture on my tongue.

"What do we do?"

Annie leaned in and kissed me. "We show her that you're not going anywhere. We give her what she wants."

"And what's that?"

"Us," Annie said. "Stay with me tonight, and in the morn-ing, the three of us will have breakfast and we'll send Janey off to school together. Will you do that, Brian? Will you sleep by my side and hold me?"

I didn't answer and I didn't need to. Annie had taken my hand, and we stood up from the swing and she guided me along the porch and into the house and down the hallway to her darkened bedroom, where, through the light of the moon that some-how knew to follow us, she lay me down on the soft bed and snuggled in beside me.

That night, our clothes fell away and our bodies became one. Later, we fell asleep with satisfaction written on our faces and love etched on our hearts.

The next morning, I woke with the sun and I was glad to see it because its presence represented how I felt, that the day held great promise and was filled with potential. I threw on my jeans and T-shirt from the night before and wandered into the kitchen. While my two angels continued to sleep, I began to fix breakfast. In thirty minutes, coffee was brewed, bacon had sizzled, and pancakes had browned. The smells that filled the house guaranteed that no one would sleep for long.

My magic worked.

Janey, wrapped in a robe and her feet in bunny slippers, entered the kitchen, her arms wrapped around her purple frog.

"It's not Saturday, Momma," she said. "Why are we having a big breakfast?"

"Because I felt like cooking one," I said.

The final remnants of sleep fell from Janey's eyes and they widened with excitement.

"*Brian!*" she squealed, running over to me and jumping into my arms and hugging me tight, a good solid welcoming embrace that erased any of yesterday's doubt.

And so I held her, and that's when I noticed Annie standing in the door frame of the kitchen, a smile on her face that surely gave the morning sun a run for its money. I felt, at that moment, that we had taken our first step toward creating something I'd wanted to start for so long—a family.

*　　*　　*

Just a few days later, July officially arrived and with it came lazy days of sunshine and spreading warmth. But summer had its surprises, too, and those included unexpected thunderstorms and even the occasional wind-driven pelting downpour. But we dealt with those as they crept up, and our days passed and our wounds continued to heal, and Annie and Janey and I continued to build our new life together. I had found within myself a new kind of comfort, and perhaps that's where I went wrong.

Settling into a routine of sorts in Linden Corners left me open and vulnerable, as though life itself were waiting for me to drop my guard. In the days since our visit to the hardware store, Janey's mood had brightened, and there was no sign of the deep worry that caused her to be so withdrawn. Annie, too, seemed immeasurably happy. Our days were filled with stolen kisses and open cuddling, with Janey joyously adding herself to the mix.

I'd also been busy out in the barn, the lumber from Chuck's store having arrived on time. I was on a deadline, self-imposed as it were, but important nonetheless. And so for four days I hid myself in the barn while Annie worked, sometimes at the antique store, sometimes alone in the windmill, and Janey helped us both when she wasn't playing by herself or with visiting friends.

Finally, my deadline came—the Saturday just after the Fourth of July. Annie had been called in to consult on a restoration project at the shop, and Janey had abandoned me in favor of a play-date with one of her numerous friends. That left me free to put the finishing touches on my surprise. It had to do with the bar, and it had all begun with Gerta's offer to hand the running of the bar over to me. Though I'd stayed on at the bar, I had yet to give Gerta a definitive answer; I was working without a contract, so to speak, and the time had come to make things more permanent.

Gerta had invited me over for dinner one night, and over a farm-fresh country dinner, she launched into another plea to get me to commit, though all the while I knew I had already accepted the job. She'd baked that scrumptious strawberry pie, and I figured it would be easiest to let her think her fine cooking had won me over. So we settled upon an open-ended run for myself at the Corner, though with Gerta keeping ownership and control.

"What we need, Gerta, is a plan, to let everyone know that Connors' Corners hasn't changed, that George's time-honored traditions haven't gone anywhere. So I've got a proposal." Then I proceeded to launch into my plan. A follow-up to First Friday, what I was dubbing Second Saturday, the same rules applying. Gerta was crazy about the idea. She immediately started getting the word out, and now, two weeks having flown like the wind, it was all anyone in town was talking about.

Now that the big day had arrived, I was ready to unveil my surprise.

I removed my treasure from the barn and loaded it into the back of Annie's truck, covered it with an old bedsheet, secured it with rope, and then headed downtown to the bar. Gerta was already waiting for me in the driveway, her face lit with anticipation. She knew something was afoot but hadn't any idea what. Surprises work best when they live up to expectation, and I had a sense this one would.

"What have you gone and done, Brian?" she asked, like a mother scolding her mischievous boy.

"Close your eyes," I said.

Good sport that she was, she complied.

And then I set up the board across the porch, making sure the sheet didn't fall off. Then I told Gerta to open her eyes, and as she did, I whipped the sheet off with a bit of flourish and there before her was a brand-new sign to be hung above the bar. The old, peeling Connors' Corners sign was to be replaced, and the new sign, freshly painted in reds and grays and trimmed with gold, read, simply, proudly, GEORGE'S TAVERN.

Gerta opened her mouth but no words came out. She held a

hand to her heart, then used her free one to wipe away a tear. Finally, she found her voice. "This is near about the kindest thing anyone's ever done for me."

She beckoned me forward and I bent to accept her tender kiss.

Just then, Chuck Ackroyd stepped out of his hardware store, crossed the street, and sidled up right between us.

"Afternoon, Gerta, Brian. What's the fuss?"

"Oh, Chuck, would you look at what Brian's gone and done?"

He looked squarely at the sign, then grimaced. "Huh. So that's what you were working on. Would've figured you'd name it after yourself."

Gerta scolded him, and I let her. "Shame on you, Chuck Ackroyd."

Probably he'd meant it as a joke, but it lacked any amount of humor. I watched as humiliation colored his skin.

"Chuck, you should be helping Brian, you know."

"Hey, I've already done my part for the day," he said, "by telling that woman where to find him."

"What woman?" I asked.

"Pretty woman," he said. "Striking. Had a set of legs, I'll tell you. She comes into Martha's about noon, has a quick lunch, and begins asking questions. About ol' Brian Duncan Just Passing Through. Sara managed to spill some info before Martha hushed her up, told her not to gossip. Me, I didn't mind helping out. Heck of a looker, Brian. Real sleek creature, clothes that said she was a city girl, you know?" He grinned with unappealing teeth. "'Cept she wasn't no girl."

"Did she give a name?" My voice had grown shaky, wary.

"Nope. All she volunteered was the fact she was looking for you. And I pointed right across the street to those upstairs windows. Said you lived there, but probably could be found at Annie Sullivan's place, first right at the windmill."

Urgency demands action. With barely an explanation or apology, I said good-bye to Gerta and raced for the truck. Then I backed out of George's and hit the accelerator. I tore through the village, folks stopping and staring, Marla and Darla especially, from their usual seats outside their stores. In less than five minutes, I'd pulled into Annie's driveway. I saw that my own car was parked near the farmhouse. Annie had borrowed it while I used her truck. She was back from work. Beside it was an unfamiliar-looking Ford Contour, a rental, I assumed.

"Annie? Annie?" I yelled, jumping down out of the truck.

Janey greeted me on the porch.

"Hi, sweetie . . ."

"A friend of yours has come to visit," she said.

She poked a finger toward the kitchen. "Where the adults always congregate." She smiled. "That's a new word, *congregate.*"

I patted her head quickly, then opened the screen door and burst into the kitchen, where I saw Annie, still dressed in the white smock she wore when doing staining, leaning against the counter, a coffee cup in hand. Sitting down at the table, dressed in New York black and also drinking coffee, was another woman. She didn't get up. Together, they were a contrast of colors.

"You didn't exactly get very far away from the city, did you, Brian?" asked Madison Laurette Chasen, sending the synapses of my brain into hyperdrive. This could be nothing but trouble with a capital *T.* Then she said, with a slightly mocking tone, "And what's all this silly stuff about a windmill?"

THIRD INTERLUDE

I knew you were a nutcase the moment you arrived in town. The way you let yourself be talked into running the bar. And now this? Yup, just plain nuts."

Chuck Ackroyd and Brian Duncan had never exactly become friends over the months, despite the fact that they both knew and loved George Connors—a common bond that failed to unite them. Still, Chuck owed him, and owed him big. Trouble was, Chuck had a hard time admitting to such a thing.

"I'm not asking you to help, Chuck. I'm just asking if it's possible—and if these plans will help."

With reluctance worn on his sleeve, Chuck grabbed the crinkled sheets of paper and said, "Well, lemme have a look."

It was the morning after Janey's visit with her mother, just sixteen hours since Annie had awakened and smiled and given them hope that all would be fine in time. Encouraged by the previous day's events, Brian and Janey decided to forge ahead with their plan, and that required a drive to town.

It was noon when Brian and Janey arrived at Chuck's hardware store—Ackroyd's Hardware Emporium—in the center of Linden Corners' tiny business district. And Chuck was just closing up the store for lunch. Brian asked if he could wait a moment, and Chuck said no, he was hungry, and so Brian asked if he could join Chuck for lunch—his treat. That certainly did the trick, and Chuck's perpetual frown settled into a mildly irritated grimace. Janey's presence helped, and together the three of them walked into the Five-O.

Brian and Chuck took up on the same side of the booth. Janey sat on her knees opposite them, and each of them had their drinks—two Cokes for Brian and Janey and a Budweiser for Chuck. They were busy poring over the plans of the old windmill. Brian kept silent while Chuck mulled them over.

"What are you boys up to?" asked Martha Martinson, as she set down the day's lunch specials—meat loaf, mashed potatoes, and green beans for the men, a burger and extra fries for Janey. A big meal at midday, but the perfect energy booster for folks with a plan.

Chuck stopped looking at the blueprints, took a big bite of food, waited for Brian to answer the question she had posed. What exactly did Brian have in mind?

So, Brian, with a quick gulp, admitted that he knew his plan bordered on the outrageous.

"Why is that?" Martha asked him.

"*Because,*" *Brian said, "I want to rebuild the windmill.*"

He wasn't sure what reaction he expected, but Martha's big round face opened wide with joy, immediately setting him at ease.

"*That's a wonderful idea, Brian Duncan Just Passing Through.*" And there was a little sparkle in her eye. "*And I know just how you're gonna do it.*"

"*How?*"

"*Not alone, I'll tell you that much.*"

Janey's voice rang out in a cheer that filled the small diner with the sound of hope, spreading smiles to everyone's faces, Chuck's, too. Janey held that kind of innocent power.

*T*hat afternoon, Janey played quietly outside while Brian continued to puzzle over the windmill's plans. He knew it could not be rebuilt by sheer will alone. It wouldn't be easy, he knew, but then he thought of Annie, desperately clinging to life, and realized anything was possible—her recovery and their future; the windmill's too.

He was in Annie's study, taking care of the matters that don't wait for tragedy to pass by, bills and other household chores. He sat at Annie's desk, filing paperwork, when he came on an envelope that struck him as familiar. Surprised, he realized the letter, addressed to Annie, was in Maddie's handwriting. Unable to check his curiosity, he withdrew the letter and began reading. It seemed the light dimmed as he read, and a mood settled over him as he absorbed Maddie's words, a pleading apology for her behavior when she'd come to Linden Corners. Her regret over what she'd done and all that Annie had lost as a result. Brian read the letter a second time and then quietly put it back where he'd found it. Maddie had said nothing to him, not the last time he'd seen her; nor had Annie. This was a silent pact between Maddie and Annie, an attempt at healing through words. Brian felt a sadness for Maddie, his thoughts drifting to happier times. But the telephone interrupted his reverie. It was Cynthia.

"It's Annie," Cynthia said, "She wants to talk to you."

"Talk? You mean . . ."

"The doctor just finished his checkup. Annie's awake and breathing on her own."

"I'll be right there," he said, and threw down the phone before he heard Cynthia's cautionary, "But wait . . ."

He passed the good news on to Gerta and Janey amidst a chorus of glee, then headed back to the hospital. Cynthia was waiting for him by the nurse's station, looking tired and worn out, despite the promising news. Brian told her to go home, get some rest. He'd stay for a while. Cynthia agreed, saying she'd wait for Bradley.

"Where is he?"

"In with Annie—he's been in there for the past half hour."

A curious expression crossed Brian's face. "What's up?"

"She won't say. The doctor was by earlier and I didn't like how he was acting. All frustrated, annoyed. Like he couldn't figure out what was wrong."

"But you said she was breathing—"

"She is. But the doctor said that only meant the operation was successful. There's still—"

He felt his elation deflate. "The damned infection."

"No one is saying anything, Brian."

"I'll take care of it."

He walked over to Annie's room and opened the door. Bradley and Annie were holding hands, and she was crying. Emotions swirled around the room, and Brian's presence only added to the blend. He swallowed hard as he knocked lightly.

Bradley turned, acknowledged Brian with an encouraging nod, and then returned his attention to Annie. He leaned in, whispered in her ear, then kissed her on the forehead. Getting up, he patted Brian on the shoulder and then went to find Cynthia. Brian and Annie were alone.

"How are you?"

"*Glad you're here,*" *she said.* "*I need to talk to you.*"

"*So I've heard. But wait—what's going on? Are you okay? What'd the doctor say today? How do you feel?*" *He asked these questions, too many, he knew, but he wanted so many answers—to why she'd summoned him, why Bradley had spent so much time there, why the doctor wasn't saying much. Then he noticed that Annie looked pale and tired and completely devoid of energy.*

"*Later,*" *she said.* "*Answers later. Just . . .*" *She paused to cough, and the cough lingered. Brian held her hand, feeling completely helpless. She had deteriorated a lot, even after yesterday's promising awakening.* "*Just listen,*" *she finally said, and again, Brian swallowed a large lump in his throat, where emotions were lodged.*

"*Lying around in a bed gives you time to think, and what I've been thinking about is Janey. She's the light of my life, Brian. The best thing to ever happen to me. She's so good, so energetic, and so little really gets her down. She's known awful tragedy already, and even though she remembers her father only slightly, she still feels a void in her life.*"

"*She's remarkable. The very embodiment of hope and resilience.*"

That made Annie smile. "*That's my Janey. She's been good, these couple of days?*"

"*A gem.*"

"*It's her birthday next month—October thirteenth. We've always had this wonderful tradition, Brian, the annual raking of the leaves. Janey loves jumping into the huge piles of leaves we create . . . just remembering last year. Oh, Brian, don't let her forget all she's come to know.*"

"*Never,*" *he said, and waited, knowing there was more.*

"*Thank you for bringing her to see me. I know it was against the rules but . . . I needed to see her, and she needed to see me. That's the only rule I know, and you knew it, too. A mother and daughter cannot be separated, not by anything, not even . . . by death.*"

"Hey . . ." Brian said. "No such talk allowed here. You're going to be fine, because we have a life to get on with, the three of us."

Annie looked away, trying to hide her emotions. At last she turned back, and the look on her face was the expression of a woman who needed to talk. There were issues to be addressed, Annie said, and she wanted to talk without interruption. Brian protested, telling her that this could wait but rest couldn't. But she interrupted him.

"This is my time," Annie said, her voice cracking slightly. "And I need you to honor it."

And he quieted, and he listened.

"Brian, when I sent you away all those weeks ago, after . . . after Maddie's visit, I asked you to figure out what you really wanted. I made it sound so one-sided, as though only you had a decision to make. But I needed time, too, because what was happening between us, as wonderful as it was, was also terrifying to me. I needed the time to really examine my feelings. And then when Janey and I came back to Linden Corners and you still hadn't returned, well, I thought you'd changed your mind, or found your answers, only they weren't the ones I was hoping for. I thought we weren't meant to be. Now that you're back, I've been thinking, wondering what it was that brought you back. What it was that originally brought you to Linden Corners—of all the places on the planet, why here, why now?"

"Because of you—"

"No interruptions," she said. "Then it occurred to me—it was Janey. The realization hit me here, in this bed, thinking and pondering the future and wondering what if. Who's going to take care of Janey? Of course, I had always provided for that; it's something a parent does, anticipating the worst—it's only practical. When . . . Dan died, certain provisions needed to be taken care of and . . . arrangements were made for Cynthia and Bradley to care for Janey. Just in case. But then you came along, and honestly, I'd never seen Janey take to someone like she's taken to you—the Windmill Man. It's a connection that goes beyond any blood re-

lation. It's cosmic; it's predestined. Cynthia and Bradley, they'll be start-
ing their own family soon; they're trying. You, Brian, Janey needs you,
and I think you need her."

"Annie, what are you saying?"

"I'm saying, Brian, that if . . . if something happens to me . . .
whenever . . . that I want you to be there for Janey, like you have been
during this time. Will you? Bradley will take care of the legal is-
sues."

So that's what they'd been discussing.

"Annie, you're going to be fine—"

She cut him off. She was a woman without a lot of time. "That's
not an answer."

Brian knew he had to reassure her, despite his fears about where
this was heading. He felt like she was giving up, and he wasn't willing
to hear that. But all she really wanted was comfort, and she had the
foresight to realize that maybe an alternate plan needed to be written.

Brian stole a glance outside, where night had fallen and the moon
had emerged, and suddenly tears were falling from his eyes, falling like
droplets of rain on her bed. He wouldn't wipe them away, he wouldn't
break his hold with Annie, not now and perhaps not ever. But he did
speak, at last, his voice clogged with emotion.

"You want me to raise Janey?"

Annie stifled tears, trying to remain strong. "None of us can alter
our destiny. Events happen; we react, we continue on. You told me,
Brian, that your friends accused you of running away. You assured me
that wasn't true, that maybe you were running to something. To some-
one. And you were right: You were running to Janey. You couldn't stop
nature, couldn't save me from what was to happen. But now we have to
face the consequences of all that's occurred. Brian, Janey was meant to
be in your life."

"Janey's such a gift, the fuel behind the sun," Brian said, himself
trying to be as brave as Annie, holding back the emotions that rippled

through his body, touching nerve endings and threatening to expose him, to reveal the heart that was breaking and melting and healing and longing all at once. His hands grasped hers, felt her warmth, fed her his strength. "Yes, Annie, Janey will be safe with me. I'll take care of her. We need each other—I know that, I feel that. But Annie, you'll be fine, too, and we'll be together, all of us."

"Thank you, Brian Duncan Just Passing Through."

"Not this time," he said.

Brian leaned in, mindful of the bruises as he gently kissed her forehead. They sat, locked together, one reassured about the future, the other terrified of the present. No one disturbed them, and before long, Annie fell asleep, leaving Brian alone with his thoughts.

How had life taken him so far? Just last year, he was on the fast track of a high-profile, well-paying job, the so-called woman of his dreams at his side. Then he became ill, he was betrayed, and his world shattered all around him. Months later, New York was all but forgotten. His life revolved around a little girl whose own world was now being robbed of its innocence, and she needed him. Someone needed Brian Duncan. Was this what he'd left the city for? Was this where he was meant to be?

Yes, he decided, because I'm already here, and a little girl—and her mother—need me. Annie is right. You can't control destiny. But you can embrace it.

Sleep came to him, then, his hands still entwined with Annie's, and he dreamed of them all, Annie, Janey, himself, together at the base of the windmill, so majestic. Then the picture blurred and images faded and suddenly Brian was alone, no Annie, no Janey, and inside his heart he felt coldness and emptiness. This picture was wrong.

He awoke with a start.

It was morning.

Brian stirred, stiff from sleeping in the chair beside Annie's bed. A feeling of disorientation enveloped him. His dream—nightmare—was gone, but he was left with lingering feelings of emptiness.

Immediately he sensed something was wrong. Terribly wrong.

He stared ahead, saw an unfamiliar sight. He rubbed his eyes to ensure that he was fully awake. He was. And he realized then that he was alone in the hospital room. Annie's bed was gone, and so was Annie.

PART FOUR

JULY-AUGUST

ELEVEN

Love—finding it, feeling it—and its wondrous power represent the height of human experience. But love is also so terribly fragile and risky. Because with love comes the possibility of loss.

These thoughts coursed through my mind as I sat in Annie's kitchen, across from Maddie. Her presence was more than simply awkward, and her condescending comment about the windmill angered me. What, I wanted to know, was she doing here? Maddie knew she'd slipped up, and I left it up to Annie how to respond. Annie remained dignified and announced that she had to take Janey up to the neighbors for some strawberry picking, and before I knew it, the front screen door slammed shut and Maddie and I were alone in Annie's kitchen.

"Was it something I said?" Maddie asked, a weak attempt at levity.

"Actually, yes," I remarked.

"She likes windmills, I gather."

"What was your first clue?"

Indeed, Annie's interest in windmills was everywhere. From the wall calendar beside the refrigerator to the series of ceramic tiles hung on the wall, to the salt and pepper shakers on the table, her kitchen was a veritable windmill museum. Maddie examined the latter two items, setting down the salt shaker so carelessly that it tipped over. She didn't bother to throw salt over her shoulder. Perhaps she should have; who knows what trouble she could have averted.

"Let's get out of here," I suggested, and I took hold of her arm and led her out the back door. "You need to see something."

Once outside, I noticed first that the grass needed cutting again, and I'd been promising to do it for the past week but had put it off while I fixed up George's tavern and completed the new sign. As we walked through the tall grass, our feet stayed dry and the rustle of the blades managed to soothe my nerves. Being around Maddie like this made me feel uneasy. I wasn't sure what to say, and I guess she didn't know, either. Still, she must have had a reason for coming, and it didn't look like she was going to volunteer that reason.

"How'd you find me?"

"I suppose you'd like me to say I hired a private investigator and spent lots of money and hours because I couldn't stand the way you left things so up in the air."

"It's not the method that concerns me. I'd just like to know."

"It was easy. John told me."

I wasn't surprised, but I was mad. She must have read that on my face, because she quickly amended her statement. "Don't blame him. I'd run into him a couple times and asked about you. He was evasive at first. Then . . .well, let's just say a situation occurred that made it necessary for him to tell me where you were."

"That's quite a mouthful, Maddie."

She nodded and was about to say something else when suddenly she stopped. We'd reached the crest of the hill, which opened onto a clear view of the windmill. Maddie was speechless for a moment; the power of the magnificent structure was that overpowering. First sight meant first love: It had been that way for Annie, for me, too, and now maybe for Maddie.

But she broke the silence and said, "Okay . . . it's nice and all, but . . ."

"Sshh, don't talk," I cautioned. "Come on; come closer."

I started down the hill but stopped when Maddie called out my name. I turned to her, a curious look on my face.

"Brian, I'm not here to look at a damned windmill. I'm here to see you."

Okay, here we were, no going back. Or forward, for that matter. We, Maddie Chasen and Brian Duncan, were face-to-face, with no excuses. I knew we had to talk. Maddie wore an expression of utmost seriousness, and I was reminded then of her forceful, unrelenting stubbornness.

"This going to take a while?" I asked.

"Depends on you, really," she answered.

I checked my watch. Three-forty-seven. Technically, the bar opened at four, and since this was the first-ever Second Saturday and I was the bar's lone tender, I figured Maddie could pull up a stool and tell me what she wanted while I poured tall ones for the locals.

I explained that I had to get to work and that she was welcome to
join me, and she agreed to come. So we set off, back to our cars, but
not before I stole a look back at the spinning sails of the windmill.
An emotion swept over me, and I tried to pin it down. Sorrow?
Fear? No, more like an emptiness, as though I needed to cherish this
moment with the windmill, because maybe it would be my last.

"Brian?"

I shook off the unsettling feeling and Maddie and I cut
across the lawn, past the farmhouse, and to our cars. Then we
headed off, Maddie following behind, to the newly renamed
George's Tavern. In fact, the old sign was gone and the new one
hung proudly; a note left behind by Gerta informed me she'd insisted Chuck be the one to put up the sign, if nothing else as a
gesture of apology for his insensitivity.

I unlocked the door and flicked the lights on, and a soft, il-
luminating glow immediately warmed the bar. I pointed Maddie
to a bar stool and went behind the counter, where a freshly laun-
dered apron awaited me. After tying it around my waist, I sidled
up to the bar and asked Maddie, "What'll it be?"

"Cute. Absolut, rocks," she said. "As if you didn't know."

There wasn't much demand at George's for top-shelf liquor,
but in preparation for Second Saturday, I'd dusted everything off,
so even my lowliest brands looked appealing. Still, she would not
be denied her choice.

"One vodka coming up," I said, then poured Maddie her
drink and slid it across the bar.

"So, Maddie, quickly, before I open the doors . . ."

"Uh, Brian . . . don't we have more time than that? This is
important—no, it's crucial."

"Doors open in less than sixty seconds," I said.

She sighed, knocked back some vodka, and said, "Oh, just
open the damn doors, Mr. Barkeep."

I headed over to the front door, turned back the lock, and

just as I was about to throw open the door for business, I heard Maddie say, "My God, look at you. I can't believe Justin sent me here to convince you to come back."

My mouth hung open as I stared back at her, but I didn't have the chance to say anything, because five guys bounded their way into the tavern and went straight for the bar, in search of the bartender. With a sudden sense of the absurd, I realized that person was me, but all I could do was stand dumbly by the entrance, apparently catching flies.

George's Tavern was so crowded by six o'clock you'd have thought we'd imported additional residents. It couldn't have been a nicer turnout, and whether they had come to honor George Connors or welcome me as the new proprietor or just plain enjoy the drink specials, the mood of the room was high. Gerta sat at a corner table, never once wanting for company. The same was said for any number of pretty young women, who found themselves paying for very few drinks over the course of the evening. The guys battled it out over friendly games of pool and darts, and sometimes the ladies stepped in to show them how it was really done. Marla and Darla were knocking back tequila shooters and told me to keep them coming; stamina, thy name is twin, I guessed. As for me, I poured drinks and pulled the tap so much my arm hurt, but the smile never left my face. A couple of times, I gazed over at Gerta, and she and I smiled at each other, and once she whispered a sweet "Thank you" that caused my heart to open up. As we hit the fourth hour, just past eight o'clock, I realized I'd yet to see Annie, who was waiting for a baby-sitter to watch Janey. I was hoping to see her around nine. And then there was Maddie, still sitting at her stool at the end of the bar, politely declining all offers for drinks, dancing, pool, and whatever else a guy with a few beers in him could think of. Chuck Ackroyd had planted himself on the stool next to Maddie. The two of them had started up a conversation about seven o'clock, and it was still going strong. I couldn't hear any of their talk, but something told me they were up to no good. Chuck wasn't my favorite person, nor I his. Team him up with my ex-girlfriend . . . well, color me paranoid, but no good could come of it.

Nine o'clock rolled around. I noticed Gerta get up from her seat and approach the bar.

"Brian, take a break. Next thirty minutes, Gerta's got the bar!"

A chorus of cheers went up over the music and any thought of protesting had simply evaporated. I took off my apron (which was filthy by then anyway) and relinquished the bar. Gerta grabbed a pint glass and yelled out, "Who's next?" in a voice that would have done a cheerleader proud. The group whooped again and I knew the party was in fine hands.

I went over to Maddie and she looked up at me. "Oh, have you got a moment for me?" There was a slight slur in her voice.

"Maybe this can wait until tomorrow?"

She shook her head. "I've been patient enough, windmill boy. Let's go. Chuck, if you'll excuse me for a short while?"

This she said with a heavy Southern accent, the kind she'd worked so hard to get rid of, the kind she used now only to get what she wanted. Chuck said he wasn't going anywhere, and the two of them exchanged winks.

"What's that all about?" I asked Maddie as I led her away.

"You don't need to know everything, Brian Duncan Just Passing Through. Just what concerns you."

"Like Justin's sending you here?"

Her face grew serious again; the playing was over. "Someplace quiet around here? Where we can talk and actually hear each other?"

"Upstairs should be okay," I said, and pointed her toward

the back room and the stairs to my apartment. As soon as I closed the door of the apartment, the noise level fell—for occasional moments, I could actually hear silence. Good, thick walls and honest construction still counted for something these days.

I offered Maddie a seat on the sofa and told her I'd be right back. In the kitchen, I threw some cold water on my face, then grabbed a couple Cokes on my way back to the small living room. I set one down before Maddie. She had brought her glass of vodka with her and ignored the Coke.

"Cute place," she said, "though not very personalized. If you plan on staying awhile, you might want to fix it up some."

"Haven't decided."

"So then I'm not too late," she said.

"Didn't say that," I said. "Okay, Maddie, you threw me a curve a few hours ago by just showing up here. But now I've gotten used to having you around. So, out with it. What do you want from me?"

Now that the moment of truth had come, Maddie seemed to have trouble getting to her point. So I prompted her.

"Come on, Maddie; it's not like you to hesitate."

"Fine. Yes, it's just as I said before, Brian. We want you back."

"We."

"Yes."

"As in . . . ?"

"Don't play games with me Brian—"

"If you'll notice, you're the one beating around the bush. Look, Maddie, we're down to twenty minutes before I have to be back at the bar. So either you spill it now or it'll have to wait—and I may not be as willing later on to listen to what you have to say."

She got the message. With a quick brush of her golden hair, Maddie straightened her shoulders and started to speak.

"What have you heard about the Voltaire Health Group lately?"

"That they're not doing too well. Stock is down, thanks in no small part to the wonder drug Tensure—which the FDA didn't seem to like. Am I close?"

"Right on the money," she said. "Unsurprisingly. I knew you wouldn't be able to leave the business world behind for this little Mayberry wannabe. Look, Brian, Voltaire is on shaky ground, sure, but they're not out, not by a long shot. What they need is a fast and amazingly top-notch publicity spin, and of course that's where we come in at Beckford Warfield. We need a plan of attack to sharpen their image and get them back on top as a leader in the health-care industry. I don't have to spell it out for you, do I?"

"No," I said, "but why don't you anyway? Given how things ended between us, I think it's best if you put all your cards on the table. Then I'll decide whether to play the hand."

"Look, it's simple. Voltaire needs an aggressive campaign. So we need the most aggressive and creative minds to figure out what that campaign ought to be. And who's the most aggressive public relations manager around?"

"For simplicity's sake, I'll go with you."

Her mouth curved upward; I'd answered correctly.

"And who's the most creative?"

"Again, to speed things up—and I figure this is the buttering-up portion of the evening—I'll go with . . . myself, Brian Duncan."

"Also the smartest."

"Now you're just embarrassing me," I said.

"Brian?"

"Yeah, Maddie?"

"Can you please stop joking? This is serious."

"Serious for whom, Maddie? You come waltzing back into my life, totally unannounced, and you start tossing compliments around like drinks before an alcoholic. Think I can't resist them, right? Well, I'm not buying 'em. And I'm also not buying your act. You know why? You sound desperate, Maddie, and that's not like you at all. You usually get what you want without the other party's even knowing you want something. So tell me what you're really after, and then maybe we'll have something to discuss."

Maddie got quiet, staring straight at me. But behind her eyes, I could see her mind at work, figuring out how to take advantage of the situation.

"Okay, it's not just Voltaire that needs the help," she said. "It's Beckford Warfield, too."

"Ah. That's better," I said. "Tell me more."

And she did. For the better part of fifteen minutes, she explained how the troubles first began when the Voltaire Group got wind that their superduper wonder drug wasn't going to be approved by the FDA and that all the money they'd already spent on the launch campaign was wasted. Their researchers had to go back to the drawing board and find out where they went wrong. The press had a field day with all this, trying to expose Voltaire as a fraudulent company, blaming them for trying to sell a product they knew was inferior. Beckford Warfield did its best to control the damage but it was failing in the eyes of the Voltaire executives.

"That's when the shit really hit the fan, Brian. Justin and I had been working night and day on the account—flew several times to St. Louis to meet with them, show them our plans, chart a course that would help them out of this mess. Trouble was, they didn't like what they saw, and . . ."

"And what?"

"They asked how come Brian Duncan was letting them down."

At the mention of my name, I leaned in closer and waited to

hear more. Maddie was hesitating again. A knock on the door broke the rising tension between us and gave Maddie a chance to excuse herself to use the bathroom. I went to the door and found Cynthia there.

"I think Gerta's getting tired, Brian. Can you come back?"

"Yeah, sure, Cynthia—of course," I said, but just then a crash came from the bathroom and I found myself hesitating. "Uh, look, Cynthia, can Gerta handle it for a few more minutes, or . . . you? I've—"

Cynthia put a hand on my shoulder, a concerned look on her face. "Is everything all right? Can I help in some way?"

"Just . . . just handle the bar for a few minutes—that would be great."

A grin broke out over her face. "I guess I could pull a tap."

"Thanks, Cynthia. Uh, hey, any sign of Annie yet?"

"She called. Janey's been winning at Monopoly, and Annie doesn't want to stop until the game's over. But she'll be here soon."

With that, she waved and headed back down to the bar.

I closed the door, then walked over to the bathroom. I knocked once on the closed door.

"There's no problem, Brian."

"What fell?"

Maddie emerged from the bathroom and our eyes locked. Hers looked red, as though she'd been crying. Or maybe she'd had more to drink than I'd thought. I wanted to ask her, but I figured she'd deny the tears, deny the drinks, too. Still, something was wrong, and it wasn't the broken water glass on the bathroom floor.

"Look, Brian, I'm sorry I came here. On the drive up, it made sense—convince you to come back to work by buttering you up, saying how we couldn't do it all without you. Justin's brainstorm, but it's not as though I tried to dissuade him, either.

I agreed to the plan, and I agreed to find you. And now that I'm here, God, what the hell was I thinking? Let's just forget I ever showed up, huh? Leave you to your new little life, and I'll . . . well, my old life works still, I guess."

All of a sudden, I felt very sorry for her, this woman I once loved.

"Look, Maddie, obviously there are some things we still need to discuss, but right now, I'm needed downstairs. So . . . look, I'm not sure you're in any condition to drive. So why don't you hang out here, get some rest, and later, maybe tomorrow, we'll settle everything?"

"No, it's okay. I've got a reservation . . ."

"Yeah, probably at the Solemn Nights. The owner is downstairs, I know, so I'll tell him to cancel the room. He won't charge you; he's a friend of mine. So why don't you curl up on the couch?"

"Are you sure?"

No, I wasn't. But Maddie was in trouble, more so than she was letting on, and I couldn't just throw her out in the middle of the night, knowing how much she'd had to drink. So instead, I managed a smile. "As the purveyor of this bar, I wouldn't have it any other way."

Then, halfway out the door, she called to me.

"Yeah?"

"Why are you being so nice to me?"

I paused. Did I even have an answer to that question? Finally, I said, "Because the past should count for something."

She nodded slightly, and I turned around and went downstairs and rejoined the party, leaving Madison Laurette Chasen to her own devices in my apartment, letting her inside a small part of my new life.

*   *   *

Second Saturday came to an official close at 1:45 A.M., with the last-call announcement and the closing of the taps. The last straggler lived up to his reputation as I shut the door behind him a half hour later. I was alone at last, and I spent the next thirty minutes cleaning up while I relived in my mind the great night that had just passed. And it was a great night, even though Annie never made it and Maddie was there. Annie had called around eleven; Janey had just gotten hold of Boardwalk and Park Place and had blood in her eye—she was going for the win, and there was no way Annie could break away. I told her I understood—and I did, actually, since I was so busy and had no time to talk. And there was the complication of Maddie's being upstairs, which I'd rather not have to explain.

Maddie was wearing one of my T-shirts and asleep on the sofa when I got back to the apartment. I kept the lights off, crossed the floor, and closed the door to my bedroom and immediately fell asleep. I was so tired I dreamed about nothing, and before long, the sun of Sunday morning was streaming in through my windows. The alarm rang out at eight o'clock. Annie was due in a half hour to pick me up for church.

I slapped off the alarm, then stretched my arms. My body still craved sleep, but I got up, figuring the only way to really wake up was to take a shower. Maddie was still asleep, and I left her that way while I showered and shaved.

I was putting the razor back in the medicine cabinet when I heard a car pull up in the driveway. With a quick look out the window, I saw it was Annie's truck, and she was just getting out of the cab when I leaned my head out the window.

"I'll be right out."

"I'm coming up," she said.

"Annie, it's okay—just give me—"

Too late. She disappeared under the roof, and the next thing I heard was her footsteps on the stairs. I was still staring out the window when Janey waved up at me. "I won, Brian. Mom landed on Boardwalk four times!" And she ended her statement with a gleeful giggle.

I waved back and dashed to the bedroom to grab some clothes. But when I opened the door, I stopped short.

"What the . . ."

"Good morning," Maddie said. She was no longer asleep on my sofa. She was no longer wearing my T-shirt. Rather, she'd made herself a bit too comfortable in my bed.

"Come on in, Brian, what's keeping you?"

And that's when Annie walked in. My bedroom was now very crowded with three people, two of them completely undressed.

"Uh . . . oh . . ." were the sounds that escaped from Annie's mouth. Then she gave me a look I'll never forget as long as I live. How best to describe it, I can't truly say, but I would bet it was similar to the expression on my face when I'd discovered Maddie in bed with that hairy bastard Justin Warfield. Betrayal isn't a look; it's a feeling. But eyes being the window to the soul, I could see it.

"Annie, this isn't—"

She cut me off, fast. "Isn't what? What it looks like? Don't throw that crap at me. Oh, Christ, Brian, I almost sent Janey upstairs to get you. That would have been . . . hell, maybe it would have been better. Brian . . ." Her voice faded then, and a tear slipped down her cheek. Her eyes focused on me as though burning a hole through me; then she turned to Maddie.

"Was he all you remembered?"

"And more. You must have taught him some new tricks, honey."

"Maddie!" I screamed.

Annie's face quivered; I thought she'd break down right there. But instead, she turned around and slammed the door behind her. I heard her scramble down the stairs and out the door. The door to her truck slammed and I heard the tires squeal as the truck tore out of the driveway. All those sounds reverberated in my head, and somewhere in the chambers of my heart, too.

I made no attempt to chase after her. She wouldn't believe any story, not at this moment, and not with me in nothing but a towel. Both Maddie and I stared at each other, speechless. The grin she'd worn in Annie's presence had disappeared, leaving a faint line of regret instead.

"I'm sorry, Brian."

"No, you're not," I said, anger fueling me. "It's what you wanted. It's what you came to do, isn't it? Get me back, at all costs? Isn't that what Justin wanted you to do? Like you told me last night, Justin stands to lose millions if Voltaire drops him. Heck, if you've been passing off work as mine, then perhaps you'll have a lawsuit on your hands, since it's not what they've been paying for."

"Brian, it's not like that, not at all."

"You know what, Maddie? I don't believe you. Get dressed, get out of my bedroom, and get out of my life."

"I'm only interested in wearing one thing," she said. "This."

And she thrust her arm out to me, spreading the delicate fingers of her hand so that I couldn't miss what she wanted me to see. There, on her ring finger, was the most beautiful diamond ring I'd ever seen. And I'd know, since I had bought it myself, so many months before.

"Whatever happened between us before, Brian, we can work it out. You love me, and I love you. We are a great team, and we're meant for each other."

"What?" I gasped. "How can you honestly say that? My God, Maddie, you just ruined my life . . . a second time. Besides, what makes you think that ring—"

"Don't even try, Brian. I recognized it when I found it in

your dresser drawer. How could I not? We picked it out together, right after Christmas. That day we walked through the snow and talked about our life together, our fantasy . . ."

"That's right, fantasy. As in not reality."

"But you bought the ring. You still have the ring."

"Maddie, forget it. Whatever we had, it's over. It has been for a while, even longer than I realized."

She gazed down at the ring, then at the rest of herself, naked beneath a bunched-up sheet, trying to cling to what, I didn't know. Maybe at that point, she was wondering, too. At last, she looked up at me, and her face was full of shock, like she'd been hit by a thunderbolt.

Our eyes locked as the truth hit her. Then, she pulled the ring off her finger and tossed it onto the edge of the bed, where it bounced before falling to the floor. Oh, that ring. Bought months ago, during another lifetime, its meaning now completely revealed.

Her hand went up to her open mouth, and a short, quick cry escaped her. "My God, what have I done?" she asked. "What have I done?"

"You've destroyed yourself, Maddie. Yourself and everything you wanted from life. And now you've destroyed my life, too."

She stared back at me, stung by the words, hurt by the truth of them.

I thought of my wondrous, beautiful Annie, so sweet, so trusting—thought, too, of the innocent way we'd met at the base of the windmill, and how that had all been ruined by the horrible scene that had just taken place in this room.

There was nothing more to say, not between myself and Maddie. But me and Annie, I hoped that what we had, all we'd shared, was somehow salvageable.

I grabbed my clothes and decided I had to at least try to repair the damage. So I left Maddie in my apartment, half dressed and fully shamed, and grabbed my car keys and dashed down the stairs. I drove as fast as I could to the farmhouse, skirting traffic laws and signs, hell-bent on finding Annie and showing her she had nothing to fear, nothing to lose.

Annie's truck was in the driveway when I got there. She couldn't have been home more than ten minutes, at most. I jumped out of the car, slammed the door behind me, and marched onto the porch. Should I knock, should I just enter? Before I could make up my mind, the front door opened and there was Janey. Her lips trembled as a tear fell from her tiny blue eyes.

"Hey, sweetie," I said, bending down to her. "What's wrong?"

She said nothing, only threw herself at me, her short arms hugging me close and tight. I held her, shushed her crying, and tried to assure her that everything was okay, that everything would be fine.

"No, it won't," she insisted, "Momma's . . . she's really upset, Brian . . . at you. I heard her. She said a bad word, and . . . why is Momma mad at you? Why, Brian? Why?"

"It's a misunderstanding is all, sweetie. We just need to talk, your mom and I. Where is she? Is she in her room?"

Janey shook her head. "She told me not to tell."

"Good—that means she's expecting me," I said, and pulled myself free. I rose to my feet and went into the farmhouse, calling Annie's name. There was no reply, no sound at all. And that was when it hit me.

"Of course," I said aloud, and went back outside, across the lawn, and down the hill. To the windmill.

Today there was no breeze, the temperature was in the mid-eighties, and the humidity was high. Still, there was no doubt in my mind that Annie was hiding out in her own studio. I ran to the base of the windmill and slipped between the silent sails.

I tried the door and, not surprisingly, found it locked. I pulled hard, but the lock wouldn't give.

"Annie! Annie! I'm not leaving, not until we've spoken."

I was staring up at the second floor, convinced that's where she was. I was right; I could see her face reflected in the glass of the window. I paced as I tried to figure out a way to get to her, but it was my mind that came up with the solution. I grabbed hold of one of the sails and inserted my foot into the latticework, then my other foot, and before long I was halfway up the side of the windmill, feeling like a teenager sneaking back inside the house after a night out. In seconds, I had reached the railing of the catwalk and I hopped off and onto the deck. I circled around until I reached the little doorway. As far as I knew, there was no lock on this second level, and I was right.

The door opened easily.

Annie sat atop her stool. But she wasn't painting. The canvas sat there covered. Instead, her arms were crossed and held tight against her body.

"Hi," I said for lack of something better to say.

"You're crazy," she answered. "What if those sails had started to turn?"

I shrugged. "Then you'd have a human windmill, I guess."

She found either the words or the image funny, since she managed a small smile. My guess was that the image of me, turning in the wind, the blood rushing to my head and then back to my feet, brought her some pleasure. No matter; I was glad to have the ice broken, and I took that as a good sign.

"Can we discuss what happened?"

"It's not going to change anything," she said.

"Maddie—she set me up. Set us both up."

"I'm not interested in discussing . . . Maddie. Brian, don't you see? It's not about Maddie, not really. It's what she represents. She's what you used to be, and what I suspect you somehow still want to be. You've had your fun, your little fantasy of running away from your real life, and now it's time to go back. Face it, Brian: You don't know what you want."

"That's not true. I want you," I said quickly.

"No, you don't. You want the image of me, the illusion. Brian, this life you've created, it's not real. Deep down, I think you know that."

"You're wrong. If anyone's looking for a quick escape from what's happened, I'd say it's you."

"That's your version of the truth, Brian."

"The truth? You want to know the truth? The truth is how I feel about you. The man I was six months ago is gone, that hurt and wounded man who ran from everything because he couldn't face things. But look at me now, Annie—I'm not running away. I've run *to* something—to *you*. I'm fighting, right here, right now, for us. Dammit, I love you, Annie."

Then there was silence between us, and I knew why. For all the time we'd spent together, atop her lovely bluff, inside this windmill, at picnics and watching fireworks and in walks through the parks, and on bike rides through the countryside, never once had I used those three tiny but powerful words, and hearing them reverberate against the wooden walls of the windmill, I was taken aback. So was Annie. Neither of us knew what else to say.

Finally, Annie spoke, and her words, I had to give her credit, were maybe more honest than mine. "I don't think you ran away from one woman only to fall in love with another. Not now, not this soon, and not with me." She paused, seeing the hurt on my face. "Oh, Brian, you and I—we got caught up in the moment, a time when you were needing solace and I was needing . . . companionship and affection and a sign that maybe I could be happy with another man. But look at what happened today. Brian, the trust isn't there, and if the trust isn't there, the love can't be.

Look, we could talk the day away and nothing would change, not where it really counts, deep inside the heart. I'm taking Janey away—for a short vacation; I think she needs it, and I know I do. We need time to think . . . about what tomorrow will bring. I believe you have some thinking to do, too. You have issues still to resolve, and Maddie's presence in Linden Corners, well, it's made all this undeniable. There can't be any more running, Brian. For either of us."

"Isn't that what you're doing, Annie, running from . . . from us?"

"Us," her breath whispered. "I like the sound of that. Us. But Brian, do you really think we're ready for what it means? Such a small word, but such a big meaning. There's still so much between you and me, issues that will keep us from really falling in love. Those issues need to be taken care of before we can see if there's more here than just a summer fling. You said just now that you love me. If that's true, Brian, then show me."

Show her. I knew there was hope yet, despite the damage Maddie had caused. "You're not closing the door, then, Annie, are you?"

"It's closed, yes, but not locked."

"So what am I to do?"

"Only you know what you want, Brian, deep inside. Now, though, you need to face those feelings, make them come to the surface, where they can no longer do you or anyone else any harm." Then she leaned in and kissed me with such tenderness. "Figure out your life, and then we can figure out . . . us."

I turned to go, then remembered a promise I'd made, one that now kept my feet from moving. "What about Janey?" I asked, my voice soft in the wind. "After what happened at the hardware store . . ."

"Janey . . . she'll be fine. The trip I'd planned, maybe it will help ease the change. When we return . . ."

"Maybe I'll have returned, too," I said.

"Lots of maybes," Annie said. "Maybe too many."

But within the word *maybe* was the whisper of another, more promising word. Between us, Annie and myself and Janey, there remained the sense of hope.

TWELVE

You know it's ninety-one degrees out there?"

"Yeah?"

"And it's only nine in the morning."

"So?"

"So, my point is that only Wall Streeters and idiots are putting on suits today. We've got a projected high of one hundred and two, and the humidity is already at one hundred percent. You're not gonna stick to the sidewalk—you're gonna melt."

John had a point, I thought, as I pulled the tie around my neck. I straightened it, then smiled in satisfaction. I reached for the jacket on the hanger, slipped it on, and checked out the whole ensemble in the floor-length mirror.

"You look great, Mr. G-fucking-Q. Christ, Brian, why are you doing this?"

"Because . . . well, because I have to. For Annie, and for Janey."

"Ah, yes, the insta-family."

"That's not fair, John."

"Fuck," he said simply.

"Nice mouth. I knew I missed you for a reason."

"Okay, pal. Sorry. Support is what you need, support is what you get." His mouth raised in a devilish grin. "You promise me every gory detail?"

"It'll seem like you were there."

There referred to the offices of the Beckford Warfield Group. The date was August 10, and it was one of the hottest days of the hottest summers New York had seen in years. Despite the objections of my best friend, I was returning to what he'd come to think of as the scene of the crime. Too bad, was my response. For the past few months, John had insisted that in leaving New York City I had run away—from my problems, from my life—and I had dismissed his remarks. So now I had returned to the city I'd fled, ready to finally confront all of my unresolved issues, and now he was telling me what a fool I was. Nice to know that the only constant in my life was John's inconsistency.

"Good luck" were John's parting words. And I'd need it. Because at ten o'clock I had an appointment with none other than the mighty Justin Warfield.

I left the apartment at nine-fifteen, giving myself plenty of time to get to Midtown. Once outside, I realized how right John was about the weather. In seconds, I was dripping with sweat. I couldn't find a cab, so I joined the masses and went down into the subway, which, while waiting on the platform, felt a good twenty degrees warmer than street level. Thankfully, it wasn't a long wait for the number six train, and I stepped into a crowded but air-conditioned car.

I had not missed the overcrowded transit system, the crush of strangers against me, or the ritual of scrambling to get to work each morning. In fact, I was grateful that I had to go only three stops. When the train screeched into the station at 59th and Lexington, I shuffled my way through the clot of passengers and then found my way to the stairs that led to the N train. I got on again—along with a teeming horde of others—and we were off, rattling down the tracks toward the West Side. I got off at 49th Street and joined the sweaty stream of New Yorkers as they headed topside. How I had lived like this day after day, year after year, was suddenly incomprehensible to me.

At street level, I headed to Broadway and 50th, bypassing the overpriced deli I'd always stopped at for a bagel or muffin on my way to the office. Food wasn't on my mind this morning. Instead, I walked along and replayed the phone conversation I'd had with Justin four days ago. He'd taken the call immediately, unctuousness seeping from every pore of his body. Couldn't wait to see me; how about tomorrow?; not doable, huh?; whenever, buddy; name the time. I did, and now it was just fifteen minutes until our face-to-face. Uncertainty paralyzed me. In all those years of playing corporate drone, no other meeting had held such importance for me, no other meeting had had so much riding on it. My future was before me. And this time, I was going to meet it head-on.

I'd left Linden Corners on the seventeenth of July, the day after Annie and Janey had gone for a vacation. Watching them go had been the hardest thing I'd done since I'd made the decision to leave New York City. Now, it was as though those two events were conspiring against me, mocking me until I could do nothing but take the reins, take control. And that was what I was going to do now. I was reminded of that last day I'd seen Annie, a day without wind and energy, a day when the sails of the mighty windmill were silent and unmoving, as though its life were on hold. Just like mine and Annie's. But there I sat, on the roof of my car—atop Brian's Bluff, as Annie had dubbed it—waiting for a breeze, hoping for some sign of life. At some point, I gave up waiting, and I left town the next day with about as much fanfare as I'd entered it, speaking only with Gerta. The bar needed a new keep.

A week alone gave me time to think as I finally made my way up the coast of Maine. Time and the open road had cleared my mind of the clutter of the past six months, and finally I knew what I needed to do. Annie had been right about one thing: I needed to resolve certain issues before we could pursue a future, our future.

I arrived on the eighteenth floor at nine-fifty and was met by a receptionist I didn't recognize and who didn't recognize me. But my name rang a bell with her, since I had a meeting with the chairman. That was the title she used, and I refrained from comment. I took a seat in the lobby, watched people walk by, and realized how much had changed in such a short time. No one looked familiar. It was like seeing a play for the second time, and even though the set was the same, all the actors were different.

"Mr. Duncan? Mr. Warfield is ready for you. If you'll come this way?"

I followed the shapely blonde down the corridor and was ushered into Justin's sanctum sanctorum. That, at least, hadn't changed—all thick woods and framed prints, very tasteful, very masculine. Those latter two descriptions could also have been used to describe Justin Warfield himself, who rose when the door opened and I was announced.

"Well, Brian, we meet again," he said, extending his hand. He was dressed impeccably, three-button suit, tie perfectly tied, black hair slicked back, revealing maybe a bit more gray than I remembered. John's statement about no one but idiots wearing suits popped into my mind, and I actually grinned. Of course, the joke wasn't that funny, since there were two idiots in the room. I stood, feeling nervous. My stomach was turning somersaults.

"Justin, uh, thanks for seeing me."

"Of course. Please, have a seat. Coffee?"

"Sure. Black," I said as I accepted the chair situated in front of his mahogany desk. Justin instructed "Corinne" to bring me some coffee, and she left the room. I crossed my legs one way, then the other. Was it as obvious to him as it was to me how uncomfortable I felt?

No sooner did I settle on a position did Corinne return with my coffee; Justin already had his, and he took a generous gulp from his mug before setting it down on a coaster.

"Your ten-thirty appointment . . . what shall I do—"

Justin cut her off. "Just let me know when he arrives. I'll handle it from there. Thank you, Corinne." He smiled devilishly, his eyebrows dancing along with his grin.

"Oh, and Corinne?"

She looked up.

"Close the door on your way out."

She nodded once, and then she did as commanded, the click of the door louder in my head than it actually was. Everything, actually, had a sense of taking place inside my head, as though this were a dream and at any moment I would wake up. Just another nightmare to count among the many others I'd had lately.

I didn't wake up. This was real and I was in Justin Warfield's office. He wore a supercilious grin like an accessory to his suit.

"Brian Duncan," he said as he took off his jacket. Rolling up his sleeves to expose those hairy arms, he took a seat and then stared across at me. He drew a pen across his upper lip, like he was smelling it. "So you're back."

"Back?" I asked. "Depends on what you mean by that."

"In New York City—and in my office. To me that means you're back, and I hope for good this time." His grin widened; I was pleased to see a poppy seed from his morning bagel stuck between his two front teeth. It reminded me that Justin was just a person, another human being, and no different from—no better than—me. Blood surged through my veins, my confidence returning.

And so I jumped into it.

"Am I back? Well, yes and no, Justin. Sure, I *am* back in New York City. But have I returned for good? No. And who's to say what's 'good' anyway, since no doubt you and I have different definitions of that word. For you, good is merely what pleases you; there's no concern for others."

He let my remarks slide off, staying as cool as the room. "I sense hostility, Brian, and I'm not sure it's warranted. Look, you asked for this meeting—that's fine. But I put off a very important client to give you the thirty minutes you requested. You've got twenty minutes left and the clock doesn't have room for any time-outs. So let's keep playing, okay? The ball, I think, is still in your court."

"Nice metaphor, Justin. I'm not sure what sport we're playing, but I think you're about to strike out." I paused, pulling my thoughts into words, remembering that the high road was best. "I originally asked for this meeting because I wanted to apologize. For my behavior this past spring. I'm sure my quitting was the last thing you expected—needed, actually—and believe me, that wasn't how I envisioned things happening. On my way over here, I thought you deserved to hear why I left as I did."

"And now?"

"What do you think?"

"What I think is this: You came to get something off your chest, and you can't leave until you do. I sense you're looking for closure, Brian. So let's dispense with the double-talk and get on with it." He checked his silver Rolex. "You have sixteen minutes."

His condescension annoyed me.

"The day you and Maddie returned from your meeting with the Voltaire executives was the same day I returned to work. I can't tell you how much I needed to come back after being so sick—being confined to my apartment—hell, my couch. Being tired all the time, not wanting to see anybody, do anything, that can drive a person crazy. So I was eager to get back to work, to throw myself into it. But circumstances, uh, intervened, and I was unable to stay on here."

"A medical condition?" he asked. "Maddie hasn't said anything about—"

"No, Justin. And contrary to the popular opinion around this office, it wasn't jealousy over Maddie's promotion, either. What precipitated my decision to leave happened before you even made that announcement. Suffice it to say I received some rather upsetting news regarding my personal life, and I let it affect my professional life. I just couldn't figure out what really mattered anymore."

"A midlife crisis, Brian? At thirty-four?"

I shrugged. "If you like."

"So you wanted to apologize and let me know . . . what? That you've got your head screwed on straight and you want to get back in the game? You want your job back, huh?" I started to interrupt him, but he cut me off. He was speaking his favorite language now, and I was curious to see where he was going with this. I had a feeling he'd misjudged the situation; he still didn't know the specifics of why I quit, and I was certain that once he did, he would change his tune.

"Brian, I'm willing to put aside your lack of consideration for my business, as long as I get you back on the payroll. What do you say—do you want your old job back?"

The expression on his face, the eagerness in his voice—there was only one response that came to me. I laughed. Outright and heartily.

"Justin, you just don't get it, do you?"

He feigned betrayal; but I knew he was faking, because I knew what true betrayal looked like.

"Okay, Brian, I'll give you the presidency and your own staff—plus the salary and the perks. Anything, Brian; just put the past where it belongs and come back to work for me."

"No, Justin." It wasn't like him to reveal his desperation, and I have to admit to a certain satisfaction of being on the receiving end of it.

"I don't understand," he said.

Was this the moment for me to finally reveal what I saw that day in Maddie's apartment? I was definitely in the power position here, and I was tempted to move in for the kill. I was about to open my mouth when Justin's intercom buzzed and Corinne announced that his ten-thirty appointment was waiting in the lobby. He looked at me squarely, then said, "Send him in."

"We're not finished," I said. "There's something else—"

Justin waved off my protests, concentrating instead on readying himself for his guest by rolling down his sleeves, unnecessarily slicking his hair back, and throwing his jacket back on. He was back in uniform, and I realized then that whoever was coming in, he was important. And I hadn't been asked to leave. A power play had been set in motion, and only at the last second did I realize how naive I'd been. Justin had to have had an alternate plan in mind in case he couldn't convince me himself. He wouldn't be Justin otherwise.

The door opened and Corinne, all perky smiles, announced

Justin's guest, a silver-haired gentleman with skin as tan as an island dweller and a suit that made Justin's look off-the-rack.

"Justin," Dominick Voltaire said, shaking his hand. Then he turned to me, smiled an incredible wealth of white teeth, and said, "Brian Duncan, wonderful to see you, wonderful to have you back. Can't tell you the scare you put into us. I trust you're back to full health, huh?" And he laughed, patting me on the shoulder like we were old pals ready for a friendly round of golf. Truth was, we'd met only twice before during those tentative days of corporate courtship. I'd been part of the team that had won them over, and from the sound of it, he thought I was still an influential part of the team. He was shockingly unaware of the actual situation.

I gave Justin a harsh glare, but he only smiled back, challenging me to say no to his job offer now. The job offer. Something was terribly wrong with that, and it hit me only then. All of his promises—the presidency, the staff, the perks—he was offering me Maddie's job. Which led to the obvious question: Where did Maddie fit into this equation? My gut provided an uneasy answer. Justin had finally overstepped his bounds, overestimating his ability to sell himself and the job.

For once, he'd fucked himself.

"Mr. Voltaire, it's very nice to see you, too, sir, but I'm afraid you're mistaken about a few things." I caught Justin's wavering expression out of the corner of my eye, saw him shake his head. He'd bypassed desperation; this was pure fear. "Justin just offered me quite an opportunity, but just prior to your arrival, I found myself in the unique position of turning down his incredible offer. I won't be returning to the company, and I won't be working on the Voltaire account."

Voltaire's affable nature crumbled, transforming him suddenly into the powerful executive he obviously was. "Warfield, what's the meaning of this? This young man is obviously confused . . ." He stopped, turned back to me. "What do you mean, 'not returning'? When did you ever leave?"

"Uh, Dominick, let's have a seat, talk this through."

Voltaire simply raised his hand to Justin, immediately shutting him up.

"Explain yourself, Mr. Duncan."

And to Justin's absolute horror, I told my story about the 'personal crisis' that led to my leaving in the spring, how I'd come today to apologize for my sudden lapse of professionalism, how I was doing it solely so I could put it past me, move on. Voltaire listened, his displeasure increasing as the story unfolded. When I'd concluded, his attention was focused on someone else. Justin had gone an unhealthy shade of white, despite his well-cultivated tan.

"Is there anything you've done in the past four months that I asked you to do?"

"Uh." Justin attempted to say something, his voice quavering nearly uncontrollably. "I did as you asked the other day—Ms. Chasen no longer works here."

Although Justin confirmed my suspicion, it had little effect on Voltaire. Maddie's presence—or in this case, the lack thereof—was the least among Voltaire's cares. He turned on his heel and said, "Mr. Warfield, I believe our relationship is severed. The attorney will handle the details—today." He didn't bid me farewell.

Justin and I were alone.

"You sabotaged me, you bastard," he said.

"You invited Voltaire into this mix, not me. So, if anyone has sabotaged anything, it's you, Justin. But if it's any comfort, nothing you could have said or done would have convinced me to work for you again. You see, Justin, I don't like it when my boss manipulates my life."

"What's that supposed to mean?"

"Let's just say that I hope it was Maddie who came to her senses—not just before you kicked her out of the company but before you kicked her out of your bed.

"Oh, and Justin? You didn't strike out. You got sacked."

That was when I took my leave, following not far behind Dominick Voltaire, but unlike the powerful business executive, who'd left angry and feeling cheated, I left with elation and a spring in my step.

It felt liberating to finally tell Justin the truth. Now I had one more mess to clean up. I had to have one last conversation with the woman I once thought I'd be spending the rest of my life with.

"I'm here to see Madison Chasen."

"Your name, sir?"

"Duncan. Brian Duncan."

"I'll call up," he said. His nametag read EDGAR, and he was probably around sixty years old, had probably been a doorman for years. You get a cushy union job like doorman, you keep it. He picked up the intercom and held up a finger to indicate each passing ring. On five, he spoke.

"Miss Chasen, a Mr. Duncan is here to see you. Shall I send him up?"

This, of course, was the sixty-four-thousand-dollar question, and apparently I came up a winner. His fingers folded in his hand, all but one, the thumb, which he left up, like a movie critic's.

"That was easy," I said, as he hung up.

"Twenty-one oh one," he instructed me, and gave me a smile.

The thing about being a doorman, you get a sense of your tenants and of their guests, and I guess he detected some sort of history between Maddie and me. Perhaps he believed in love. Or perhaps he was just a nice guy. He waved me over to the elevator, and in seconds I was speeding up to the twenty-first floor.

Maddie, John had told me, had moved, two months after she'd gotten the promotion at Beckford Warfield, into this posh building on the Upper West Side that had amazing views of Central Park. As I soon discovered, there were only two apartments on this floor, and they must be decent-sized—and expensive. For a second, I wondered if Maddie would still be able to afford it. Then the door opened.

Maddie was dressed in shorts and a halter top. Her silky hair was neat, as were her makeup and her smile. Her eyes—those were another story, one I was familiar with. I saw in them much sadness and regret.

"Hi," she said.

"Hi," I said back.

"I heard you'd come back. To the city."

"John looking out for both of us again?"

She shook her head. "Nope, someone at the office. She e-mailed me, said you'd been by to see Justin this morning."

I checked my watch. "A mere three hours ago."

"So then you heard."

My head bowed slightly, as though I'd heard someone had died. "Yeah."

"Yeah, that's about all you can say."

"Look, Maddie, can I come in? Maybe, we could—"

"Talk?"

"We need to, don't you think?"

She opened the door fully, letting me in. "Yes," she said simply.

Once inside, Maddie closed the door and escorted me through a vestibule and into the living room. The place was spacious, tastefully decorated with all-new furnishings and artwork. I recognized none of it from her previous place; clearly she'd taken to her new position at Beckford Warfield with zeal, elevating her lifestyle to one that befitted a corporate executive making a nice six-figure salary.

"Wow," I said. "Nice digs."

She settled down on the plush sofa and folded her feet beneath her. I took a seat opposite her, in a fancy wing-back chair. For a second, I looked out the window, saw her fabulous view of the park and beyond. Airplanes were approaching LaGuardia.

"How's Annie?" she asked.

"Okay, I guess. We're, uh . . . let's just say we're taking a break," I said, perhaps a bit too defensively, but glad, too, that she'd broached the subject. This was a meeting in which nothing could be held back, not feelings, not emotions, and not the truth. Wounds healed, and in time you needed to remove the bandages. Sometimes with one swift pull, the pain fierce but ultimately short-lived. This conversation would probably be like that.

"I'm sorry, Brian. What I did—well, it was unforgivable."

"Maddie, it's okay . . . now. When I was still in Linden Corners, I was mad and I couldn't understand how you could be so destructive. To make Annie think I'd cheated, betrayed her. I didn't know you had it in you to be so cruel." I paused, and the only sound in the apartment came from the central air-conditioning system.

"It's not over, Brian, between you and Annie—I can feel it," she said, and then, somewhat to herself, added, "I never should have listened to that jerk."

"What jerk?"

"That guy—at the bar. He's the one who told me how to screw things up with you and Annie. 'Just make her think he's sleeping with you again,' that's what he said."

Chuck. It had to be Chuck, because only he knew the kind of reaction a cheating lover would have on Annie. At least I now knew what Chuck and Maddie had talked about at the bar. I squelched any anger I felt toward him, realizing now was not the time.

"He manipulated you, Maddie. But don't expend any more energy on him now. Besides, one situation at a time, okay?"

"Is that what I am—a situation?"

"I think what you are—what we are—is unfinished business. You've apologized to me for, well, for screwing up my relationship with Annie. I've come to apologize, too, for leaving you without any explanation."

"Brian, we don't have to go there . . ."

"Actually, we do. Because I can't move forward until I settle all the issues of the past. I can't let New York City go until I come clean."

"Sounds final. You mean—"

I nodded. "I'm not staying. John's taken over the lease on the apartment and he's busy selling my stuff—the old furniture, things I put in storage back in March. I'm just here to close this chapter on my life. I have to. Before I can go home."

"To Linden Corners?"

I smiled, ever so tentatively. "Yes."

"If it will help, I'll talk with Annie, tell her—"

"Maddie, it's not necessary, really," I said, and then I asked her about the job. "What happened?"

She let out of a sigh of exasperation that only slightly masked her bitterness. "Simple. We were going to lose the Voltaire account, which meant millions of lost revenue for Justin. They wanted you on the account, not me, and so I was given an ultimatum—get you back . . . or else. If I succeeded, Justin would pawn me off on another account and you'd be the sole executive on Voltaire. But, what he didn't say—though, knowing Justin, it was easy to guess—was that if I failed in my mission to bring you back, then I'd be out on my ass. I had no doubt that was what would happen and that Justin would do his best to blackball me in the industry. So I did what I could to get you to come back to work. I think I must have been deluding myself—it wasn't Justin who said 'any way possible.' That was my own thinking. I was trying to hold on to everything I'd worked hard for—the job, this apartment. God, it all seems so irrelevant now. But at the time, it was all I lived for, and it meant ruining the life you'd worked so hard to create. The . . .love you found with Annie. Brian, I've been foolish . . ."

"Maddie, you're not the first person to get so wrapped up in your job. Hell, a year ago, I would have been right there with you. Ambition attracted us both. But Maddie, I want you to know that I don't blame you, not for anything that's happened. That's what I came here to say. It's time to bury the past, so we can move on."

"Separately," she stated, with a slight hint of a question mark on the last syllable of the word. As though maybe there was some possibility of our reclaiming what we'd lost. But I nodded my head, confirming that what we had was gone, that yes, we were moving on separately.

"Brian, there's one thing about this whole mess you never knew—"

I cut her off, quickly. "The past, Maddie. Leave it there."

She realized then what she should have guessed all along. That I knew about Justin and her. Tears sprang from her eyes and she tried her best to wipe them away, but others followed. She covered her mouth with her hand. "That's why you left—oh, God . . . but . . . how, Brian? We thought we were being so smart, so . . . God, I felt disgusting after it happened. But I couldn't stop it, not without jeopardizing all I'd worked for . . . you do know that, Brian, don't you?"

I went to her and I held her and soothed her, assuring her it was good to have everything out in the open so we could both move on. After a few minutes, she regained her composure and wiped the last of her tears away. I got up to leave, and she didn't try to stop me. At the door, I turned to her and found her standing right in front of me. I stared into those lovely blue eyes of hers, saw in them the spark that had once drawn me to her. That was when I knew she'd be fine, that she'd survive and go on and find another job and another love and a new life. I told her so, and that's when she leaned in and pressed her lips to mine. Our kiss held, and it was almost as if each passing second represented each month we'd spent together, until finally we'd run out of time and our lips parted.

I turned to leave and I heard my name.

"Go find happiness," Maddie said, then managed a smile that could only be called bittersweet. "Go back to the windmill."

I'd been so busy repairing the wounds to my heart in all these past months that I'd forgotten about the hepatitis that had started this whole thing. So I took advantage of being in the city to drop by the doctor's office for an examination and blood test, hoping for the prognosis I'd sensed anyway—that I was healed.

Three days after my appointment, the phone rang. I was busy amidst a sea of packed cartons; I was nearly fully packed and ready to finally move out of my apartment. I was fully expecting it to be my doctor. It wasn't.

"Hello?"

"Brian?"

"Yes, this is Brian."

"Brian Duncan?"

"Yes. Who is this?"

"Brian, dear . . . it's Gerta. Gerta Connors."

My heart swelled as I recognized her voice, at the rush of memories it brought back. George and the porch and Sunday dinners with sweet strawberry pies for dessert.

"Oh, Gerta, how are you?"

"Fine, dear, simply fine. Folks in town, though, they're awfully thirsty. Linden Corners without the tavern, well, it's not the same. Brian, are you coming back?"

I looked at the packed cartons, at the empty walls, heard the silence within those four walls. "Yes, Gerta, I'm coming back."

"Goodness, that's wonderful to hear. Because I need your help. See, I've come up with this idea for the Labor Day weekend. You know, most folks are off on Friday and Monday, and they're eager for the long four-day weekend. So here's what I've been thinking. You remember First Friday?"

"And Second Saturday, sure."

"Well, we're having a Third Thursday, and I need you here, to help behind the bar."

The Thursday before Labor Day, that was only a week away. Suddenly, I couldn't wait to see Gerta again—and the other fine folks of the town I missed so much. But most of all, I longed to return to Annie's world, the quiet mornings at the farmhouse, the tender nights in her arms, of finding again the joy that Janey instilled within me. And of course, the windmill. There was no way I could resist the call of Linden Corners.

"I'll be there, Gerta, you can count on it."

We made a date to meet for lunch on that Thursday to finalize plans for the night's festivities. I resisted, though, asking about Annie. What Annie and I had to say to each other, well, the phone wasn't the way to do it. It had to be face-to-face, open and honest. So instead, I simply said good-bye to Gerta and set down the phone. I needed to get on with my packing.

Finalizing my plans to leave New York took four more days, which flew by, and before long, it was Wednesday morning, late August, and I was saying my good-byes to John, my best friend, my sole support through this tough time.

"Come to Linden Corners, John. Come visit."

"As long as you don't make me get up early to milk cows," he said.

"Jerk. I'm not a farmer."

He showed me a smile and said, "I'll see you soon, farmer boy."

A belly laugh filled my car as I pulled it out of the garage and headed off. There was one last stop to make before I left the city limits.

On 47th Street, I parked the car, got out, and walked down the street to Eli's Jewelers. And it was there that I pulled from my pocket the engagement ring I'd bought for Maddie those many months ago. It was the last reminder I had of my previous life, and it was time to let it go.

Eli said he'd be right back and went, again, for his paperwork. Again I had the store to myself; there were no happy couples poring over rings; no reminders of what might have been. While the old man was in the back, I took the liberty of looking around. The old man returned, eyeing me carefully as I pointed to a diamond set between two aquamarines that were exactly the color of Janey Sullivan's eyes. Our business together took longer than I expected, but that was fine. Some things are worth the time, the effort.

"A new start?"

I nodded. "Yeah. 'Cause you know what, Eli? Life goes on. You face your battles, and you win. You—"

And he interrupted me. "You tilt at windmills?"

He grinned at me, and I returned the grin. Then, vowing this was my last visit to his shop of dreams, I left with my future in my pocket—and my future before me.

I'd finally stopped running away.

THIRTEEN

I remember my first time in Linden Corners. The way the windmill caught my eye and sparked my imagination—and how I had become transfixed. Time seemed to shift and the troubles of the past were no more. All that lay before me was the future, and where it lay was in the wondrous land of this windmill.

Today, though, with New York City hours away by car and millions more by mind, I approached Linden Corners. A dark, foreboding sky lay before me. It looked like a summer storm was imminent, and immediately George's face came to me. He'd revered—and feared—these storms. Still, the rain couldn't dampen my spirits, not when I was nearly home.

Six months ago, I had driven over this now familiar hill, and this time, I knew what to expect: the windmill.

Today its sails spun, and as I'd done before, I pulled over to the side of the road, hoping to recapture the mood and the feeling. I got out of the car, climbed atop its hood, and crossed my legs, and just stared at the slowly turning slats, at the darkened windows. In my mind, I relived the moments I'd shared with the powerful old windmill. No cars passed me, there were no interruptions; time just stood still.

As I sat there, as though I were watching a favorite movie, a vision came running over the hill, a running figure who stretched out her arms and raced into the wind. My heart leaped at the thought of seeing Janey once again, only this time I realized my wingless angel wasn't Janey but Annie herself.

And I could hear her laughing, laughing in the wind.

The rain started then. A drop here, a drop there. The humid air swept past me, thick and clinging. Annie seemed oblivious to both as she continued to run down the hill—and between the churning sails of the windmill. Then exhaustion overcame her and she dropped to the high grass. She was still laughing, and she still hadn't noticed me.

How appropriate that we had parted here and that we would meet again here, where our future together would begin.

I jumped from the hood of the car and crossed the road. And I began to walk toward Annie and her windmill.

"Now I know why Janey thinks she can fly," I said.

Annie, still lying in the grass, turned at the sound of my voice. When she saw me, her words failed her. So I filled the silence.

"Hi," I said.

"Brian."

"Yeah."

"Don't say—"

"I know—don't say 'yeah.' It seemed appropriate."

"You're . . . back?"

"Not back. I'm here. Now. And if you'll have me, I won't be going anywhere."

"No more Brian Duncan Just Passing Through?"

"Brian Duncan Here to Stay."

"Well, I know a good real estate agent," she said. "If you need a place to stay."

"You tell me."

She didn't answer, not immediately, but she did pull herself up from the grass, not bothering to brush herself off. She came toward me, her footsteps hesitant. So I bridged the distance myself, and soon Annie and I were face-to-face, only a breath of air separating us. We both waited for the next words, whatever they might be and from whichever of us they would come, but neither of us knew what to say.

I reached up and stroked her rosy cheek, still flush from her dash down the hill. She craned her neck, kissed my fingers. And then I pressed my lips to hers and the sensation I felt was like the first tender kiss we'd shared that Memorial Day evening back at Connors' Corners. A beginning then, a new beginning now.

"I missed you," I said, "incredibly. You and Janey."

"And the past?"

"Where it belongs," I said. "Annie, New York City is over. The final chapter has been written. It's time to start a new book, the story of a windmill and the woman who loved it—she and the precious little girl who both inspire my world. I can't wait to see Janey—where is she?"

"At a friend's house. She's at an overnight play date. A bunch of girls, their last summertime romp before school starts up."

"Meaning . . . we're alone?"

Annie nodded, a sly smile on her face. "Gerta told me you were coming . . . home. So I hoped—"

"I haven't even been to the apartment. My first stop was you."

"Come, then," Annie said. "Let me show you my windmill."

Annie led me through the door and up the winding staircase and into her studio, and it was there that the past was finally laid to rest. And the future was blessed with the belief that love, in all its passion and all its glory, could not be denied.

That night, we never left the windmill.

And that night, the storm moved in, the wind howling through the windmill's giant sails and out on the open land. Inside, though, we were safe, together, like we were meant to be.

At eight the next morning, with Annie opening up the antique shop and Janey still at her overnight play date, I returned to my apartment above Connors' Corners—now called George's Tavern. I dropped my bags, and before long, I was unpacked and back in the bar. I was immediately overcome by a musty smell and a quiet that had seeped into the walls. The taps were dry and the glasses even drier, and it occurred to me that Gerta had shut down the business completely during my absence. I found further evidence of this in the coating of dust along the brass bar and atop the tables. The jukebox was unplugged and silent. Darts had been left in the corkboard, and the chalkboard still said WELCOME TO SECOND SATURDAY.

"Well, this is unacceptable," I said to the empty room. The first thing I did was plug in the jukebox and get it going. Toad the Wet Sprocket's "Fly from Heaven" filled the room and encouraged me to get down to work.

So I toiled about the bar in the morning hours, the jukebox drowning out the sound of the rain that was still pouring down from the skies. After a couple of hours of work, I decided to venture out, to pick up supplies for that night's party. Then I'd go meet Gerta for lunch at her home. So I got in my car and drove down to Hudson and spent a good piece of my savings and a couple hours of my time before I noticed I was running late for lunch.

The rain had let up, but above me, the sky was a slate gray and getting darker and blacker by the minute. It was almost one in the afternoon, and I was beginning to feel uneasy. On this wickedly humid day in late August, there was little doubt that what was coming was a serious storm. I watched the trees and high green grass alongside the road waver in the wind. It wasn't here yet, the storm, but it was coming, quickly.

I flipped on the radio to hear what the local weather forecasters had to say. After a few songs and commercials, the fast-talking disc jockey turned to topical news and weather. The temperature was in the high nineties, humidity one hundred percent, and thunderstorms were expected to sweep through the Hudson River Valley about midafternoon, with violent, dangerous lightning probable. Stay indoors—and stay tuned—the DJ suggested, and then, his irony in check, he played Bananarama's version of "Cruel Summer."

Twenty minutes later, I found myself cresting a small hill, and my senses were rewarded with the wondrous sight of the windmill. It was hard to believe that it was only last March—nearly six months ago—that I'd first seen this marvelous structure that was at once so familiar to me but still so very foreign. Pictures of Annie flooded my senses, of the nights we'd shared, weeks ago and just last night, too, and for a second I couldn't imagine her anywhere but in that windmill. But I knew Annie was at work, even though a light seemed to be on inside.

And I was now officially late for my date with Gerta. Third Thursday didn't begin for another four hours and there was still a lot to be done in preparation for it.

But as I drove through downtown Linden Corners on my way to Gerta's house, I was struck by how empty the town was. The Five-O was locked up and the lights were turned off. Down the street, Chuck Ackroyd's hardware store was equally deserted, and I began to wonder if something had happened in Linden Corners during the few hours I'd been away. Maybe it was a dream, and I began to wonder if this place even existed at all: It felt as though I were in the middle of a ghost town.

I didn't like this, not one bit. Where was everyone? I left the downtown area and headed down the county road toward the Connors house—maybe with this storm brewing, Third Thursday was canceled. The drive took little time, and soon I was parking in Gerta's driveway and making my way up her front steps. I knocked once, waited, knocked a second time. There was no answer.

Leaving the porch, I circled the grounds looking for any sign of activity, of life, and came up empty. Only Gerta's car was there, parked in the garage. As I went back to my car, I heard the distant rumble of thunder and looked around as far as I could see. All I saw was a coming blackness, perhaps the blackest sky I'd ever seen. A flash of lightning laced the clouds with ribbons of yellow.

It occurred to me that the residents of Linden Corners had, fearing the coming storm, gathered in a safe place. Which meant either a church basement or a school, the only two places large enough to hold the whole community. Back in the car, I pulled out easily onto the empty road and headed back toward the town, watching the storm as it came even closer and closer. I flipped on the radio and caught the DJ in midreport. Even so, it was simple to figure out his message.

"... severe thunderstorm watch is in effect through six P.M.

tonight. The National Weather Service is advising everyone to stay indoors. Dangerous lightning and strong winds are expected." Then, before he went to commercial, he urged everyone to stay tuned because he'd be back with more updates and some "great music" to get us through.

I flipped off the radio and concentrated on the road ahead of me. The DJ had a good idea—stay indoors, stay safe—and I resolved that if I didn't find anyone at the church I'd return to the bar and wait out the storm alone.

But once I arrived back in the village, I drove around the back of the church and found a parking lot filled with cars. Mine joined the others, and I got out and ran fast toward the rear entrance of the old-fashioned brick building, getting doused on the short trip. I grabbed the door handle and it opened easily. I was soaking and was met by a blast of cold air. How great it felt after the humid air outside. I followed the sounds of voices down the stairs and into the spacious basement. There must have been a hundred people there, families with children and lots of folks whose faces I recognized, all busy with something. Some listened to the radio, others had a television going in the corner, and the kids were busying themselves with video games or board games or were just plain running around.

"Brian—over here, dear!"

I'd found Gerta, or, more accurately, she'd found me. I waded through the crowd, seeing her arm waving like a beacon. She hugged me tight, which, I have to admit, sent waves of emotion up my spine.

"It's so good to see you," she said, giving me a hard look, as though looking for a clue as to what had happened. "Welcome home. I'm so glad you found us. You haven't been with us through one of these storms. They come every once in a while, and we all gather here or at the school. Whichever is closest."

"How'd you get here?" I asked. "Your car—"

"I took care of her," I heard from behind me. The voice belonged to Chuck Ackroyd. I turned to face him, trying my best not to pound the shit out of him, considering how he'd manipulated Maddie into coming between me and Annie. In Gerta's presence, though, it was an urge I had to bury. Instead, I flashed him a fake smile but acknowledged him no further.

"So, what's this storm—a hurricane or something?"

"Nor'easter," Gerta said, "which can be worse. Especially given the kind of heat we've been having."

"It's the same in New York City."

"You were back in the city?" Chuck asked.

"For a short while," I said. "Had to rid myself of the apartment, you know?"

A stricken look crossed his face, which was exactly my intent. He excused himself and went to see if he could be of help somewhere else. Hopefully somewhere in Siberia.

I followed Gerta through the room, scanning the assembled folks for any sign of Janey or Annie. I came up empty. Perhaps they were at the school. Or—a light went off inside my brain as I recalled the light I'd seen inside the windmill a short while ago—perhaps Annie had gone back there. But why? I dismissed the thought; she wouldn't be there with a storm like this brewing. Suddenly a crash of thunder rattled the windows, and my gut churned with nervous energy. I had a bad feeling about this storm; maybe it was my inexperience with them, since everyone else seemed calm, even unconcerned.

Gerta stopped at the television, where the local weatherman was detailing the path of the storm. From what he said, the northern portion of the Hudson River Valley was going to be the hardest hit, with possible power outages and the touching down of lightning bolts. He couldn't repeat himself enough: Stay indoors. And again, an unsettling feeling overcame me.

"Gerta, have you heard anything from Annie?"

A puzzled look crossed her face. "Well, surely she's here, somewhere. Just a half hour ago I saw little Janey playing with some other children," she said reassuringly. "Relax—it'll be over soon. Though it does look like nature has put a damper on our Third Thursday—not much you can do but listen when God speaks up."

She took a seat then and settled in to wait out the storm.

I told her I'd be back, and I waded through the room, asking after Annie and Janey. No one had seen Annie, but Marla the twin said she'd seen Janey with a couple of other kids upstairs, playing in the vestibule. I dashed up the stairs two at a time, bypassing folks who were coming down the stairs with trays of piping hot food, a small town's answer to riding out a storm. It smelled good, making me realize I hadn't eaten all day. But food would have to wait. My heart was near bursting knowing Janey was nearby. I needed to know she was okay.

There were five kids running around the altar, and I suppose on any other day Father Burton would have put a stop to it quickly, but today the kids had the run of the place. Janey, I saw, was among the happy group, oblivious to the coming storm.

I called out Janey's name, and she stopped short and peered out from behind the lectern.

"*Brian!*" she cried loudly, and as she came running toward me, a loud clap of thunder shook the room and I turned with sudden surprise, only to be knocked off my feet as Janey came racing into my arms. The two of us fell to the floor in a happy reunion. This little bundle of joy, my God how I'd missed her presence, her exuberance. She was a true gift, and for a moment I felt a sadness at having lost her even for a brief amount of time. But here she was, giggling and laughing, an infectious combination that got a similar response from me.

"You came back, just like you said you would. Brian's home! I knew you'd come home," she said, barely pausing for breath. "That's what I kept telling Momma, that'd you'd be back."

Before I could respond, another clap of thunder roared through the church. Then the sound of shattering glass shook the room. There were a few cries of shock, and someone yelled, "Look out!" I looked up to see shards of stained glass heading my way— Janey's way.

"Get down," I shouted, and then threw myself over her. My body covered Janey just in time as pieces of glass fell all around us, bouncing on my back and my legs but luckily not piercing either. I listened for the brief shower to end. Then I raised myself from the floor and grabbed for Janey.

"Are you okay?" I asked, checking her over for any cuts or bruises. She seemed to be okay.

"Wow," she said, and then, with the hint of the devilish grin I'd come to love, she said, "See, you can't ever leave me, Brian. You're always saving me!" And then she giggled again. I knew she was just fine, probably better than I was.

I looked up then at the broken window and saw pieces of a tree branch sticking through the open space, felt rain coming in, and felt the wind as it whipped through the smashed window.

"We can't leave the window like that, can we?" a man shouted.

"What choice do we have?" someone else asked.

Behind me was Chuck Ackroyd, who suggested we board it up. "With planks of wood from the hardware store."

"You can't go out in that . . ."

To my surprise, Chuck was headed out the door, and I took off after him, thinking he was crazy to go out in the midst of the storm. I caught up to him, grabbed his shirt to pull him back. He resisted.

"Either help or don't," he said. "But don't stall."

I made up my mind fast. "Okay, I'm going with you."

For a second we both hesitated, as though the idea of our working together was incomprehensible. It was us versus the storm, we both realized, and there was no time for anything else.

I was ready to leave when Janey came running up to me, asking me not to leave.

"I've got to help Mr. Ackroyd," I said. "But I'll be back."

"Okay—but Brian, bring Momma back with you."

So what I sensed was true. Annie wasn't there.

"She said she'd meet me here, Brian. She was closing up the shop and heading for home. Can you go and get her?"

Annie, alone at the farmhouse, or worse, inside the windmill. Definitely, she was inside the windmill. And that was not the safest place to be.

"Yeah, we'll go to the store and we'll get your mom, too. Until then, be good, huh, sweetie?"

Chuck threw open the front door of the church, only to be pushed back by a fierce gust of wind. But we persevered, running through the stinging sheets of rain until we reached his truck. He pulled out of the lot and drove the three blocks to the hardware store, both of us assessing the damage already done to the village square. There were downed trees and large puddles of rain and street signs waved wildly. I prayed they were secure in the ground.

We turned onto Main Street and quickly came to Chuck's store, and his first reaction said it all.

"Shit."

The front display window was shattered and the wind was ripping through his store, causing who knew how much damage. Lots, I figured. Neither of us said a word; we just stared ahead, uncertain what to do. Finally, I said, "Forget the church window. You can't beat this storm."

"Yeah," he said, "you said it."

We were about to leave when out of the truck's window I

noticed another truck parked in the lot. It looked terribly familiar, and an unsettling feeling overcame me. Then a beam of a
light caught my eyes. The beam was coming from inside the
store.

"Wait, Chuck—someone's inside the store."

"What the hell . . . hey, that's a flashlight beam."

He hopped out of the cab. I joined him.

We ran to the store, seeking what cover we could from the
torn awning over the front entrance. Forsaking the keys, Chuck
jumped into his display case and entered the store the convenient
way—at least it was now. That was probably how the intruder
had entered as well. *What intruder?* I thought. Hell, it was Annie.
Again, I followed, shrieking out a series of hellos that weren't
heard; the fury of the storm swallowed my voice.

I sought out the beam of light, running through the aisles,
while Chuck went to check on the other entrances and exits. I
continued to call out and finally I got a reply.

"Who's there?" she asked.

"Annie!" I screamed at the top of my lungs.

Her mouth opened, but if words came out, I couldn't hear
them.

I ran to her. "Are you crazy—what are you doing out in this
storm?"

"I needed supplies. I needed help."

"Help? For what? Annie, you need to get over to the church.
Janey's waiting for you. Come on."

I reached for her windbreaker, but she pulled away.

"I'm not leaving—not yet!"

"Why? What's going on?"

"I need rope. Coil. Something that's strong."

"Strong? Why? What are you going to try to tie down? In
this storm, it'll never hold anyway. Just forget it, Annie. Come
with me, back to the church. Janey needs you."

Her maternal concern stopped her for a second. "She's fine? Janey's okay? Her friend's mother brought them to the church okay?"

"Yeah. Except she wants her mother," I said. "Annie, what's going on? What are you doing here?"

"Brian, don't you get it? It's the windmill. I'm afraid the storm's going to damage it. I can't have that happen, Brian. It's too much, don't you see? I've lost too much in life. I can't let the windmill be destroyed. It's what keeps me strong—strong for Janey." She paused, and in that moment her eyes became fierce, determined. "Brian, it's the windmill that brought you to me."

She'd shaken me to my core, the determination in her voice cutting off all rational thoughts I might have had. My brain ceased to work, save for images of that windmill, and for a second I saw it in complete ruin and realized I couldn't allow it to happen either. Annie's dream was now my dream, too, and we couldn't let it be destroyed.

"Come on. Let me help."

Not even twenty-four hours earlier, Annie and I had renewed our love inside the windmill, and I think she realized, now, that it was no longer just her windmill but ours.

"If you're helping, then let's move. There's very little time left," she said, scrambling down the aisle until she'd found what she was looking for. Grabbing both a coil of thick wire and another of taut rope, a hammer and heavy metal spikes, she started toward the exit and stopped at the registers in the front.

Chuck, who was there assessing the damage, waved her on. "You'd better get out of here or you'll never make it back to the church in time. Your items are free."

She thanked Chuck and turned to me, her impatience evident. "In the car. Come on, time's wasting."

I shook my head and followed Annie out of the store and into the fierce storm. The wind immediately whipped her hair into her face and nearly knocked her down. It was clear that the storm was intensifying, fast. I helped Annie to the cab of the truck, and she started the engine. She looked ready to leave without me, but before she had a chance to do that, I grabbed the passenger door and jumped in beside her.

"Ready?" she said, her lips curled upward. She was enjoying this.

"Annie Sullivan, you're crazy."

"No, Brian. It's about loyalty. The windmill saved me years ago, and it continues to save me, almost daily. I can't let it stand alone and unprotected."

Just then another gust of wind passed us, rocking the truck like it was a ship being tossed on the waves.

"Then we'd better go now, before the wind carries us to Oz," I said.

"Now who's in a hurry?" she said. Then she tilted her head toward the hardware store. "What about Chuck?"

"I think he can fend for himself. Come on—let's go save our windmill."

I'd made her smile, and she leaned over and kissed me fast before putting the truck in gear and then pulling out onto the road. The truck barreled down the empty roads, swerving occasionally to avoid a fallen tree branch or, in one case, a whole tree. Annie missed the turnoff for her driveway, continuing down the main route, and I realized she meant to drive directly to the windmill. And that's exactly what she did, hopping the shoulder and peeling her way over the great lawn. In the near distance, the windmill still stood. Despite the incredible wind outside, though, the sails weren't moving. My face scrunched up in puzzlement.

"I secured the sails when I heard the weather report earlier. I was inside—I wanted to finish your painting, and so I secured the lock inside the cap. It's a safety device, to keep the sails from turning too quickly—from allowing nature to take total control of the sails."

"So then why the rope?"

"Because the lock may not hold—not in this wind. Just an hour ago, the weatherman said we could have gusts of up to eighty miles an hour. I'm not taking any chances, not with the windmill."

"What will the ropes do?"

"I want to secure them to the ground. Hopefully, between the lock and the ropes, the sails will stay put."

I gave her a doubtful expression.

"You have a better idea?"

I had to admit I didn't. That still didn't give me confidence in her plan. But I was going to help her, no matter what.

She brought the truck to a stop about a hundred feet from the windmill, and before she stepped back out into the storm, she turned to me. Rain, maybe sweat, dripped from her forehead and her hair was drenched and lying flat against her scalp. She looked amazing.

"What?" she asked me suddenly.

"What what?"

"You're staring at me."

"Can't help myself there."

She had her hand on the door handle. "Yes, the windblown look is terribly attractive."

I should have laughed, since sarcasm was unusual coming from Annie, yet what I felt wash over me was a sudden sadness, as though all we'd been through, the friendship, the love, the time apart, the coming home, all of it was now on the line. This was the moment we had been heading toward, and our next steps would dictate our future.

"What's the matter, Brian?"

"Are you sure we're doing the right thing?"

"Brian, you came back to me yesterday, told me you were fighting for something you believe in, something that means the world to you. Well, I'm doing the same thing."

I saw her swallow heavily, like it hurt. You can't make your emotions slide away. We both knew that. Silence enveloped the cab, and for a brief moment we were oblivious to the storm raging outside. Then, in one blast of wind, the truck again rocked and our eye contact was broken.

"I'll get the supplies," I said.

As I reached for the length of rope, Annie jumped out of the truck. The wind nearly knocked her over, but she braced herself against the side of the truck in defiance. She yelled something to me, but I couldn't hear what it was. So I joined her outside in the storm, and together, we went running toward the windmill, getting soaked to the bone as we pushed against the wind. I had certainly never seen a storm of such power and certainly had never been in the midst of one.

"This is crazy," I shouted into the wind, and my words were met only by Annie's laugh. She was invigorated, alive, and her sense of purpose found its way into me. I laughed at her recklessness. "You're crazy."

She waved at me as she reached the windmill. Thrusting open the door, she went inside and wiped away a fountain of water from her hair and face. It pooled on the floor, and I stepped in it as I followed behind her, shutting the door behind me. Lightning lit the black sky for a split second, and then thunder rumbled directly overhead.

"Are you sure about this?" I asked, coming up behind her.

"No time like the present," she responded. "Okay, here's the plan: I'll head upstairs and throw the rope down to you. Don't forget to lace it through the slats; that will help secure it."

I shook my head. "Only one thing wrong with that plan—I don't want you spending all that time outside on the catwalk. It's too dangerous, Annie."

"No more dangerous—"

"Annie, for Janey's sake, stay inside as much as you can."

That stopped her for a second, and I hoped she was reconsidering this entire plan.

"I'll do my best."

She took the rope and wound her way up the spiral staircase, as I waited on the main level for her okay. She yelled down that she was in position and so, steeling myself against the elements once again, I scurried out of the relative safety of the windmill and into the insanity of the storm. Immediately the wind whipped at my body, and I slipped in a puddle of mud. Picking myself up quickly, though, I made my way to the base of the windmill, where the sails, dormant when we'd arrived, now threatened to shake loose of their holding winch and fall victim to the uncontrollable forces of the wind. I just had to have faith that Annie's plan would work; I, too, hated the thought of the windmill's being damaged.

"Brian—catch . . ."

I spun into action, climbing up the sails like I'd done weeks ago, winding the rope through the latticework. Then, when it was fully woven through the sails, I tied a knot and then grabbed from my pocket one of the metal spikes Annie had taken from the hardware store, and with the hammer I pounded the spike into the bottom part of the windmill itself because the ground was too sopping to let me gain any purchase. I pulled at it, tightening the rope until I felt it grow taut while Annie yanked from the other end, securing her end around the mechanism inside the windmill. I gave her a high five, letting her know my end was done.

"Mine, too!" she screamed. "We did it, Brian—look!"

And I did look up at the windmill's sails—and saw that they

were truly immobilized. Annie's theory had proven true—at least for now. Now all we could do was hope that the wind would let up soon.

"You did it, Annie—you were right," I shouted up to her, happily twisting in the wind, ignoring the rain and the sharp pellets of hail that battered my body. Who cared? Annie and I had triumphed over nature, over adversity, and wasn't that really why I'd come back to Linden Corners? Annie was all that mattered, she and Janey, and I had to let her know it, now. Fumbling in my pocket, I found the small jewelry box I'd aquired from Eli's Jewelers yesterday. It contained a ring that was meant for only one woman. A different ring for the right woman.

I stared up at Annie then, watching as she double-checked the tautness of the rope, thinking what an angel she looked like. I saw our future, a time that would bring three people together as a family. I called up to her, got her attention, and in a sudden rush of adrenaline and emotion, my arms thrust into the air, the ring box flat against my open palm, I said, "Annie . . . this is all that remains of my life in New York. I bought it there and brought it here, beside my heart. Marry me, Annie, I love—"

My declaration was cut off. She never heard the last word; neither did I. A huge rumble of thunder ripped the sky, nearly shattering my eardrums as it passed directly overhead. Then lightning flashed down, once, twice, and then a third time in a streak of electric yellow that reached down from the heavens and struck the ground near my feet. Its force threw me to the ground and then I heard an awful cracking sound. I saw the sails begin to move, felt the rope give way and whip wildly out of control, slapping down hard in the muddy ground.

Then I heard a scream. I wiped rain from my eyes and watched in numb horror as the windmill's wooden sails, suddenly all ablaze, came separated from the holding winch and tumbled to the earth with a crashing roar. I tried to get up, slipped again in the mud, recovered, then raced over to the blazing heap of burning sails. Fire still sizzled over the wooden slats. I looked up to the ledge where Annie was standing to make sure she was fine. All I saw were flames engulfing the top of the windmill, flickering far and high, fueled by the wind. What I didn't see was Annie. Frantically, I ran around the windmill, looking for any sign of Annie, but came up empty. Panic overtook me, and I was screaming her name at the top of my lungs, over and over, running and running until I came around the mill and saw a flicker of yellow on the ground, buried beneath the wrecked pile of wood that had, seconds ago, been the sails of the windmill. I knew what it was immediately, and awful dread filled me. That yellow was Annie's windbreaker. I ran to her, recklessly tossing away broken pieces of wood until I could reach her. She lay facedown on the ground. She wasn't moving. Dammit it, she wasn't moving—that was all I could see, all I could wrap my mind around.

"Annie, Annie, talk to me . . . please, Annie, let me know you're all right. . . . Oh God . . ."

I felt a jolt at my back—the touch of another person—and I jumped in surprise. A quick turn of my head, and I saw it was Chuck.

"Call an ambulance," I yelled. "Now!"

"What happened?" he asked.

"Never mind, Chuck—just get help—get it now. If you care for anything or anyone, for God's sake, help me."

Chuck ran off, and I was left feeling alone and helpless. I couldn't touch Annie out of fear that I'd hurt her further, so I merely sat beside her while the rain and the hail and the wind blew past me and thunder and lightning raged overhead. There was nothing I could do, not now. Annie was beyond my help.

I slunk down in the mud to wait, staring up at the charred remains of the windmill, then down at the silent figure of Annie Sullivan, the woman who had loved the windmill, the woman who had forever altered my life, for the good, for the better, for always.

FOURTH INTERLUDE

Nurse!" Brian shouted into Annie's empty room.

Brian opened the door to the hospital room, his heart beating quickly, his palms sweating. Fear crack led up and down his spine like water on a hot pan, as though his dream were coming true, that Annie was gone, truly gone.

"Nurse!" he yelled again, and this time he got an answer.

"Mr. Duncan, ssshh," the duty nurse admon-

ished him from her station across the hall. She was probably sixty, had gray hair, and reminded Brian of a stern teacher. He found himself obediently quieting down, but then found his resolve again. He approached the nurse and demanded to know where Annie Sullivan was. Was she all right?

"Mr. Duncan, take it easy. Mrs. Sullivan was taken from her room early this morning."

"Where did they take her?"

"They've taken her for further tests. Please, take it easy."

"I'm sorry. It's just . . ."

Just what? That he dreamed the worst possible scenario, and then he awoke to find the room empty. Premonitions like that usually spoke the truth.

"She'll be back soon," the nurse said, trying her best to comfort him. "The doctor's just being cautious. That's a good thing."

Yeah. But needing to be so cautious, that wasn't.

Brian was still frightened, and he found himself on the pay phone, calling Cynthia and Bradley, Gerta, too, urging them to get to the hospital and to bring Janey with them. Then Brian settled down to wait, for the Linden Corners version of the cavalry to arrive, for the doctor, or better yet, for Annie to return. He sat with his head in his hands, his hands clasped together in prayer. Even though the nurse had tried to be reassuring, Brian knew it wasn't good news if a patient was taken from her room during the night. Something had happened. Something had gone wrong.

The infection.

Brian remembered the doctor's words. They couldn't be sure. But dammit, why not?

The wait, it turned out, wasn't long.

Twenty minutes passed before Brian sensed someone standing before him. Taking his hands from his face, he looked up and saw Dr. Savage standing there, his face drawn.

Brian ran a hand across his face, as though that might wipe away the worry he felt.

"Doctor?"

He hung his head, then sat beside Brian. Their shoulders touched, a small comfort. But it wasn't enough.

"We're very concerned, Mr. Duncan. It's as we feared. Annie has developed an infection, one we're doing our best to fight. Medication is our only defense, but she's not responding to it. I'm sorry. All we can do now is wait. She'll be back in her room within the half hour and you can see her then."

"Dr. Savage, what are you saying? That—Annie could die?"

"Speculation is useless, Mr. Duncan."

That, Brian found, was not the encouraging answer he'd hoped for.

Just then, Cynthia turned the corner, and seeing the scene unfolding before her, the drawn expression on Brian's face, the doctor sitting beside him, she stopped in her tracks. She couldn't move. Janey, who was at her side, broke free and raced forward, sensing a feeling in the air and not liking the feeling at all, and she threw herself into Brian's arms.

Tears fell, his, hers, theirs. Two lost souls consoling each other.

Brian looked at the doctor and said, "We have to see her."

We. Meaning he and Janey.

It did not go unnoticed that today, there were no objections from the staff about a minor in the ICU.

"Hi, Momma," Janey said, kissing her mother's cheek.

"Hi, baby," Annie said, her voice weak. Her face was sallow, and her eyes looked unspeakably tired. They'd been together forty minutes when Annie propped herself up and beckoned Janey to move in closer. "I want to tell you something, okay?"

"Okay."

"You, Janey Sullivan, are the most precious thing ever—the most wonderful person I've ever met, the best daughter a mother could ever have. And seeing as though you're the best girl ever, I want you to promise me something."

The little girl gulped. She knew this was serious and so she listened hard.

"Listen to Brian. He loves you very much."

"I love him, too," Janey said.

"You're so lucky, Janey, so loved. Remember that. You are loved. Now, come here, sweetie."

Janey leaned in close and let her mother embrace her. She looked determined to hold on forever. Brian watched from the door, giving them space but hearing every word that was spoken between them. Annie grew tired and she at last released her daughter, but not before kissing Janey's trembling face.

"Let your mom rest, sweetie," Brian said, moving closer.

"One more hug," Janey said.

And so there were further hugs and promises and expressions of dreams, and eventually Brian led Janey out of the hospital room. She joined Cynthia in the waiting room. Brian returned to Annie's bedside.

"You have a promise to keep, too," Annie said.

"No problem there," he said, kissing her cheek. "Rest easy. And know, Annie, that Janey isn't the only one who is loved."

"That makes two of us," Annie said. And then, her voice barely a whisper, she pulled Brian in close. "We haven't talked about . . . what you said—asked, just before the accident. Brian, you meant it, didn't you?"

A mixture of emotions ran circles around his heart as he realized she had heard and remembered his proposal, and before he could let another moment pass, he told her yes, yes, of course he meant it, more than anything in the world, and as if to prove it, and know-

ing that actions do speak louder than words, he withdrew from his pocket the ring he'd kept with him since that fateful day of the storm.

"Will you wear my ring?" Brian asked Annie, and through tears that rolled down her pale cheeks, she nodded.

Brian lifted her hand, careful of the tubes and bandages from the IV, and slipped the diamond-and-aquamarine ring onto her finger. It fit snugly, as though it truly belonged there. It sparkled, even in the fluorescent light of the hospital. Still, it paled in comparison to the spark of life Annie suddenly gave off.

"Thank you for asking to marry me. Thank you for . . . becoming part of my family. Thank you for all the good times Janey will see. I . . . I never returned the words. You know, the ones you said just before my accident . . ."

"Sshh—it's not necessary."

"But it is. I love you, too, Brian."

Brian's tears fell as he held the woman who had agreed to be his wife, held her until she fell asleep. He stayed with her all day, holding her hand, feeling her pulse, watching as she drew each breath. She did not appear to be in pain and he supposed that was one saving grace in all this; she didn't appear to be suffering, at least not in a physical way. Visiting hours slipped away and the nurses encouraged him to go home, to go take care of that precious little girl. But he wanted to stay with Annie. Janey and he, they had a lifetime together. Annie, he sensed, needed him now.

And so he stayed.

That night, shortly before the midnight hour, Annie awoke to find Brian still at her side. She smiled and, in a faint voice, thanked him for staying with her.

Just then the windmill clock Brian had brought from home sounded and the sails spun twelve times.

"A new day," Brian said.

"And see, the windmill still turns," Annie said, and then she drifted back to sleep. Brian did the same, still holding her hands.

He wasn't sure when it happened, but he awoke with a jolt, only to discover it was still dark outside. Morning had not yet come. Still, a stunningly bright light shot across the sky, a shooting star he imagined, and then, quickly, fearfully, he turned to Annie.

She looked peaceful, at rest.

And that's when he knew. Annie was gone.

"I love you, Annie Sullivan."

He stayed with her a while longer, holding her as the tears fell.

That next day, as a bright sun blazed across the sky and the crisp feel of autumn rode in on a wave of wind, a beaten and defeated Brian Duncan returned from the hospital.

News of Annie's tragic death spread through the community, and many of the residents of Linden Corners had gathered at the Sullivan farmhouse. They had come with food in their hands and love in their hearts, but maybe more importantly, they had come to work. The sights and sounds before Brian's eyes were miracles—the steady sound of hammers pounding nails, saws cutting lumber, men and women hard at work, rebuilding the windmill.

They had come to honor the woman who had brought them such joy, the woman who had filled their lives with countless lessons in love. She had come to Linden Corners and had come to love the windmill. And they knew that the windmill, which lay in ruins still from the storm, must again live, must turn with the gentle caress of the wind. There was no time like the present. Tomorrow came with no guarantees.

Brian stood atop the hill, watching as Martha and Gerta and all the other wonderful folks he had met—even Chuck—rallied around him. The plan, as conceived in the attic by a little girl full of hope, as deemed possible at a tiny diner known as the Five-O, as ordained by a young woman who came to a town and instilled within it a sense of friendship and love, the great windmill restoration project had begun, a lasting tribute to the woman who loved the windmill, the woman they had all loved.

EPILOGUE

Seasons came and seasons went until countless years had passed and the men who had crafted her, labored in the hot sun to build the magnificent windmill, were like the wind itself, blown into the past, into the memories we coin as history. As for the windmill, it was allowed to fall into disrepair for too long a time, and the once-heralded landmark—a classic token to a lost era—became nothing more than an eyesore to a generation that no longer embraced its ancestry. There was talk, and not just once, of tearing down the old windmill.

Until she came along, the girl who loved the windmill, and restored it to its former beauty, and grace. Again the wind would pass through its spinning sails, a familiar friend returned to once again define an otherwise lost landscape. She thought it sacrilegious to deprive the windmill of its true purpose, and by instilling within the building a spirit all its own, she breathed vibrant new life into the community around it. She could never know, never imagine, though, that her love for the creaky old structure would inspire a sense of mutual caring and nurturing—even love—among the townsfolk. But it would, even in the face of awful tragedy and sorrow. The windmill would generate an invisible power of healing and would bring together two most unlikely souls.

Just as the mother had revered the windmill, so, too, did the daughter.

"Brian, come on, bring the rakes. We've got work to do!"

Janey stood at the top of the hill behind the farmhouse, dressed in blue jeans and a purple turtleneck, her windbreaker wrapped around her waist. Her hands were positioned on her hips and exasperation was written on her face. That and the hint of a smile.

"Yes, ma'am—here I come."

I emerged from the barn, huge wooden rakes in each hand. For a second I held a pose, looking like the male half of a contemporary version of *American Gothic,* but now I was a single parent as opposed to part of an elderly couple. Janey came running up to me and grabbed one of the rakes.

"Let's go," she said, and began to dash down the hill and across the leaf-strewn lawn.

A month had passed, summer departing and autumn officially rushing in with a breath of cold air blowing down from the north. Everywhere in the Hudson River Valley were signs of the coming winter: Trees were ablaze with orange and yellow and brown leaves; the wind cradled the delicate branches, and the dying leaves fluttered to the ground.

Today, a crisp October day, was the annual leaf raking. It was also Janey's eighth birthday, and we'd planned a quiet celebration. The wounds from Annie's death were still fresh for all of us, especially Janey. Many a night had passed when Janey's sleep was peppered with tears, and I would sit by her side until she'd fall asleep. Sometimes I sat by her the whole night long, there if she needed me. But together, we were persevering.

Today, I hoped we could find some joy. We needed some.

From the lawn, I saw a familiar car drive up, saw Gerta Connors step out, a wicker picnic basket on her arm and a smile brightening her face. She, too, was ready to build new memories, eager to share in the annual tradition of the raking of the leaves.

"Gerta, thank you for being here, for sharing this day with us," I said, then pecked her cheek. "Here, give me that. Let me carry it."

"Nonsense," Gerta said. "I can handle it just fine. You and Janey get cleaned up. I'll set up—by the windmill, right?"

"Absolutely. We'll join you in a few moments."

I called a halt to the raking. Huge piles of leaves were gathered in various locations on the giant lawn, and Janey was already busy jumping off a small ladder and landing in the soft mounds of leaves, all the time laughing, laughing, laughing. Her joy was infectious. The wind picked it up and whirled around me and Gerta until we were all feeling that anything, even happiness, was possible.

Gerta spread a thick flannel blanket on the cool ground, and I secured its corners with heavy stones. Placing the basket on the checkered blanket, Gerta then settled down, tucking her legs beneath her. She urged little Janey to her side. I joined them, and together we made an unlikely threesome, one that had known too much genuine sorrow this past year. But we were a determined group, determined to head toward the future, fueled by memories of happier times, filled with hope for tomorrow.

And so our feast began, and we dined on sandwiches and soda and, yes, Gerta's strawberry pie for the adults, chocolate cupcakes dotted with sprinkles for Janey. I took a moment to light a single candle atop one of the cupcakes, which burned brightly until Janey blew it out. Then she ate the cake with relish.

A strong breeze suddenly blew across the land, ruffling Janey's hair, tickling her nose. She let out an exclamation of surprise and then turned to stare up at the windmill. Its sails turned, then turned more, an endless revolution that drew her up from the blanket and into a twirl all her own, her face wide and bright and electric.

"That was Momma," she said, dancing. "Momma came to wish me a happy birthday. And now it is, it truly is!"

I went to her, hugged her, wiped a tear from the corner of my eye. This girl, how she inspired me with her bravery and hope. She missed her mother; she always would. But she would be fine—because Annie lived inside Janey, in the memories she had created with her, and in the memories Janey and I would share.

Ultimately, Annie lived each day through the sheer power of the newly restored windmill, and no one could ever silence her spirit or silence the great and giant windmill that once again spun its magic—today, tomorrow, and forever.